DIE
FOR
YOU

DIE FOR YOU

International Bestselling Author

MONICA JAMES

Editing: Editing 4 Indies

Interior Design and Formatting by

T E.M. IPPETTS
BOOK DESIGNS

www.emtippettsbookdesigns.com

Follow me on:
authormonicajames.com

OTHER BOOKS BY
MONICA JAMES

THE I SURRENDER SERIES

I Surrender

Surrender to Me

Surrendered

White

SOMETHING LIKE NORMAL SERIES

Something like Normal

Something like Redemption

Something like Love

A HARD LOVE ROMANCE

Dirty Dix

Wicked Dix

The Hunt

MEMORIES FROM YESTERDAY DUET

Forgetting You, Forgetting Me

Forgetting You, Remembering Me

SINS OF THE HEART DUET

Absinthe of the Heart

Defiance of the Heart

ALL THE PRETTY THINGS TRILOGY
Bad Saint
Fallen Saint
Forever My Saint
The Devil's Crown-Part One (Spin-Off)
The Devil's Crown-Part Two (Spin-Off)

THE MONSTERS WITHIN DUET
Bullseye
Blowback

DELIVER US FROM EVIL TRILOGY
Thy Kingdom Come
Into Temptation
Deliver Us From Evil

IN LOVE AND WAR
North of the Stars
Fall of the Stars

REVENGE IS SWEET SERIES
Crybaby

HEART MEMORY TRANSFER DUET
Heart Sick
Love Sick

KISS OR KILL SERIES

Bad for You

Die for You

STANDALONE

Mr. Write

Chase the Butterflies

Beyond the Roses

Someone Else's Shadow

Love Hard

Love Harder

Like a Boss

CONTENT WARNING:

DIE FOR YOU is a **DARK ROMANCE** containing mature themes that might make some readers uncomfortable. It contains strong violence, sexual assault, trauma, child abuse, murder, profanity, drug use, criminal activity, blood gore, blood play, and some dark and disturbing scenes.

There is no cruelty to animals.

This twisted tale is not intended for the fainthearted.

PROLOGUE

"**Y**ou're in so much trouble, *tesoro mio.*"

Calling her that is habit, a very *bad* habit, one which I should break, but with Valentina, old habits die hard. Although it's been five years, she's a bad habit I don't think I'll ever kick. Looking at her now and knowing all the things we've done to one another over the years doesn't change the fact that I still want her.

I hate her.

I honestly do.

But the fucked-up thing is that makes me crave her even more.

Our relationship has always been complicated. I think we've always hated one another more than we've loved. But for two fucked-up people, the hatred has us appreciating the love so much more because you cannot have one without the other.

Valentina is covered in blood.

The blood of one of my men.

She did this to make a point.

She did this to be seen.

So the question is, what does she want?

Why has the rabbit come out of hiding?

"I've heard you loud and clear," I say, closing the motel door behind me. "What do you want?"

I don't bother putting out my cigarette because I don't plan on being here long. It's better this way because bad things always seem to happen when Valentina and I are alone.

And considering the last time I saw her, I fucked her so hard so she'd never forget who she belongs to, it's best if we don't dally.

Yes, it was a stupid, dishonorable thing to do, but it's pretty evident Valentina is bad for me, and I'm bad for her, which is why I've stayed away.

Well, I have for the most part. Seeing her again after so long is like a kick to my solar plexus, and I somehow have forgotten how to breathe.

And she knows it.

That arrogant smirk reveals she knows that no matter who I'm with or how many miles are between us, she will always get under my skin.

"What do you want, Valentina?" I ask again.

She runs her pointer finger over the tip of the bloody blade, that sly grin tugging at her sinful red lips. She sashays her hips as she walks over to me, a ploy she learned from the Antichrist to lure in stupid men.

Just the thought of Gianna Ricci has me wanting to hurt something. It's because of her that we're here.

I thought Valentina would see the light, that she would see Gianna for the lying psychopath she is. But sadly, all I see is more of Gianna in Valentina.

It shouldn't surprise me since Gianna is her mother. A fact Valentina does not know. Well, I don't think she does because if she did, I doubt she'd be here, doing her bidding.

The million-dollar question is, why haven't I told her?

Gianna and I are the only two people...alive, who know the truth.

The person who told me this bombshell is dead, thanks to Gianna. She killed Aldo Cattaneo in cold blood because she knew he was the only person who could bring down her empire by telling the truth. And she believes her secret died with him.

How wrong she is.

Aldo knew that if Valentina found out the truth, she would

destroy Gianna for lying to her. Aldo wanted to adopt Valentina as he knew the power she held. She has Ricci blood running through her veins. She is a Mafia princess who can change the world. He wanted her on his side.

But Gianna got to Valentina first, poisoning her.

That is why I haven't disclosed the truth, because with wisdom comes power. This is the collateral I have over Gianna, and I plan on exploiting it when the time is right. Five years seems like a long time to find the "right time," but I've been wrestling with my moral dilemma since I found out the truth.

Disclosing to Gianna's rivals that she had a daughter puts Valentina in danger. She's a sitting duck, ripe for the picking for those who wish to blackmail Gianna because she was the one who taught us love makes you weak.

And for once, she was right.

I'm still trying to protect Valentina, which makes me a fool. She's proven time and time again that she doesn't care for me, like when she buried me alive, tampered with my car brakes on an icy night, or when she framed me, leaving me to rot in a Tijuana jail.

But I suppose I've given as good as I got. I did plant an explosive in her car, sank her boat while she was out at sea, and I did trick her into becoming a stripper named Honey Bee.

We've played this game of cat and mouse over the past five years, and secretly, I've allowed it because it gets me off.

The violence.

The blood.

It's the only thing that makes me feel alive.

That, and my love for Valentina.

And that is the only reason we're still alive. We've had ample opportunity to kill the other. But we don't because our love runs deeper than revenge.

It shouldn't, but it does.

And that makes us both weak, weak for the other.

It seems Gianna's lessons were wasted on both Valentina and me.

Until one of us cracks, this will be a vicious cycle we both refuse to break.

Her signature scent of cherries kicks me straight in the face. But I keep my cool.

"You know what I want."

"No, I really don't. I stopped knowing that a long time ago."

She steps closer.

I don't waver.

For now, anyway.

"Surrender."

"What's behind door number two?"

She ignores my quip. "You cannot win. Our empire grows stronger. Not just here. But abroad as well." Her Italian accent is thick, thanks to her living in Italy.

Not that that was her choice, as she's a fugitive on the run.

I yawn in response because I've heard it all before. "Gianna shipped you off to Italy because it was easier than having to deal with you here. Stop making her a martyr. She's the villain here."

"I chose to go to Italy, where I have prospered. I found who I am and what I am capable of."

"Oh please…" I roll my eyes because what in the ever-living fuck is this bullshit? "This sounds like a chapter out of *Eat. Pray. Love*. Stop fooling yourself. You were sent away because of what you did. If only you fucking listened, things would have been so different. But now look at us. On opposite teams, and for what? Your loyalty to a heartless bitch?"

"You ungrateful bastard. She did everything for us," Valentina snaps, her cheeks turning scarlet.

"Are you kidding yourself right now? She's a liar and a really fucking horrible human being. You're the only person who can't see that."

"We owe her our lives."

I've heard this all before, and my reply will never change. "If only you knew—" But I hold my tongue as I've said too much.

"Knew what?"

I don't reply, which infuriates her.

"And you expect me to trust you?" She snickers, shaking her head. "Gianna has never lied to me."

"Oh, wake the fuck up! Look what you've turned into."

"And what's that?" She folds her arms across her chest in defiance.

With measured movements, I lean over her shoulder and snuff out my cigarette in the glass ashtray behind her.

Her breaths begin to quicken.

I pull away slowly, our faces inches apart. Peering up at me from under hooded eyes, she parts that lush pink mouth, the tip of her tongue curling under her top lip. She's doing this to bait me because, like always, the line between love and hate blurs.

"Aldo wasn't a fit leader. He was weak. His men saw his inability to lead."

"You sound exactly like her."

"And for that, I'm proud."

The room grows smaller because it seems...off.

"You're here because you want something. What is it?"

She swallows past the lump in her throat. A subtle action but one that doesn't go unnoticed by me.

"I'm here because I need you to give up. Gianna is planning a takedown so large, Lennon, you will not survive it."

A laugh escapes me. "I'll take my chances. Besides, the past five years have been nothing but a fight for survival for us both. I won't back down. And neither will Bria."

The change in Valentina is clear. Her hatred for Bria still runs deep. Whether it's jealousy or admiration, I'm still not sure.

"She is no one."

"Watch your mouth," I warn, my tone firm.

"Or what? The truth hurts, no? The only reason she is protected is because—" But Valentina soon stops herself, and I know the reason that is.

But regardless, I decide to torment her because I enjoy seeing that fluster creep up her long neck and paint those cherub cheeks red.

"Because? What's the matter? Cat got your tongue?" I lower my face into Valentina's, uncaring for her personal space.

She stands her ground, but I'm getting under her skin.

"Could it be because she's smart, experienced, and a skilled fighter? Not to mention beautiful, so beautiful in fact she's been able to lure your men to their knees…before she takes their heads."

Low blow, but Valentina has no right to bad-mouth Bria. Not only has she been loyal to me since day one, but she is also…

"It's because she's your wife!"

And then there's that.

Valentina and I will never have a happily ever after. Too much has happened to forget. There were never any expectations or promises between us, and being on opposing teams makes it hard to maintain a relationship with the enemy.

Falling in love with Bria wasn't on my bingo card, but here

we are.

It was a slow burn because, regardless of what Valentina did, it always felt like a betrayal to open my heart to anyone but her. But as time progressed and she tried killing me any chance she got, it got a little easier to let her go.

Now, I cling to the memories, and perhaps a part of me is a hopeless romantic living in a fantasy world where we can coexist, where we both change and can be together.

But reality soon takes over when Valentina attempts to stab me in the shoulder with the knife.

I quickly block her, slapping the blade from her hand. "Really?" I mock, getting into a fighting stance just as she does. "Anyone would think you weren't even trying."

She smirks, circling me, eyes never leaving mine. "For old times' sake, I guess. Call me nostalgic."

And this is why I can't let her go.

The chemistry between us hasn't subsided with time. If anything, it's only grown. But you can't base a relationship on the fact that someone gives you butterflies. That we're trying to kill one another every chance we get seems to erase the warm and fuzzies.

I need to remember she's the enemy here, and not my overpowering need to grab her by the throat and pin her to the wall.

And that's not an issue as she retrieves a throwing star from her sleeve and tosses it at my head. It embeds into the wall behind me.

She missed on purpose, which piques my interest. Then I realize she is here not because of Gianna, but for something else. This has nothing to do with our fight for power and control, but rather…something that affects us both.

But the question is, what is it?

What is so important to her that she would risk coming back to America? And why does she save me when she could have killed me ten times over? She wants me alive for a reason.

What reason is that?

"What have you done, *tesoro mio*? What have you done?"

Valentina's demeanor changes when she realizes I now see she is guarding a secret, and her purpose for coming here is to divulge what that secret is.

But she got cold feet at the last moment.

Before I can ask anything further, she tasers me.

Dropping to the floor, I don't fight the electrical current passing through me because I fucking deserve it. I lowered my guard, which is always a dangerous thing when Valentina is involved.

She stands over me, watching me seize.

"Kill…me." I manage to press past the pain. "Because once I find out the truth…I *will*…kill you."

Her face pales, and her mask finally slips.

It seems Valentina and I are now at war for another reason, and whatever the reason, it's enough for her to risk it all by coming here.

"You have to catch me first." Those are her parting words as she amps up the voltage on the Taser and disappears from my life…again.

CHAPTER 1

VALENTINA
FIVE YEARS AGO

'm alone in this beautiful Sicilian farmhouse, surrounded by hectares of land which are prosperous with olive trees. The views are nothing but a serene green landscape of rolling hills and lush vegetation.

I don't know who my neighbors are because there are none as far as the eye can see. I'm isolated and secluded. I finally feel at home.

I've been here a week.

I've slept like the dead for six of those days.

My body and mind were beyond fatigued. Every time I woke, I remembered where I was and why I was here. My soul slipped into self-preservation mode and retreated into the darkness, where I could forget.

Today is day seven.

It's the first day I have been able to get out of bed longer than to use the bathroom and grab a drink of water. The house is huge. I haven't even explored a quarter of it, but I guess time is on my side because that's all I have.

I'm here because I can never go back to America.

I knew the consequences of my actions when I ended that piece of shit's life. However, the crime of killing Father Merry is worth the punishment because, given the choice again, I would make the same one.

Gianna put me on a plane, and when I arrived in Sicily, a driver was waiting for me at the airport.

We didn't speak.

He simply grabbed my duffel and drove me here.

There are no phones.

No internet.

I don't even see a car.

I am totally off-grid, and I know that's with intent.

It's safer this way.

Gianna and I know that the fewer people who know of my arrival, the better it is, for now, anyway. Because it's expected of me to take over where Gianna cannot. She's hunted here, thanks to Aldo. That bastard deserves the fate he got.

Gianna trusts me to look after the family business here. I will ensure that I don't let her down.

As I peer over the balcony while sipping my espresso, I can't help but think that life is a roller coaster. I have done some god-awful things. I have killed and enjoyed doing it. And I know I will kill again. The things done to me in my past don't excuse my behavior.

But perhaps there is a God, after all, and this home, this serenity, is my compensation as such for what I endured. Whatever the reason, I don't question it because, for the first time, I feel at peace.

Father Merry is dead.

Gianna is finally free of Aldo.

And I am safe.

There is only one thing missing.

And that's Lennon.

Our last exchange confirmed that we are now enemies, and this time, it's for good. We fight on opposing teams, and I don't think we will ever be on the same side. I wish it were different because being apart from Lenny, I miss him so much.

He's been a significant part of my life, and regardless of my faults, he has always been there for me.

But not this time.

I am truly on my own.

Well, that's not entirely true when I hear a dog barking in the distance. The noise grows louder until who that bark belongs to ends up in my back garden.

A black-and-white dog runs around the olive groves like he owns the place. He's clearly been here before.

I quickly make my way down the stairs and out through the kitchen. The moment he sees me, he comes running toward me, his pink tongue lolling from the corner of his mouth.

"Hey, boy," I coo as I crouch.

The dog crashes into my arms, licking my face excitedly.

"Who do you belong to?" I ask, unable to contain my amusement.

It almost feels foreign to laugh.

"Are you hungry?"

He barks happily.

Just as I stand, I hear a branch snap. On instinct, I turn and throat punch the young man behind me. He clutches his throat, gasping for air. I'm about to poke out his eye when the dog runs over to the man and anxiously circles him, ensuring he's all right.

It's apparent this man is the dog's owner, and I just throat punched him.

"Oh my God, I am so sorry," I say, trying to help him. He waves me off, backing away as he gasps for air.

Not that I can blame him. I did just attack him.

"You shouldn't trespass." I try to reason that my actions aren't totally unhinged. But to keep a low profile, I can't be punching people in the throat.

Note to self…

A string of Sicilian leaves him when he eventually gets the air back to his lungs. I have no clue what he's saying, but it's evident he doesn't mean any harm.

"No Sicilian," I say with a smile.

Although I know Italian, the Sicilian dialect is foreign to me.

"No English," he replies with a thick accent.

Whether I'm lonely, or maybe the company is a distraction from the thoughts in my head, I make a hand gesture asking if he would like a drink.

He nods and waits for me to lead the way, seeing as I just attacked him. I doubt he wants a repeat performance of that. So I turn and walk up the stairs. The steps are hot, and it's only now that I realize what I'm wearing, and it's not much.

Sleep shorts and a tank. And that's all. No underwear. No shoes. And my hair is a snarled mess. Not that it matters. I don't plan on seeing him ever again.

I look around the large kitchen, wondering where the glasses are kept. I've been drinking straight from the tap, which is uncouth. I suppose I should try to act semi-human if I'm to oversee Gianna's business.

I open and close the cupboards, hunting for glassware. I eventually find them and open the fridge, and I'm surprised to find it stocked with food and drinks. No doubt, Gianna's doing.

Even thousands of miles away, she's still looking after me.

I reach for the bottle of juice and pour us each a glass. I offer it to him and only just realize how tall he is. And how blue his eyes are. They contrast with his black hair. His handsome face is chiseled and covered in a five-o'clock shadow, which emphasizes the cleft in his chin.

He appears a little older than me. Maybe twenty-two. Not that it matters, but why am I suddenly wondering what his name is?

He sips his juice, watching me over the rim of his glass.

It's quite comfortable being in his presence. There is no pressure to talk, seeing as we don't understand each other.

"*Mi chiamo Nico.*"

"I'm Valentina. What's your dog's name?"

He arches a dark brow, clearly not understanding me.

I reach for a white bowl and pour some water into it, then place it on the floor for the dog. Nico understands when I point at the thirsty K-9.

"*Lupo.*"

I smile as I pat the dog's scruffy head. "Hi, Lupo."

He barks in response.

Nico finishes his juice and places the empty glass in the sink. "*Grazie.*"

"*Prego.*"

Nico's eyes widen, but I wave him off with a smile. "I know Italian. Sicilian, not so much."

He nods politely, oblivious to what I said. But I like it. I like that we don't understand each other. We merely coexist with no burden of making small talk.

I do wonder what his backstory is.

I wonder how long he's lived here and if he or his family knows of Gianna.

The thought of knowing more about Gianna is tempting because she's still as much of a mystery now as she was when I first met her. But it also feels like a betrayal of her trust.

Lenny's judgmental voice sounds in my head. *"Why are you so loyal to her?"*

Truth be told, I don't know.

She saved us when no one else did, when no one would take a chance on two misfits like Lenny and me. She protected us and showed us affection in the best way she could. I accepted that she isn't someone who shows love the way most do.

But her actions prove she cares.

If she didn't, I wouldn't be here.

What I did was my choice, and it was a stupid choice at that.

But I couldn't stop myself.

I was sick of waiting.

I was sick of being weak.

I was sick of my childhood memories controlling me.

Yes, I am now a fugitive on the run, but ironically, I have never felt freer than I do right now.

No one knows who I am.

Or what I've done.

"You can't run away from who you are."

It seems my father's voice follows me wherever I go.

A part of me begins to fantasize about what it would be like to start over in a place where I am no one. I started my life this way and wanted more, but now I somehow want that simplicity once again.

I could be like everyone else and blend into a society I've never been a part of. I could get a nine-to-five job. I could gossip to my girlfriends about my loving boyfriend, whose name is Tom, and our three Bengal cats.

I could be normal.

"Who are you fooling? You can never be normal."

He knows me better than I know myself, and the reason for that is because he *is* me. Perhaps, I don't hear my father, but rather, it's my own conscience.

Memories of Father Merry's mutilated corpse hanging from

the crucifix flash before my eyes, confirming what I know to be true—I can never be normal, and honestly, I don't want to be.

Things here are slow-moving, and eventually, I will get bored. Thoughts of a normal life make me want to vomit, and I can't help but want to set something on fire for something to do.

I'm so messed up. And the only person who loved me and accepted me, flaws and all, is a billion miles away.

My heart aches.

I miss him.

I miss him so fucking much it hurts.

I'm homesick. Rather, I'm Lenny-sick because he is my home.

Toying with the black crystal around my neck, which hangs from the necklace Lenny gave me for my birthday, I realize that I don't know what it feels like to live life without Lenny. Although we argued half the time, I knew he'd always be on my side…until I left.

I have no doubt he meant his parting words. And the next time we see one another, one of us will be gravely hurt.

I don't know how I got here, but this is my life now. I have no one, and I've learned it's better this way.

Nico says something and leaves, taking Lupo, not that I blame him. I'm hardly any company.

I wonder about Cat. Did he perish in the fire? He was my only friend, and I couldn't even protect him.

I truly am alone, and for the sins I've committed, I deserve the solitude. So I accept my fate.

I am no one…once again.

CHAPTER 2

LENNY

This house is fucking beautiful. And we're safe. But the fact that it's Aldo's house feels all shades of wrong because Aldo is now nothing but ashes, burned to death in the house that was never my home.

Lewis sleeps in one of the many guest rooms. Still exhausted, he's sleeping away years of abuse from his bones.

Bria sits behind me, stroking Cat in a catatonic state.

And me, I'm standing on the balcony, staring into the darkness wondering what the fuck I'm supposed to do.

It's taking every ounce of strength I have not to jump on

a plane and find Valentina. I found out from one of Gianna's men that she'd been shipped off to Italy to take over Gianna's enterprise, but he didn't know much more, which is why his torso is weighed down and sits on the bottom of the ocean. His other extremities are scattered at random locations, never to be identified.

This is my life now.

Bria hasn't spoken a word since we fled. That was a week ago.

I don't feel sorry for her because no one wants pity, but I am sad she lost her dad. He was a great man.

His last words will forever haunt me.

"Her mother is…Gianna. Gianna is Valentina's mother."

Clenching the baluster, I vow that Gianna will pay dearly for what she's done.

She knew who Valentina was from the very beginning, yet she treated her like a stranger, nothing but a pawn in her game. She trained her own daughter to be a lethal weapon.

What sort of mother does that?

My mother was hardly a saint, but what Gianna has done is psychopathic.

I don't know what I'm supposed to do with this information. I can't tell anyone, as Valentina will be in danger. Regardless of what she's done, the need to protect her remains.

I want to be with her, but I can't if Gianna is still alive. If I kill her, Valentina will hate me, so I'm stuck.

Damned if I do. And damned if I don't.

The only way for Valentina to listen is to show her what a lying snake Gianna is, because now that I know the truth, I plan to use it to my advantage. I'm going to let Gianna hang herself. And she will.

She thinks she's got off scot-free now that Aldo is dead. But I know the truth. Ironically, she trained me, and now, I'm her rival.

What a silly move on her behalf because I know her strategies. I know the way she fights. And I know how she conducts business. I could ruin her with my eyes closed, but I won't because she will always have one up on me.

Valentina is her secret weapon.

That's the reason she adopted us both. I was always meant to be Gianna's insurance policy.

It all makes sense now why Aldo wanted to adopt Valentina first. He knew this would happen. He knew the power she would hold. And Valentina isn't even aware of the power she wields.

I'm stuck between my head and my heart. I save the woman I love, sacrificing myself because, without solid evidence that Gianna is her mother, Valentina will kill me for insinuating such a thing. Or I go up against her and leave it to fate and let the better man win.

She knows how I fight.

As I know how she does.

There will be no winners.

Just a blood feud that will stem for years because neither of us will back down.

I tried to save her, but now...I must save us both because I won't give up on her. Just like when we were kids down by the lake, I will push her to the point of breaking in hopes she sees the truth.

And in the meantime, I hope Bria doesn't kill her first.

"Get up," I order, turning around.

Bria sits with her knees drawn up to her chest, cuddling Cat. Her eyes are bloodshot, her pink hair thrown into a limp ponytail. She's wearing an oversized tee and no shoes. I understand she's grieving, but there's no better way to get over pain than by facing it head-on.

"We're going to fight."

That gets her attention, and she finally meets my eyes. Something inside her has changed. Bria was never innocent. But the way she views the world has changed. Losing her father will shape Bria into someone she never thought she'd become.

But death does that.

And so does revenge.

Soon, nothing else will matter than avenging her father and righting all the wrongs done to her and her legacy, and the first person in her sights will be Valentina.

Valentina knows how to fight and will beat Bria with her eyes closed. I need Bria to be able to defend herself because she's on my side.

Valentina chose her side, and it's not mine. So, for now, Bria and I fight together to bring down the woman I love in hopes to save her.

"Don't make me ask you again."

She doesn't have the energy to fight, and her curiosity gets the better of her when she stands.

"Leave Cat."

She does as I say.

We walk in silence through the house until we reach the basement. But this isn't any typical basement. This is a martial arts sanctuary.

It's decked out in heavy bags, sparring gear, and every weapon needed to train a skilled fighter.

Scanning over the weaponry on the brick wall, I reach for the rattan kali sticks. Something easy to test her skills.

I toss it at Bria, who catches it with confusion in her eyes. "To survive, we must fight. We must fight with our heads, not our hearts," I say, circling her.

She turns with me, ensuring her back is never turned. But she leaves herself open, which is her first lesson. I whack her in the ribs.

A pained grunt leaves her. "What the fuck?" she cries,

clutching her side.

"That was lesson one. Never let your guard down."

"Lesson number one? I didn't realize I was here to be schooled."

As she's mouthing off, I spin and thump the stick into the back of her knee. She buckles forward.

"Lesson number two. Don't talk back. A smart mouth will get you killed."

"Lenny, fuck off!"

She's angry, which will be her downfall. I show her how so when I connect with her stomach with the end of the kali stick.

Her anger turns to full-blown rage as she charges at me, swinging her stick like an amateur. It takes me three seconds to disarm and slam her back against the padded wall. She tries to buck me off, but I place my forearm over her throat, subduing her.

Her green eyes are on fire. "You've proved your point."

"I wasn't trying to prove a point. It was a test to see if you could fight. You failed."

She eyes me something wicked.

"Good, use that anger to win a fight. But never rule with your emotions. They will get you killed."

How I wish Gianna wasn't right in that lesson she taught us, but she is. Emotions make you weak. They force you to do things you might not usually do. I'm a perfect example of this.

"My emotions died with my father," Bria spits. "Now, your little girlfriend suffers the same fate."

It's a low blow, but I don't let her verbal stab affect me because that would defeat the purpose of this exercise. And besides, I did promise Bria her vengeance.

"You don't stand a chance against Valentina. She would beat you blindfolded with both arms tied behind her back. We'll train every day until you're ready. You do what you're told. You don't question my decisions. You don't talk back. Are we clear?"

Bria snickers.

"I said"—I press down harder on her windpipe—"are we clear?"

I don't release her until she eventually nods.

She gasps for air when I do.

"This isn't a choice either of us made. But this is our life now. We either fight or concede."

"There's no way that bitch Gianna is getting away with what she did to my dad."

Finally, we agree on something.

"So where do we start?"

Picking up her fallen kali stick, I toss it at her. "Again, and this time, fight me like you mean it."

Her eyes narrow, and I can see she loves to hate me right now, which is good. This is the only way to be because I too lost myself when Valentina left. I have nothing left but hate.

It seems Gianna taught me something after all.

Bria and I trained until she could no longer stand.

I'll give it to her—the girl has guts. Something I always knew. But now, she has something to prove. She understands the legacy she carries because the Cattaneo name holds much respect and power. And now that Aldo is dead, it's open season on us.

We're merely seen as kids trying to fill the shoes of a great man. Every man and his dog wants what is rightfully Bria's. The only other reputable leader is Gianna. And it'll be a cold day in hell before she takes this empire to make it her own.

Which is why I'm sitting at Aldo's desk, snooping through his laptop.

I need to play catch-up and fast because our leadership *will* be challenged. And when the time comes, Bria and I must be ready.

I've found Aldo's suppliers—both legal and illegal—and contacted them to organize a meeting to ensure they know who I am and what will happen if they fuck me over. Aldo's crystal ruse was fucking genius, and I plan on carrying on with his brilliance.

I've called a meeting tonight with Aldo's men.

Although they pledged their allegiance to me, I know there is talk of a coup. I'm also certain some men have jumped ship and are now on Gianna's side. These are the men I plan to make an example of.

With the important bases covered, I am left with the folder named *Bellezza*.

I know this is everything Aldo has on Valentina. It touches me that he calls her such a name, while her mother instead encouraged her first kill when she was merely a child.

I move the cursor over to the file and click on it.

The hundreds of files and images load, and it's like a spinning top of Valentina's life flashing before me. I get lost in her eyes, the sad eyes of Valentina as a child, of when I met her. I think of the atrocities of what was done to her, and although it's not an excuse, I understand why she's wired the way she is.

She's been taught nothing but hate. But then I think of the love she showed for Cat and me, demonstrating she isn't all bad. That is why I fight for her even when she doesn't defend herself.

Once the files stop loading, I click on the one dated the year she was born. When I do and see a baby, bundled in a pink fleece blanket with soft dark hair, I close my eyes and take a deep breath. I need to compose myself.

How could Gianna do this to her?

She was an innocent child. It's nature versus nurture because Gianna made her this way. I have no doubt that, born to different parents, Valentina would have flourished and not been plagued with the demons that eat away at her soul.

I open my eyes and continue my search.

What shocks me, however, is that Aldo seemed to believe that Valentina's father, serial killer Patrick O'Loughlin, was not actually her father. Aldo knew who her mother was, but it seemed he was on the hunt for Valentina's biological father, as this would help him convince Valentina of the truth.

All I have is a name: Francesco.

But who is he?

I see the family tree he had pieced together and notice a Sister Margarette. This was Valentina's supposed mother, which we know is bullshit. However, it appears that there is indeed a Sister Margarette who was friends with Gianna.

I have the photo evidence to prove it.

Sister Margarette *was* a sister at the orphanage, which explains Father Merry's obsession with Valentina. Father Merry clearly had a hard-on for Sister Margarette. So Gianna dropped Valentina off at the orphanage doors, pretending that Valentina was Sister Margarette and Patrick's daughter because it appears the sister did fall for the serial killer, but she never had his child.

Gianna exploited the sister's immorality to cover her ass and abandoned Valentina, but why?

Why didn't she want Valentina?

Was she doing it to save her own skin?

Or could it be perhaps she was doing it to save Valentina?

Valentina's entire life has been a lie.

And I finally have the evidence to prove it. Perhaps no blood needs to be spilled between Valentina and me after all.

I have this proof in front of me, and I also have the whereabouts of Margarette—Orchard Parks State Hospital.

No doubt, she was put in here by Gianna to cover the truth, and because of Margarette's sins, she went willingly as penance.

Valentina would have gone to see Margarette, believing this was her mother. So why didn't Margarette tell the truth?

I suppose there's only one way to find out.

Gianna has manipulated every situation to suit her and to control her own daughter. She is worse than I ever imagined.

Angered, I slam my fist onto the hard desk, seething.

How can someone be so fucking evil?

The door opens, and Bria pokes her head in. I slam the laptop shut because I don't want her to see any of this. No one can.

If she notices my strange behavior, she doesn't let on. "It's time to go."

Looking at my watch, I realize she's right. I have been in here for hours, lost in Gianna's web of lies.

"Everything all right?"

"Peachy," I reply, unable to keep the irritation from my tone. She doesn't push.

We make our way toward the garage, where we have our pick of luxury cars. I decide on a black SUV.

I fired Aldo's driver because I intend to keep my circle small. I don't trust anyone, and every man and woman has to prove themselves. If I suspect they're a rat, well, there are no second chances. This is the only way to gain respect.

Bria is quiet. But it's clear behind that silence that her mind is deafening.

Bria was brought into my world for a reason. I'm not one for coincidences. If it wasn't for her, I wouldn't be here. The fact she was stealing her father's drugs and selling them for a profit helps us out. No one can know she was stealing, however, because this would reveal weakness on Aldo's behalf and portray Bria as disloyal.

But she has the knowledge that I lack, and we need that to succeed.

I don't care why she was stealing from her father. That was another life ago. Now, both of us must leave our old selves behind and rebuild to stay alive.

We pull into the old chocolate factory where I first met Aldo—seems fitting.

The nefarious scene is set in this derelict neighborhood because anyone who enters these streets doesn't want to be seen. We mind our business and don't cause any trouble. It's a code that works because, like every person here, we're all delinquents.

We make our way into the crumbling building, and it surprises me to see a lot more men than anticipated. Word has spread, and it seems we're under the microscope.

Tonight is a test for us all.

We're being closely scrutinized and sized up. Some men nod in respect, while others snicker among themselves at the two kids who are supposed to take over from a man who was respected and feared. Our reign will be challenged by those who think they're superior.

Or by those who think they know better because of their age.

But little do they know that the shit I've lived through and the things I've seen make me feel a thousand years old.

And tonight, I'll prove that to them.

I don't carry any weapons because anyone can assert their authority by waving a gun around. No, I intend to gain respect the old-fashioned way—through fear.

Bria and I stand before a group of about thirty. The chatter dies down when I simply wait for them to shut the fuck up.

I eye each man, assuming each one is a foe, not a friend.

"I don't care who you once were," I commence with. "Or the part you played in Aldo's business. Aldo is dead because he was careless. He died because he led with his heart. Love makes you weak."

Gianna's teachings are correct when it comes to war, and I hate that I sound like her, but I was taught by the best.

Bria stiffens beside me but doesn't speak.

"Lesson number one: If you are vulnerable, your enemy will exploit that for their gain. You are all disposable. Don't think you're special, because you're not. I will replace you with some other chump who has something to prove. No matter how determined you are, there is always someone hungrier, someone who will betray their own grandmother for the only thing that matters in this world—money.

"Gianna Ricci is our enemy. She stands between total control."

"Isn't she your mother?" One asshole up front snickers.

He's young. At a guess, early thirties. He looks like he should be teaching kindergarten in his chinos and crisp white shirt, not out here with us malevolent bunch.

"Gianna adopted me, yes, but is she my family? The answer is no."

"How do we know you're not working together? Seems a little convenient that you enter the scene and Aldo is killed."

I stare him dead in the eyes as he's doing this to get a rise out of me. "What's your name?"

He wasn't expecting that question and looks at his friend for support.

Walking toward them, I tower over both weasels. "You need

your friend to speak for you, is that right? Or perhaps you're that fucking stupid you don't even know your own name."

His nostrils flare. "My name is—"

He never finishes his sentence because I punch him straight in the jaw.

He staggers back into the men behind him, but they push him forward, not wanting a part of his rebellion.

"Deaf and stupid, it seems. I don't care what your fucking name is. But seeing as you can't shut your mouth, I'll call you Donkey."

Donkey from *Shrek* seems like an appropriate nickname for this know-it-all.

He wipes his bloody lip with the back of his hand as he comes back to a stand.

"So let's try that again. What's your name?"

The man inhales through his teeth, but eventually, he concedes. "Donkey."

I grin. "That's right. You're Donkey, and don't ever forget it. Lesson number two: Don't ask stupid questions."

His acquaintance steps away from him, showing me that his friend is no friend at all. Other men grin, thankful they're not in the firing line. But little do they know that Donkey has passed the test while the rest of them have failed.

And because of that, I choose him to be my right-hand man.

"We run this business my way. It's time for change. I know how Gianna works. And I plan on using that to take the bitch down. Each and every one of you is on probation. Betray me, and I will take your fucking heads.

"There are no second chances. You fuck up, you deal with the consequences. So choose wisely. I ask for loyalty, and in return, you will be rewarded greatly."

The men are quiet, and that's because they're weak. I suspect most will attempt to overthrow me. Or some will try to make a deal with Gianna.

Troubled times are ahead.

But I'm ready.

"Although I don't care about you, don't mistake that as me not knowing who you are...or who your family is."

The silence is deafening. You threaten a man's family, and they'll listen.

"We're done for now."

The men look confused, like they were waiting for an epiphany. But there is none.

Tonight was for me to weed out the strong from the weak and for the men to see I am someone not to be fucked with.

This is personal for me, and with Valentina gone, I have nothing left to lose.

The men soon realize I'm serious and quickly scatter, no doubt to discuss whether I'm a suitable leader or not. But I don't care what they think.

"Donkey."

He walks toward me apprehensively and waits for me to speak.

"Congratulations, you now work directly with me."

It seems he's taken lesson two on board as he doesn't ask any questions.

"You're going to gather the names, addresses, and information on all these men. Think you can do that?"

He nods.

With that, Bria and I walk back to the car since there's nothing more to say.

CHAPTER 3

VALENTINA
ONE MONTH LATER

I t's amazing how quickly I've fallen into a routine.

I wake at dawn.

Go for a run.

Eat.

Train.

Sleep.

And repeat.

I've not ventured past the property line because I don't feel the need to explore, and that's because I'm happy.

Once a week, a box of groceries sits at my door.

I have everything I need.

A part of me does wonder, however, when Gianna will call on me because I sense this silence isn't forever. Knowing Gianna, this is one of her tests.

So I simply wait for instructions.

She has conditioned me to think this way, which, being away from her, I now see is wrong. But I don't know any different. And I have nowhere else to go.

I've run for miles and am completely famished.

As I walk toward my home and the familiar feel of gravel beneath my sneakers crunches in time with my steps, I realize that for weeks, I've not heard my father's voice. The silence has been welcomed. Out here, there is nothing but me.

And the longer I stay, the more it feels like home.

I see the wooden box of groceries at my door like every Monday past. I wonder what produce Gianna has organized for me.

Picking up the box, I take it inside and set it on the kitchen counter. I remove the perishable items and place them in the fridge. I hum along to the Italian music playing softly from an old radio I found. I never switch it off because the noise gives me comfort, perhaps tricking myself into thinking I'm not alone.

And just like that, I'm not.

"*Ciao.*" Nico knocks on the back door. He waits for me to invite him in, seeing as the last time he turned up unannounced, I throat punched him.

I stand with a bunch of carrots in my hand, staring at him. "Hi," I finally say.

Lupo comes charging in, jumping up on me and licking my face happily.

Nico smiles and enters.

I don't know what it is about him, but I don't feel he's a threat. He just seems like a...normal young man. Nothing like Lenny.

My heart does a tiny flip-flop just thinking of his name.

Angrily, I toss the carrots into the fridge because thoughts like that will only get me hurt.

Or more hurt, if that's even possible.

Once I turn, Nico slides an envelope across the white marble counter. My name is written on the front.

I swallow past the lump in my throat.

The day has come.

I eye him and the envelope.

Have I mistaken him for a friend when he is in fact a foe?

He reads my suspicion and quickly reaches for something in his brown leather satchel.

On instinct, I lunge for the knife block, but soon stop in my tracks when he retrieves a small book. He rifles through it and turns to a page, staring at it intently.

He licks his lips before saying with a thick accent, "Postman."

I'm impressed that Nico went out and purchased a translation book. He could have used his phone, but perhaps he likes living off-grid too.

That one word puts my mind at ease because he isn't the one who wrote the letter. He is simply the deliveryman.

I stare at the envelope like it will detonate at any moment because, without a doubt, this is from Gianna. It's time to do what I came here for. But the thought turns my stomach.

And I don't mean in the figurative sense.

I mean that literally as I run to the sink and throw up.

Nausea so brutal suddenly overcomes me, I waver on my feet and would have fallen if not for Nico catching me.

Usually, I would shrug any help away, but I literally cannot stand, so I allow Nico to lead me into the living room where I lie down on the velvet couch. Nico places a knitted blanket over me.

How fucking embarrassing.

I don't need a man looking after me, but as Nico returns from the kitchen with a juice in hand, I push aside my pride and accept his help. I slowly gulp down the juice in fear it'll come back up.

So far, so good.

Nico crouches by me and places a hand to my clammy

forehead. "*Ospedale.*"

But I frantically shake my head.

I understand that word, and that word is hospital. There's no way I'm going there.

"No, I'm okay. Just tired."

Nico looks at me confused, so I reach for the book he left on the coffee table and scan through it until I find the word for tired.

"*Stanca.*"

He nods, and I realize this tiny book is our only way of communicating. How incredibly old-school. I love it.

Nausea and dizziness hit me once again, so I slump back down into the cushions, groaning as I place my forearm across my eyes to block the morning sun.

If this is my response to a single letter, then how am I expected to carry out what Gianna demands of me? Have I lost my nerve because this simple life has shown me that this is what I secretly crave?

I surrender to sleep because those questions are ones I don't want to face.

Now, and perhaps ever.

I wake to the smell of something delicious, which surprises

me, considering I was throwing up my guts not that long ago.

Opening my eyes slowly, I see that it's dark out. I must have slept the day away.

Lupo sleeps on the floor beside me, which means Nico is still here.

This is so out of character for me to let my guard down this way.

I don't like it.

Coming to a slow sitting position, I brush the hair from my face and am thankful the nausea has subsided. It troubles me that I reacted that way.

What's happening to me?

Peering around the room, I see that the golden crucifix ornament I threw into a drawer sits on the mantel once again.

It's the cue I needed to remind myself of who I am and what I have done.

Angered, I stand and charge into the kitchen to tell Nico to mind his business and to get out of my house. That religious relic has no place in my home because there is no God. But what I observe has the anger in me simmering because Nico has cooked me chicken soup.

He places a soup bowl onto the neatly set table.

A large ceramic bowl with oranges printed around the sides sits in the center of the table, filled with freshly baked bread. Olives, cured meats, cheese, and fruits complete this feast, and

I suddenly feel undeserving, seeing as I was about to kick him out.

He smiles when he notices me.

Why does he do that?

I don't understand.

Lenny never used to smile at me that way. Perhaps it's because we never really had much to smile about. Both foreigners in a world that chewed us up and spat us out time and time again. All we did was merely attempt to survive, clinging onto the other in case we drowned.

But with Nico, those feelings aren't present. I don't know what I feel because I've never experienced it before.

Nico pulls out a seat for me.

Now is the time to tell him to get out and never return, but I find myself doing the complete opposite and sitting down. I peer at the food in front of me. It does look good. My empty stomach growls, demanding to be fed.

I run my fingers over the mismatched silverware and realize this is the first meal I've sat down for. Yes, I was fed and fed well at Gianna's, but did we ever sit down at a setting such as this and have a "family" dinner?

No.

I usually ate my meal, standing at the kitchen counter, alone.

Everything in Gianna's house was perfect and had a place,

unlike Lenny and me.

I never had an issue with it because I didn't know any better. But now, presented with this scenario, I see that under that perfection, things were so distorted.

What is wrong with me?

Why am I suddenly nostalgic, thinking of all the things I never had? Realizing all the things I was made to do because Gianna didn't want us to be human. To be human, we were to feel, and to feel, she couldn't…control us.

An epiphany hits, and I see Lenny in the corner of the kitchen, casually lighting a cigarette. *"I told you so."*

So my father is now replaced with Lenny. I *am* going fucking crazy.

The imaginary Lenny is still able to evoke butterflies and make me feel things I shouldn't.

I'm not sure what I'm supposed to do with this revelation. I don't even know if it's how I feel.

Everything is so muddled.

My head is a mess.

"This is the first time you're away from her, away from her poison. You know the truth, tesoro mio."

Imaginary Lenny is still a pain in my ass, I see.

Nico sits across from me, watching me closely. I feel incredibly rude, so I smile. Well, I try my best not to scowl as I reach for the spoon.

The soup is delicious.

With my hunger returning, I guzzle down the soup and wipe away any remaining liquid with pieces of crunchy bread. I don't stop eating until my bowl is clean. And it's then that I realize I still have company.

Sheepishly peering up at Nico, I feel my cheeks redden. This just confirms that I'm not accustomed to eating in the company of others. I expect him to excuse himself and run out the door, never to return.

Instead, he pushes the plate of meats and cheese to me. "*Mangiare.*"

He just told me to eat. Not that I need the encouragement.

But I watch as he wraps a piece of prosciutto around a slice of melon and places it into his mouth. He licks away a droplet of juice from his bottom lip. The way he savors it, I assume it's good. But I've never tasted such a strange combination before.

He does the same again, but this time, he offers it to me.

I accept without hesitation, and when I taste the sweet and salty combination, I understand what the fuss is about.

"Is good?" he asks.

"It's very good," I reply around a mouthful of food.

He laughs, appearing happy I have enjoyed his cooking.

My first meal with another wasn't a complete disaster after all.

It's after midnight by the time Nico leaves.

Once we clean the dishes, we sit in silence, listening to old Italian music on the back porch. It wasn't uncomfortable. It was…nice.

However, now that he's gone, reality sets in, and I sit in my bed, staring at the envelope on my lap. *This is why I'm here*, I remind myself. This was never a "get out of jail free" card. I'm here to pay back my dues.

"You owe her nothing."

"Shut up, Lenny," I mumble, annoyed that even hundreds of miles apart, he's still annoying me.

It's the push I need as I slide my finger under the seal and open the envelope. I unfold the piece of paper and take a deep breath.

It's an address with a date, a time, and a name.

Madam Gazella.

That's all.

No further instructions.

It seems I can only outrun my past for so long.

The silence was nice while it lasted.

I barely slept because every time I closed my eyes, all I saw was that address. I gave up on sleeping and decided to go for my morning run. Halfway through, however, I turned back because my legs felt heavy, and I wanted to throw up again.

Once upon a time, I enjoyed the silence, but now, it grates on my nerves.

I really could use Google Maps right now because I have no idea where I'm supposed to meet whoever I'm meeting at the provided address. The meeting is tonight at eight o'clock.

My serenity is long gone, and my stomach is in constant knots. My hand trembles as I fill a glass with water from the tap.

What is this response I'm experiencing?

I've not been taught to feel, and now it seems as though all those repressed feelings are bursting at the seams. Has everything I've done, everything I've experienced, finally caught up to me?

I feel Father Merry's mouth and his hands all over me.

I see my mother's terrified face when she saw me. She saw me as nothing but a monster.

But at the forefront, I remember saying goodbye to the man I love with every beat of my heart.

I'm so fucking broken, and I don't think I'll ever be healed.

I'm merely holding on to pieces of myself in hopes that I don't fade away.

Nausea tackles me once more, and I race to the bathroom with my hand over my mouth, only just making it in time. I heave and heave, hoping to dispel some of this bitterness within. But it only burns.

Tears cascade down my cheeks as I slam my fists against the toilet bowl, screaming in agony.

My head and heart battle against each other because I don't want to feel; I've been taught not to. But my heart has ruptured, and each memory tears at my core.

"Don't care whether you live or die? Think of this moment whenever you fool yourself into thinking that is true."

Memories of Lenny holding me underwater assault me, and I finally understand the lesson he wished for me to learn. I had switched my emotions off for so long, and now the switch has been flicked, and I can't turn it back off.

"I hate you."

"No, tesoro mio, *you hate yourself that you don't."*

I sob uncontrollably, allowing myself to grieve for the first time in my life. I cry a lifetime of tears because this is the only way to move forward.

I purge myself until nothing is left to give, and only when my tears dry do I lift my head from the toilet bowl.

My throat and stomach are raw, but I feel better.

I will never be healed from what I've experienced, but I must say goodbye to the old Valentina because I am no longer that person.

What my future holds, I do not know.

What I do know is that I am stronger than the things that tried to beat me. I have the scars to prove it. I need to let go of who I was and who I loved and embrace this new life. I've been given a second chance. This is my new home.

This is the new me.

Flushing the toilet, I wearily stand and look at myself in the mirror. I vow to my reflection that from this day forward, I'll never forget who I am and the power I hold.

I am Valentina Ricci.

And here, I will rule.

Lenny's reflection stands beside mine, those eyes pulling me in as they always do.

But to move on, I also must let him go.

He is the past. And no matter my love for him, love will never be enough.

I turn the faucet to hot and watch as the mirror fogs up. Lenny's face fades by the second.

"You cannot forget me, tesoro mio. *I am a part of you."*

"I can try," I reply to make-believe Lenny, watching as his image is nothing but a ghost.

The pain in my heart is unbearable, but I think the pain will forever be there as a reminder that Lenny was real; that what we had was real.

The pain is a reminder that, for a small fraction of time, I loved and was loved in return.

And what a bittersweet memory it'll forever be.

I swipe my palm down the mirror, wiping Lenny away.

All I see now is the face of someone I was always destined to become.

I dress and feel remotely better. Perhaps this is what closure feels like.

I still have no idea how I'm going to get to where I need to be tonight. It's time I rejoin the land of the living and get myself a cell. Or at least access to a computer.

Until then, I need to rely on a Good Samaritan.

I slip into my white sandals and tie back my hair as it's a warm night. My appearance is that of any other girl my age. But I am nothing like them.

The moment I step outside, I tip my face to the heavens and inhale the clean air. If I'm going to live life as a criminal, then what better place to be?

I realize this is the first time I've left the property. The land my home is on is big enough for me to run circles around and still not cover the entirety of it. So as I get closer to the steel gates, a sense of anxiety overcomes me.

But I quash it down because I have a job to do.

Once out of the gates, I scour my surroundings and commit everything to memory. The street is dead quiet, and as for neighbors, there are none. However, I continue my journey because Nico has to live nearby. He is the only person I know, so hopefully he can help.

Even though everything is unfamiliar, I don't feel displaced. Perhaps it's because with a new place comes new memories, ones where no one knows who I really am.

I follow the gravel road for what feels like miles until I hear the revving of a motorcycle. I follow the noise, hoping that my hunch is right.

Nico comes and goes on foot, which means he must live close by. Not to mention Lupo wandered into my yard like he owns the place. This must be his neighborhood. And when I stand at the bottom of a driveway and peer at the small but charming farmhouse, I'm glad I trusted my gut.

Nico is tinkering with his motorbike, oblivious to me admiring his very naked chest. I wasn't expecting him to be packing that six-pack and broad shoulders. But I guess that's because I wasn't really looking.

However, now that I am, I'm not sure I can look away.

Lupo gives me away as he barks happily.

Nico peers up to see what the noise is about, and when he sees me, he waves with a smile.

I stop gawking and wave back before walking up the

driveway. The brick house is modest, but the fruit trees surrounding it are simply beautiful. I assume by the farm machinery that this is Nico's work and residence. I wonder if he lives here with his family. Or a partner.

"*Ciao*," he says, wiping his greasy hands on a rag. His chest is slathered in smudges of oil.

"*Ciao*," I reply, ensuring I keep my eyes on his.

Our inability to converse soon loses its charm, and I decide to use Google Translate ASAP.

Reaching into my pocket, I show Nico the note with the address. "Can you take me here?"

He looks at his watch and nods.

A relieved sigh leaves me.

He makes a hand gesture that he's going inside.

I gesture back that I'll stay here and wait for him.

We stand staring at one another, both openly checking the other out.

He is tall, dark, and Italian—of course he's handsome. But he doesn't set every part of me alight with a look alone.

I quickly look away, embarrassed and feeling guilty for looking at another man.

Baby steps, I remind myself because my love for Lenny won't disappear overnight. But when Nico walks inside, I wonder if my love for Lenny will disappear at all.

I pat Lupo as I wait for Nico. I feel uncomfortable all of a sudden, which proves I fooled myself into thinking I could try this normal on for size.

Nico returns a moment later. Thankfully, he had gone inside to put on a shirt. He offers me a helmet. I look at it, then back at him, confused.

He gestures that the helmet is to be put on my head, as he believes my confusion stems from not understanding the role of a helmet.

"No car?" I ask, mimicking turning a steering wheel.

He shakes his head.

He gets on the bike and looks at me, waiting for me to sit behind him. But honestly, I don't know what to do as I've never ridden a bike before. He extends his hand, and his eyes reflect nothing but kindness.

I read no ulterior motives. I really need to arrive at this meeting on time.

After putting the helmet on my head, I place my hand into his and accept his help as he guides me onto the back of the bike. I don't know what to do with my hands or body, to be honest. Nico guides my hands to rest around his waist and encourages me to shuffle forward and press my chest to his back. He rubs his fingers over my knuckles kindly, assuring me that I'm safe.

Once I'm settled, the engine roars to life, and he turns with precision. Giving the bike two revs, he zips down the driveway, gravel spurring up under the wheels. Lupo barks excitedly, following us until Nico turns onto the street and roars down it. I grip him tighter because I can now see why he encouraged me to hold him like a spider monkey. Holding on to him is literally the reason I haven't fallen off. I didn't realize how much you need to trust the driver because it's what stands between you and death.

Nico takes the turns with ease, and once I no longer fear for my life, I appreciate this beautiful landscape before me. Sicily is abundant with fruit trees, the vibrant colors standing out against the backdrop of dormant volcanoes in the island's mountainous landscape.

As we drive down a narrow road that wraps around a mountain, I close my eyes and grip Nico tighter. His abs ripple from his laughter. I like the way that feels.

If I didn't need to hold on to him, I would let him go because I don't like these feelings he's evoking in me. It feels like I'm betraying Lenny.

However, I think about Bria and Lenny together and how he didn't seem to feel guilty for making me watch him with another woman, a woman who I know has feelings for him. The memory still burns, and I wonder if they're now a thing.

Gianna did kill Bria's father and Lenny's mentor, so the need for revenge will bond them. It'll have them depending on each other and existing in their own little world. I should know because once upon a time, I was a part of Lenny's world.

Now, we are worlds apart.

The ride into town takes about thirty minutes. I try my best to remember all the important landmarks because this is the first and last time I'll rely on anyone. Nico turns a corner, and when we arrive at a street market, I wonder if perhaps we're lost.

But when he finds a spot to park and kills the motor, I realize we're here.

The sight before me is that of a vibrant street market. The backdrop is the main street. It's lined with old white buildings that appear to be three-story apartments. The occupants are out on their balconies, sipping a glass of wine or smoking a cigarette over the balustrade, taking in the bustle below.

Vendors are spread out as far as the eye can see, their striped umbrellas a burst of color and fun. The stalls sell every fresh produce you could ever want, as well as clothes and ornaments. The smells are a blend of spicy and sweet.

I cautiously get off the bike. My legs resemble jelly as my feet touch the ground. I take off the helmet and unfasten my ponytail to shake out my hair. Once I'm done, I pass the helmet to Nico, who I notice is staring.

I have no idea why, but I ignore him because I only have twenty minutes to find the elusive Madam Gazella in the sea of people.

With no time to waste, I quickly enter the bustling street

and decide to walk up and down it. Surely whoever I'm meeting will stand out in some way.

The lively market is filled with excited patrons who sample local food and explore this culture-rich place. I don't realize Nico has followed me until he reaches for my hand.

I stop dead in my tracks and peer down at our union, then back at him.

"*Venire.*"

He yanks on my hand and leads me through the throngs of people. It appears he knows where he's going, which sets off alarm bells. Maybe he is involved after all?

I can deal with the aftermath later because this is one of Gianna's tests. If I fail, I know she won't be happy.

Fairy lights line the street and are entangled around the poles of the stalls, setting a romantic mood. A colorful artwork of umbrellas turned upside down hangs on strings coiled between two buildings. Everything is magical.

But with each minute passing, I can't help but feel claustrophobic. My stomach begins to churn, and I feel vomit rising.

No, not now. I beg my body to withstand this test, and I promise to treat it better come morning. But for now, I just need to find Madam Gazella.

And when we turn a corner and venture down a section which isn't as busy as the rest, it seems I was right. Nico does know who she is. Just not in the way I thought.

Ahead is a blue tent with a third eye and a crystal ball printed on the side. And in gold letters is the name Madam Gazella.

Is this some sort of joke?

Gianna wants me to see a fortune teller?

I let go of Nico's hand and signal to him that I won't be long.

He nods and doesn't question why I have a meeting with the town's clairvoyant. He reaches into his back pocket for his wallet and offers me a fifty. I want to wave him off, but I'm not sure what to expect when going into the tent.

So I accept. "I'll pay you back."

He smiles and leaves me to face the unknown.

As the clock tower chimes eight times, I enter the tent and am greeted with a black velvet curtain. A bottle of disinfectant spray sits on a small wooden table, accompanied by handwritten instructions in Italian with English translations underneath. It requests that those entering disinfect the soles of their shoes and their hands before proceeding beyond the black curtain.

I do as the sign asks.

Once I'm done, I part the curtain and am greeted by an elderly woman sitting at a round table. A stack of worn tarot cards and a crystal ball sit in front of her. She wears a silk scarf around her head, but wisps of gray hair peek through.

It takes all my willpower not to roll my eyes because this

hocus pocus stuff is nothing but a fraud to con people out of their money. But I smile and enter.

She points at the chair opposite her.

I sit and wait, unsure of what to expect.

I notice the large gold crucifix around her neck and the evil eye bracelet she wears. It smells of incense in here, the type used at Mass. Memories of Father Merry arise, but I push them aside.

She reaches across the table and takes my hands. Peering down at the union, I look at the contrast of our hands. Hers are weathered while mine are infant. Each line represents a life event that happened to her, denoting the life she lived.

I wonder what mine will look like when I reach Madam Gazella's age. Or the better question is, if.

She closes her eyes and appears to concentrate as she rubs her thumb across the back of my hand.

Soon, Italian spills from her, and I frown, disappointed because I don't understand a word.

Just as I'm about to speak, she opens her eyes and stares at me. "You've been brought here for change. And that change must come through death."

I understand her broken English just fine, so I don't question if I heard her correctly.

"Enzo Cattaneo is who you must conquer to succeed."

I recognize the surname immediately.

This is a relation to Aldo.

Madam Gazella lets go of my hands and reaches under the table to produce a cell. She slides it across the table to me. "There is a number programmed. Call it tomorrow. He will tell you what to do."

And that's it.

I wait for more, but Madam Gazella nods, hinting our meeting is over. I wonder what role she plays in all this. She only seems to be the messenger.

I don't ask any questions because Gianna taught me better than that.

Reaching into the pocket of my dress, I produce the fifty euro.

She accepts.

I go to stand, but she grips my wrist and turns my hand over. She appears to be reading my palm. I humor her because I am a non-believer, but what she says next turns my stomach.

"A lifelong commitment."

I arch a brow, confused. "Pardon?"

"The sickness you feel, it's the commitment. *Bambina.*"

The blood drains from my body because I know what *that* word means.

But that's not possible.

She's wrong.

Snatching my hand away, I shake my head. "No, you're

wrong."

But Madam Gazella stands firm. "*Una ragazzina. Un miracolo.*"

Again, I know what she's saying, but I refuse to believe it.

"Thank you," I blurt out before running from the tent.

The moment I'm outside, I bend in half, and with hands on my knees, I take three deep breaths to calm myself.

It doesn't help.

There is no way she's right. She's a fortune teller reading palms at a flea market, for fuck's sake. She's wrong.

My mind is racing, and there's only one way to settle that.

I quickly make my way through the patrons who are casually browsing. Must be nice not to have a care in the world. When I see the stall I need up ahead, I realize I gave all the money I have to Madam Gazella.

But this is an emergency.

Thankfully, the store clerk is busy serving a group of tourists who all wear I LOVE ITALY T-shirts. I wish I could share the sentiment.

When I see what I'm looking for, I subtly peer around to ensure no one is looking, and with skills only a criminal possesses, I swipe the product swiftly and walk away. I feel awful for stealing and make note of the store name on the tent. I will return to repay them when I can think straight.

Thankfully, the bathrooms are ahead, and I practically run

to them. Once inside the small cubicle, I do my thing and wait.

"She's wrong," I whisper over and over.

I sit on the toilet, holding something in my hand which may as well be a grenade, and when it changes before my eyes, I go numb.

It seems Madam Gazella isn't a bogus fortune teller, after all, because she was right.

"The sickness you feel, it's the commitment. Bambina.*"*

And that commitment will change everything, and that's because…I'm pregnant.

CHAPTER 4

LENNY

Orchard Parks State Hospital is supposed to help people. But being here for five minutes has me wanting to claw my face off.

Medicated zombies roam the halls. They shuffle their slippers along the linoleum with a vacant stare on their faces. Their eyes are dead.

How is being locked away in here good for anyone?

So when the orderly unlocks the door and I see a woman restrained to a single bed, I realize that this place *isn't* good.

I enter, and when the door slams shut behind me, I take

that as Margarette is not a threat. But of course, she isn't. She's tied to the bed with no place to go.

I instantly feel pity.

Regardless of her sins, no one deserves to be treated this way, shackled to the bed like a neglected dog. Seeing her this way only fuels my hatred for Gianna. It's because of her that Margarette is here.

She doesn't move, and if not for the shallow rise and fall of her chest, I would think she's dead. I approach the bed. She still doesn't stir.

I didn't prepare a speech. I just knew I needed to come here and ask questions.

However, looking at Margarette's comatose state, I doubt I will be getting any answers.

"Hi, Margarette. My name is Lennon. I was an orphan at Saint Maria's. I know your friend, Gianna Ricci."

Bingo…

A slight flicker of her eyelids reveals she heard me, and I've struck a nerve.

I pull up a chair and sit by her bedside.

Margarette is the only person who has damning evidence against Gianna. She is the only person who can help me save Valentina.

However, she may well be in a coma.

"I don't care about your past. All I care about is saving the girl who came to see you. Her name is Valentina, and she is Gianna's daughter."

No recognition, but I know she can hear me.

"Gianna lied to Valentina, claiming you were her mother. That's why I'm assuming she was livid when she came to see you. I need your help. I need you to tell me the truth. I need to know who Gianna was and why she would do such a thing.

"Was she your friend?"

Margarette stares vacantly at the ceiling.

I must get through to her. Leaving here without answers is not acceptable. But how do you get through to someone who looks more dead than alive?

I suddenly realize there is only one way: the way that connects us and makes us human.

Love…

"Regardless of what he did, you really loved him, didn't you?"

The silence is deafening as I wait for some kind of response.

"Valentina believes him to be her father, and you, her mother. Can you imagine what that does to a kid who believes her father was a serial killer and her mother a nun who fell in love with him?

"She believes you abandoned her on the steps of the orphanage. Help me show her that she is worthy. That she is someone worth saving.

"Because like you, I will do anything for the person I love.

"Please, please help me save her." It's my final plea.

I wait for some kind of revelation, that perhaps life will cut me some slack.

But Margarette remains still.

I hang my head low and grip my hair in frustration. I thought this would help convince Valentina who Gianna really is.

But now, I—

That thought never comes to fruition because if I believed in miracles, this would be one.

I snap my head up when a hoarse groan leaves Margarette. She is looking at me, like really looking, her eyes begging I hear her because I don't think many have.

Jumping up, I lower my ear to her mouth as I don't want to miss a thing. All I hear, though, is jumbled gibberish.

"I don't understand," I say, pulling back, beseeching her to try harder.

Her mouth gapes open and closed like a fish out of water, and it's only then do I comprehend why she can't speak.

She has no fucking tongue. A tiny stub is where it once was.

"Did Gianna do this to you?" I probe, seeing as the only way to communicate is for me to ask the questions.

She nods slowly, tears filling her empty eyes.

"I'm so fucking sorry. But I'm going to make this right. I'm going to get you out of here."

She begins screeching and thrashing on the bed. The orderlies come running into the room, syringe in hand.

This is far worse than I thought.

Margarette knows Gianna's secrets, which is why Gianna took her tongue. Another person falling victim to that fucking bitch.

The need to destroy her is stronger than ever, and I finally have the proof. Margarette, coupled with Aldo's laptop, has all the evidence I need to show Valentina who Gianna really is.

Valentina can't come back to America, which means I have to go to her.

Bon voyage…

I need to get my affairs in order so I can fly to Sicily in two days. Impulsive, I know, but this shit show won't get any better. I don't have a game plan as such, but all I know is that I need to present Valentina with the damning evidence and hope she finally sees the truth.

She is the link to end this feud once and for all.

The question is, what happens if it does end? Do I want to be in control? Aldo's business won't stop just because I do, which means the responsibility falls to Bria. She is more than capable of ruling, but a part of me doesn't want to give this up.

I finally feel like I have a purpose in life.

An honest, law-abiding life was never on the cards for me. So in a sense, I feel as if this opportunity is my destiny. It also gives me the power I need to ensure I end Gianna's reign, as well as her life.

A donkey enters Aldo's former office, which is now mine.

I look at him, wondering what the fuck he wants.

"I did knock," he says, reading my annoyance.

"What do you want?"

He closes the door behind him.

He knows better than to sit unless invited to. "Alfonso is a rat."

And this is one of the things I like about Donkey. He doesn't believe in sugarcoating.

When I asked him to compile all the data on my men, he did so within three days. We were able to dispose of a handful of traitors, thanks to his meticulous research skills. It seems Alfonso didn't get the message when I stated disloyalty will not be tolerated.

"How?"

"He's a scout for Gianna."

I curl my palm into a fist on the desk. "What has he done?"

"He has informed her of our latest shipment of crystals arriving at the docks tonight. Word on the street is that she is planning an ambush to steal our cargo. She's also trying to turn our suppliers against us, saying that a boy rules where a man should."

A laugh escapes me. "Let her see what this boy can do, then."

Donkey nods. "How many men do we need?"

"Five."

He arches a brow, but doesn't contest the small number I've requested.

"And ensure Alfonso is one of them."

Donkey doesn't dally and leaves me alone to digest this news. It shouldn't surprise me that Gianna has infiltrated my team. But she's done me a favor. She has helped weed out the deceitful weaklings who will suffer for their choices.

A dishonest man is someone you cannot trust because loyalty is everything. Even if I'm forced to start from scratch, I would rather a small, loyal group of men than a large posse of traitorous cowards.

Tonight, Alfonso will be made an example of.

Gianna will be there tonight as this is her first attack, and she will want to see how I respond. But she doesn't realize I now know her secrets, which will be the end of her.

Once tonight is done with, I intend to fly to Italy and bring Valentina home—kicking and screaming if I must.

And I really hope that she does…

I've left Bria at home, much to her disgust.

But someone needs to be there in case Gianna decides to change things up and attack when she knows I won't be home. She is cunning and smart. I would be foolish to underestimate her. I must bide my time.

But flying to Italy has left me with the dilemma of who I can trust this empire with. Bria can't do it on her own, which is why Lewis sits beside me. This isn't ideal, but my brother has wasted enough time. Yes, the hand he was dealt sucked, but now, it's time to reclaim his life and start living.

I don't know if this is the right step, though, because an ex-junkie around drugs is probably the worst way to test his resilience, especially since it's still early days.

But I've decided to throw him into the deep end and see if he can swim.

Even though we're blood, we're merely strangers. He's broken, and I'll do everything in my power to help him heal.

Conversation is nonexistent between us.

I don't know what I was expecting, but I thought he would be happy to get off the streets. But as he stares vacantly out the window, I wonder if maybe he's too far gone.

Regardless, I won't give up on him. My baby brother is

inside there somewhere, and I will find him. For now, we have to reconnect and build trust.

I park the car close to the docks and kill the engine, but I don't get out. I scope out my surroundings, looking for anything out of place.

The warehouses seem eerily quiet. Most are likely a ruse, just like Aldo's store. Because who would suspect a shop selling crystals and fucking lavender incense would be anything but a haven for people who dance around a bonfire during a full moon while charging their crystals and manifesting world peace?

It's actually genius on Aldo's behalf.

Thanks to Gianna, this is another thing I must take care of before I leave for Italy.

Peering over at Lewis, I realize I just found his first job. "What do you know about crystals?"

I hate that it appears he's in a constant, disjointed state. It's like I need to repeat myself after everything I say because he wasn't listening the first time I said it.

He slowly turns his cheek to look at me.

It still pains me to see him so gaunt and so…ghostlike. It's like this person wears my brother's face, but he's nothing but a stranger.

"Meth?" he asks.

I clench the steering wheel, refraining from acting on

instinct to reach out and slap him. "That shit is your past, all right? Leave your habits there. This is your life now, away from that."

Lewis shrugs, such a noncommittal gesture. "You haven't changed."

"What the fuck does that mean?"

"Thinking you can control everyone around you."

"Excuse me? If only you knew the shit I've been through to find you!"

"I was fine where I was!" he yells, unsnapping his seat belt and getting into my personal space.

I don't waver because this is good. His passion shows that he isn't completely lost to me.

"Fine? You call turning tricks for gear fine? Because me, I call that pretty fucked up!"

"I never asked you to come find me."

"You ungrateful brat," I spit, our faces inches apart. "You want to go back out there, then? You want to be a slave to some vile predator who would sell you for five bucks? Is that what you want? You want to be an addict to the junk you inject into your veins? Is that it?"

Lewis's eyes fill with tears, but fuck him. This is the real world, and it's time he stop being a little pussy and remember who the fuck he is.

"Because I'm giving you one chance and one chance only.

If you don't want to be here, then leave. I won't stop you. But there are no second chances—so choose wisely because I swear to God, blood or not, I will fucking kill you myself if you betray me."

I press the button to unlock the car doors.

Lewis mulls over what I just said, and once he realizes this is no joke, he backs down.

I wait for him to jump out of the car, fleeing into the night.

But he doesn't.

"Good. Now, let's get to work."

We get out of the car and keep to the shadows as we walk toward the docks. The sky is pitch black. It seems even the moon has gone into hiding, not wishing to witness what's about to transpire. I know Gianna is here.

I can feel it.

But like the coward that she is, she'll wait and hope that I destroy myself, saving her the trouble.

It'll be a cold day in hell when I let her outsmart me again.

The red hue from the cigarette Donkey is smoking alerts me to where he is waiting behind a cargo container. The five men wait with him, Alfonso being one of them.

When they see me, they nod. No words are spoken.

No one engages in small talk.

Tensions are high.

Alfonso peers down at his gold watch.

"Got somewhere better to be?" I question, lighting a cigarette.

Alfonso rolls down his sleeve. He doesn't reply. But his anger is apparent.

I'll give him something to be angry about in ten or so minutes.

But for now, I focus on the task at hand when three men walk down the docks toward us.

These are Aldo's men and have been for quite some time. They're a small, loyal group, and Aldo's notes have stated that they haven't fallen victim to Gianna's charm. She's tried to undercut Aldo many times, but they've always kept their business with Aldo. They're smart businessmen, which is why I need them to remain loyal.

This shady scene is out of every gangster movie—men hidden in the shadows, wishing to exert their power and proving who has the biggest cock. Which is why I am certain Gianna is here watching, hoping I fail so she can swoop in.

She's nothing but a scavenger.

The men approach me. It's clear I'm the leader, as I'm flanked in protection.

"I'm Lennon." I extend my hand, introducing myself.

"Tian."

"Kong."

"Matias."

They're wary, which has me trusting them because it's obvious they know nothing about me.

"We heard about Aldo," says Tian. "We are happy to continue the arrangement if you are."

I nod.

I don't trust anyone, and bringing new people into the mix leaves me open to defeat. Even dead, I trust Aldo's judgment more than most people.

Kong's dark eyes narrow. He's sizing me up. As he should because, for all he knows, I'm the one who ended Aldo's life.

Matias is the muscle. He is built like a brick shithouse. He steps forward and passes Donkey a black duffel, and in return, Donkey offers him a Nike gym bag.

The exchange is quick.

The three men nod in a sign of respect, which is as anticlimactic as it comes, but that was just the appetizer. Now, it's time for the main course.

They turn to leave, and when I see Alfonso's shoulders depress with a sigh of relief, I know now is the time for me to reveal what sort of leader I am.

"Aldo was a man of honor," I commence, which has the men stopping dead in their tracks. "He kept his circle small because in this world, who can we really trust?"

Lewis shifts beside me because, brother or not, I sure as shit do not trust him.

The three men turn around to face me, and their body language divulges they're ready to fight if need be.

"You can't trust anyone," says Tian, looking me dead in the eye.

"No, you can't, which is why those untrustworthy need to be made an example of."

The air is thick because of whom I stand among. We're all sinners. This could apply to anyone, and it does. No man is more worthy than the other because here is where the wicked thrive.

But it's time I make an example of those who challenge me.

"I don't believe in delaying gratification, which is why—" I turn to look at Alfonso. "I am going to cut out your spleen and fucking feed it to you."

It takes him a moment to realize I'm serious.

He frantically looks at a building to his left, which is such a rookie move, as he just confirmed my hunch as fact.

"Gianna!" he screams, running to the warehouse.

Donkey doesn't hesitate and pulls out his gun, shooting him in the thigh.

He drops to the ground, howling in pain.

If I were capable of liking anyone, Donkey may be an all right guy.

Alfonso drags his body along the ground, and a zigzagged trail of blood follows him. His legs are useless, which is why I stroll without haste to where he is desperately lugging his body to safety.

He peers up at me when I stand in front of him, arms folded.

"Please, I'm sorry," he splutters, and I have secondhand embarrassment for his cowardice. "I didn't have a choice."

"We all have a choice," I calmly state, tossing my cigarette to the ground, inches from his face. "You just made the wrong one."

I butt out my cigarette, only to kick Alfonso in the face seconds later, instantly breaking his nose and sending three teeth somersaulting through the air.

His anguished screams don't make a lick of difference. He was a dead man walking the minute he sided with Gianna.

Yanking his head back by his hair, I look him dead in the eye. "What does she want?"

"Please," he sobs hysterically, begging I show mercy.

But I am done being played. "You have three seconds."

"I have a family."

"One."

"Please! I'll do anything!"

"Two."

"All right! She wanted me to steal Aldo's laptop!"

"Why?"

"I-I don't know. I swear it! All I know is that she wants to destroy you."

"How?"

"She said…she said, in the end, you'll destroy yourself with the people you love."

Exhaling slowly, I compose myself because this reminds me of all the fucking lessons she "taught" us when we were kids.

"Where is she?"

Seeing as her house burned down, I need to know where she is and what she has planned.

Alfonso tries to shake his head, but I hold him tight. "I won't ask again."

His breaths are stunted, and the fear is reflected in his eyes. He knows this is the end in one way or another. "She's at—"

But his sentence will remain forever unfinished because although I am still holding his head, it's no longer attached to his body. It's been blown to bits by a high-powered rifle. The bottom half of his face is no more.

Peering down, I see I am merely holding the top of his skull. His eyes are wide open, forever frozen in this macabre moment in time. Blood gushes from the open wound.

Lifting what's remaining of Alfonso's head, I present it for all to see. "Nice to see some things haven't changed, Gianna. You're still nothing but a coward."

She destroys anyone who gets in her way. I wonder why I'm still standing.

Tossing Alfonso's head into the river, I nod at the three

men.

They return the gesture, a sign of respect which I earned tonight. I wanted them to see that I am not someone to be fucked with. And by Gianna's actions, they were able to see she is far from honorable.

I'm about to leave when I notice Lewis is gone.

I don't bother with formalities as I take the bag from Donkey and quickly go in search of my brother.

I instantly regret my decision to bring him along as I now see that, regardless of our blood tie, he will never be loyal to me. Too much has happened. Therefore, I need to be smart because I know Lewis will betray me if given a better offer.

And my suspicions are confirmed when I turn the corner and see him talking to Gianna.

He averts his gaze guiltily when he sees me, while Gianna merely smiles a cat-who-got-the-cream grin.

It takes all my willpower not to shoot her where she stands. All this would be a lot easier if I did, but I can't, and that's because she's the only person who knows where Valentina is.

Alfonso's words hit harder now because this is a prime example of me being held hostage by Gianna.

"I wish I could say this was a pleasant surprise, but that would be a fucking lie. You're so obsessed with me," I quip while lighting a cigarette. "Perhaps you need to get yourself a hobby? I hear Australia is nice this time of year. Maybe you can get in touch with your spirit animal and wrestle a crocodile or two."

Sending her away to the farthest country from here sounds divine. Too bad it's just a pipe dream.

"Sarcasm? I taught you better than that."

I can't help but scoff. "You taught me to be a heartless killer. Come to think of it, it's probably the only valuable lesson you ever taught. And now you think you can do the same to my brother?"

Lewis takes a step away from Gianna.

But the damage is done.

Gianna won't be happy until she destroys everything I love. She knows she can't break me, so she will let me do the job for her.

"I'll go wait in the car." Lewis excuses himself, understanding my patience for him is wearing thin.

Gianna wears her usual attire of all black. From afar, she is a beauty, but up close, she is far from beautiful.

"How about you stop playing grown-ups and give up? It's embarrassing," she says, examining her red nails.

"Well, I wish you'd fuck off and die, but we can't have it all."

I can do this all day.

"We need to come to some agreement, Lenny. You cannot win."

My cheeks billow as I blow out a cloud of smoke. "Watch me. You forget who raised me, *Mother*."

Her back straightens when I drop the term of endearment. But in this case, it's anything but. "If you're so eager to see me dead, then do it. I'm giving you a free pass."

It's tempting, but she knows that I can't.

Until I know where Valentina is, I need Gianna alive. Once I convince Valentina of the truth, I will then exact my sweet revenge.

This is the reason Gianna is giving me this "free pass."

"You're nothing but a liar," I spit, unable to look at her smug face a second longer. "I *will* find Valentina. And when I do—"

"You'll what?" Gianna challenges with a smirk.

It's apparent she is unaware that I know the truth. And I prefer to keep it that way as it gives me the upper hand.

So for now, I have to suck it up and remember the bigger picture—no matter how badly I want to toss Gianna into the river and hold her head under the water, only to bring her back up and repeat.

"Just as I thought," she concludes. "I think you've forgotten she left because she wanted to. She stays away because *she wants to*."

"She stays away because she's afraid," I counter, refusing to play these games.

Gianna levels me with those cold eyes. "If that's true, then go ask her yourself."

A cold shiver passes over me because I know she's serious.

But what's the catch?

"Go ask her, and you'll see the person you're so intent on saving does not want to be saved. Then perhaps you'll give this up and allow the adults to do their job."

It takes all my willpower not to slap her. But insults reveal I am getting under her skin. If I wasn't, I would be a headless corpse like Alfonso. But she needs me alive for some reason, and I can only guess that reason is that she is nothing without me.

She needs my men on her side, and that won't happen, even if she kills me. This fucked-up world has some sense of respect and honor, and Gianna knows that I am respected because of Aldo. She is still seen as his enemy. Therefore, her empire will crumble without mine.

Ironic, isn't it?

We both need the other to get what we want.

"What's the catch?" I ask.

Gianna steps closer to me while I remain perfectly still. "No catch. I will tell you where Valentina is. All I ask is that you consider my offer."

"What offer?" This suddenly feels like I'm shaking hands with the devil.

"I never wanted to work against you, Lennon. I raised you to work *with* you. Imagine how powerful we could be if we were on the same team. We would be unstoppable. Nothing but royalty."

I didn't think she could shock me anymore, but I was wrong.

What in the ever-living fuck is going on?

"We will *never* be on the same team."

Gianna's ruby lips curl into a sinister grin. "We'll see."

Before I can push her aside, she places her lips to mine and kisses me chastely. There is no love or passion to the gesture—this is the kiss of death.

I watch helplessly as she turns to leave because when my phone chimes, and I see it's an address in Italy, it seems that no matter how many steps I think I'm ahead, Gianna will always be at the forefront, taunting me.

CHAPTER 5

VALENTINA

I don't look any different.

But I certainly feel different.

I suppose I should be relieved that my strange behavior is linked to my hormones.

But I am not.

How can I be?

I can't bring a child into this world.

My world.

I wasn't taught to be a mother.

I was raised to be a killer.

Nausea threatens to take me down, but I'm so used to it, I close my eyes and wait for it to subside. Once it does, I place my hands over my flat belly and look at my naked reflection in the bathroom mirror.

How is this possible?

This doesn't feel like a gift.

This is a curse.

With a mother like me and a father like Lenny, this child is bound to be evil.

But when I think about her conception and how she was made with nothing but love, I wonder if maybe she's not a curse, but a miracle instead.

I want to protect her and give her the life I never had.

But how is that possible?

She will be subjected to the horrors of my life and the dangers that face me every single day because of my actions, which led me here.

I now have a little someone depending on me to keep them safe when I can barely keep myself safe.

Cupping my belly tighter, I quash down the tears because I won't give her the life I had. I will try my best to be the mother I never had.

She was unplanned, and this throws a huge curveball my way, but I'm all she has. I know what it feels like to be unloved and question your worth, so I vow here and now that I won't do that to my *angioletto.*

"Lettie," I mumble under my breath.

It seems perfect as it's in the same vein as her father's name—a father she'll never know.

My little angel has a name.

I've been alone my entire life, but no more.

Lettie is a part of me.

And she is a part of Lennon.

It's impossible not to love her.

Guilt swarms me because Lenny has a right to know that he's going to be a father. But how do I break this kind of news when we're not speaking? The last time we saw each other, he made it clear that our reunion, whenever that may be, would not be a happy one.

But would this change things?

Maybe Lettie will reunite us, and we could be one big happy family.

I scoff at the notion because Lenny and I only know conflict. And besides, I don't want our daughter growing up in a world where her life is at risk.

She will be collateral to many.

Therefore, no one can know she exists.

If it was uncovered that Lenny and I had a child, a Mafia princess, then the bounty on her head would be priceless.

No one can know of her existence. I will keep her safe here

in Italy. I can never return to America. A hard truth but it's one I must accept. Everything happens for a reason, and that is why I came here—to save my child.

Something deep down in my belly tells me to keep her a secret from the world, Gianna included. A protection so fierce overcomes me, something I've never felt before. I decide to listen to intuition, and I can work out the rest along the way.

"Ciao, Valentina, sei a casa?"

Quickly slipping into my robe, I splash some water onto my face so I look semi-human and meet Nico in the kitchen. The smell of freshly brewed coffee is one of the only things that doesn't turn my stomach. A fact Nico is aware of.

He takes one look at me, and his reaction says it all.

"Nice to know I look as shit as I feel," I say, while Nico arches a brow, confused. "Oh right, you don't understand me."

Even though he doesn't, he can read my body language and knows I'm being a huge bitch to him, which is unwarranted. He has been nothing but nice to me, so I have no right being so rude.

I don't think I can blame baby hormones on this.

He doesn't press and instead pours me a shot of espresso.

No cream or sugar. The Italians take it black.

I drink it in one mouthful and am thankful when it doesn't come back up.

Nico downs his coffee before washing his cup out and

leaving it by the sink. He makes it clear that he's leaving, and I don't blame him after my antisocial behavior.

I instantly feel bad.

"Do you want to go into town? I can make us dinner," I say in a rushed breath.

Nico turns to look at me while I point out the window and gesture with my hands to my mouth.

Thankfully, he understands my charades and nods.

I have no idea why he's so good to me. But I will try my best and return the favor.

Quickly excusing myself, I go to my bedroom and slip into some underwear, a yellow summer dress, and sandals. I tie my hair into a messy bun and don't bother with any makeup. Looking into the mirror, I shrug because this is the best I got.

Reaching for my bag, I quickly check the cell Madam Gazella gave to me. I haven't called the number like instructed. I had other pressing matters to deal with.

But I will make sure to call it today.

Once I head back out into the kitchen, I see Nico waiting outside by his motorbike. It's a beautiful day, and the sun bounces down on him, highlighting him in a way that evokes a longing that hits me hard. Yes, Nico is an attractive man, but this desire is different.

I suddenly feel myself getting wet just by the sight of him.

His white shirt sticks to him like a second skin, leaving

nothing to the imagination as every taut muscle is on display. His skin is sun-kissed, and his hair is styled in just the right way to give him that sexy bedhead look.

Every part of me is aroused, and it terrifies me. I have never felt this way for another man before.

Nico turns and catches me watching him through the window.

My cheeks instantly blister.

I lock the back door and walk toward him. But something off to the right catches my eye.

It's a bicycle.

Nico points at it with a smile. "For you," he says with a strong accent, which just makes the gesture even more special.

I want to refuse, but truth be told, this bike is a godsend as it gives me a means of transportation. I don't have a driver's license, but even if I did, I can't afford a car. So this is perfect.

"Not new," he explains, but I don't need new.

The faded blue bike has some rust, but its wheels are sturdy, and the cute little woven basket at the front adds a rustic touch.

Many people ride bikes here because of the winding, narrow roads, so I will fit in, which is what I want. Besides, most people underestimate those who ride a bike. It's the perfect disguise.

"Thank you," I say and stand on tippy-toes to kiss his cheek.

He freezes, which makes me realize what I just did.

It was innate, but I suddenly pull away, embarrassed for the

PDA.

However, Nico softly grips my wrist, rubbing his finger over my suddenly racing pulse.

We lock eyes, and I see it—he feels this too.

Our chemistry is hard to ignore, and regardless that we're lost in translation with one another, our bodies speak the same language. And right now, my body wants to be closer to his. I don't know what it is, but he makes me feel...safe.

Deep down, I know that's because he doesn't know the real me.

If he did, he wouldn't want anything to do with me.

I remember that when I gently remove my wrist from his hold.

Whatever passed between us disappears, which I am thankful for because I can't forget who I am. But more importantly...I can't forget what I have done.

It's a lovely Sunday morning, and if circumstances were different, I would appreciate the beauty. But I'm being followed.

The market in town is packed with people. Locals buy their fresh produce, while tourists take it all in. It's the perfect place to go unnoticed.

But I was trained by the best, and I know the middle-aged

man wearing a white shirt with the sleeves rolled up and brown pants isn't here for the infamous cannolis.

He's here for me.

Friend or foe?

I don't know.

But I will soon find out.

First, however, I need to ditch Nico.

He has been enjoying the market, talking to locals, and buying enough food to feed an army. I did say I was going to make us dinner, but that's the least of my concerns now.

We stop by a fishmonger who waves eagerly at Nico.

This is my chance.

Nico introduces me, and I smile politely before saying, "*Toilette.*"

Both men nod, and the fishmonger points toward a brick building that is far enough away not to rouse suspicion.

"I won't be long."

Nico nods, and I casually walk toward the toilet, ensuring I make eye contact with the stranger.

There's no point playing coy.

He could have remained incognito, but he wanted me to be aware of his presence.

He follows subtly as we duck and weave our way through the unsuspecting shoppers. They are oblivious. Must be nice to live a life where you're not constantly looking over your shoulder.

Thoughts drift to Lettie.

I don't want this for her. I don't want this to be her legacy, which is why I decide that once I do this for Gianna, I'm out.

I will repay my debts, then I will make a life for me and Lettie—away from all this.

Maybe I can start fresh?

But I know I can never run too far from my demons, as they are never far behind.

Once I reach the bathrooms, I turn the corner, away from prying eyes, and wait for the man. He appears a moment later.

I don't fear him because if he wanted me dead, I would be.

"Who are you?" I ask, not bothering with formalities.

"I was expecting your call," he replies in a strong Italian accent.

So it's his number that is programmed into my phone.

"Well, you saved me a call. What do you want?"

He has the audacity to laugh. "Gianna warned me about you."

"In that case, I'm sure she also told you that I have no patience."

It's amazing how easily I slip into this persona, and I soon realize I am two people—I just don't know who I like best.

"I am Vince, your contact here in Sicily. Gianna wants to keep you hidden, just for now. You are her secret weapon."

It's hard not to be a touch insulted that Gianna merely sees me as collateral she can use for her gain.

"Enzo is Aldo's brother, and he will do anything to get his revenge. We must be careful. No one suspects you, which is why we will win."

"And what exactly do we win?"

Vince arches a dark brow. "Power," he states like I'm some imbecile for not knowing this.

This suddenly seems so insignificant in the greater scheme of things. Gianna wants power, and all I want is to ensure the safety of my child.

My priorities have shifted, but I remember not too long ago basking in the power and revenge of when I ended Father Merry's life. So I can't be judgmental of her priorities.

But that doesn't change my mind.

I want out.

"What do you need from me?"

"Enzo isn't like his honorable brother. He likes pretty… things."

Vomit rises for another reason this time.

"Get close to him, learn his secrets, and then…you kill him. Once this is done, Gianna can come back to Italy, and you may choose what life you want to live."

I'm taken aback as I never thought this option was on the cards. But it seems Gianna is giving me a choice.

But I don't have a choice.

I will do what I must to protect Lettie. And to do that... Enzo must die.

The sooner I succeed, the sooner I can leave this life behind.

I do this for my daughter.

I do this for myself.

"Where can I find him?"

"I will send you the details. Perhaps you should go shopping and buy something"—he looks me up and down, unimpressed with my attire—"nice."

It's on the tip of my tongue to tell him to go fuck himself, but I nod instead.

Without anything further to say, I make my way back to Nico, my mind racing. When he sees me, he gives me a bouquet of wildflowers.

I don't deserve this. I don't deserve any of this.

But as I realized, there are two of me, and this Valentina simply smiles.

The other me, however, claws at the confines of my chest, screaming to get out because blood will be spilled by my hands once again.

And only then...will I be free.

Nico and I are sitting at the dinner table, the radio humming low in the background.

I made meatloaf and a huge serving of the different produce we purchased at the market. The cannoli Nico bought looks delicious, but my appetite is shot.

I can't stop thinking about today's encounter with Vince.

I am pleased I finally have direction, but Gianna made clear I am to be Enzo's mistress so to speak. I am to do whatever it takes to get close to him. The thought makes me feel sick.

But his death brings me freedom.

What choice is there?

The flowers Nico bought me sit in a crystal vase in the middle of the table. Such a sweet gesture, one I don't deserve, seeing as I'm strategizing the quickest way to do what Gianna wants.

Nico reaches into his pocket, and I'm surprised to see a cell. He types something and holds the phone out to me.

I soon hear a robotic voice say, "The cannoli is sorry."

Pursing my lips in confusion, I look down at my plate and see I have massacred the ricotta.

A laugh escapes me.

It seems Nico purchased a phone from the market today. It's an older phone, but it has a translation app on it. Nico doesn't seem like the type of guy who has socials, so I wonder if he got this for me.

The thought touches me.

I gesture for him to pass me the phone.

I type out my reply and switch the language so it'll translate into Italian. "I'm the one who is sorry. I'm not much company."

Nico frowns, shaking his head, and gestures for the phone back. He frantically types and presses a button. The robotic voice sounds. "Please don't say sorry. You're the best company I've had in a very long while. You can talk to the farm animals for only so long."

I burst into laughter.

Nico is funny. I never thought so. I guess this allows me to understand his personality better, and so far, I like it.

I ask for the phone. "Why are you so kind to me?"

Nico mulls over my question.

His brows knit together as it seems he's weighing up what to say. He sighs before typing out something that is the beginning of the end.

"Because I like you," says the robotic voice.

"Why?" I ask, genuinely curious.

He doesn't need the translator to understand me as he frantically replies. "Because you are good...even if you don't believe it."

I don't know what to say.

His kind eyes are too much, as are his words, and I stand abruptly as I need air, but in my haste, I accidentally spill the half bottle of wine all over Nico's white shirt.

He jumps up, but the damage is done.

"I'm so sorry!" Grabbing a napkin, I dab at his shirt, but this will stain if we don't soak it. "Take off your shirt."

He hesitates, but with fumbling fingers, I unbutton his shirt. Each button reveals a sliver of hardened, olive skin. Once the final button is undone, I have to remember to swallow because his pecs are perfectly shaped, and the sprinkle of hair running from his chest down to his belly button just adds to his masculinity.

He has a tattoo of a tree down the side of his ribs, which seems to emphasize his ripped abs.

I want to bury my face in that soft chest hair and take a big whiff because he smells so damn good.

Nico offers me the shirt, and I snap back to reality, taking it sheepishly.

I race to the laundry and take three calming breaths. Gripping the trough, I will my heart to calm down and stop acting like a lunatic.

My hands shake as I place his shirt into a bucket of hot water and a stain remover powder.

"Chill the fuck out," I whisper to myself. "If he knew what you did, he wouldn't be saying the things he does. Remember who you are."

Hardly the pep talk one would usually want to hear, but it

works.

As I reenter the kitchen, Nico stands topless, collecting the plates. A man who cleans up after himself.

Honestly, how is he single?

I wonder what his backstory is. He seems too good to be true.

My eyes drift to the front of his pants, and I see his jeans are also stained.

"I can soak them too?"

He looks at me, and I point at his pants.

He seems to wrestle with his decision, but eventually, he unfastens the top button. As soon as his zipper is halfway down, I hear a voice that is heaven and hell in one breath.

"Is this a private party, or can anyone join?"

Surely, I'm hallucinating.

Perhaps the fumes from the chemical cleaner got to my head, and I am delirious. But as he comes to stand behind me, his signature fragrance kicking me in the solar plexus, I know that Lennon is really here…and he is really going to kill Nico.

Spinning around, I place my hand on his chest, stopping him from lunging forward. Our eyes lock, and it feels as if time stands still. I hadn't realized how much I missed him until now.

I was resigned to the fact that I may never see him again.

But here he is, looking like the epitome of every bad boy wrapped into one tall, muscular alphahole.

His hair is mussed, and he hasn't shaved in days. But I still want to eat him alive.

"Miss me, *tesoro mio*?"

That term of endearment slays me. It always has. But that smug smirk of his, tugging at that sinful mouth, pisses me off.

It's the dose of reality I need as I shove him away while he chuckles.

"Get out," I order, but it's half-assed because I don't mean it.

I have never wanted anyone to stay more than I do right now.

I suddenly feel faint as my stomach roils. It's not a bad feeling, but I can't help but think it's Lettie—our baby responding to her father's voice.

Lenny watches me closely as he knows me better than I know myself. "What's wrong?"

"Other than the fact that you're here, ruining my life?" I quip, hiding under sarcasm.

"Oh please, Casanova over there doesn't really seem like the best conversationalist." He juts out his chin at Nico.

I forgot he was here.

That's how badly Lenny affects me.

Turning around, I soften my face because Nico doesn't deserve any of this. I reach for the phone and type out a reply.

"I'm sorry, Nico. I have to talk to my friend alone. I will be all right. I will see you tomorrow."

Nico's attention bounces between Lenny and me.

Lenny laughs hilariously. "Fuck me. Is this how you communicate? I guess you'd both be really good at charades, though."

"Lennon, shut up!"

Nico steps forward, which earns a low growl from Lenny.

Playtime is over.

"You heard her, dipshit. You've outstayed your welcome. Zip up your pants and leave. I'm giving you one chance and one chance only. You best take it."

Nico's nostrils flare, and he clenches his fists by his side.

Lenny simply scoffs in humor. "You look fucking ridiculous. Put on a shirt, for fuck's sake. This isn't WWE."

Nico, however, doesn't see the funny side to any of this and advances, primed on hitting Lenny.

"No!" I scream because I know this will not end well—for Nico.

Lenny pushes me out of the way and smacks Nico in the nose. Blood instantly pours from it.

"Lenny!" I cry, pressing a linen napkin over Nico's nose.

Lenny jumps up onto the kitchen counter, unperplexed as he reaches for an apple from the fruit bowl. He chews it as he watches me nursing Nico.

"Should have listened," Lenny says, pointing his finger at Nico. "Or maybe I should have used your translator?"

"This isn't funny."

"It's a little bit funny. Fucking *testa di cazzo*."

It's on before I can stop it as Nico shoves me out of the way and charges for Lenny. I trip over the bottle of wine on the floor and end up crashing into the wall. It's an accident, but Lenny doesn't see it that way. He launches off the counter and headbutts Nico, who stumbles backward.

Lenny doesn't give him a chance to gather himself before he grabs him by the front of the neck and he shoves him into the refrigerator, choking him. Nico slaps at Lenny's fingers, but I've seen Lenny fight—Nico doesn't stand a chance.

I find my footing and jump onto Lenny's back, hoping to stop him from choking out Nico.

It doesn't work.

Lenny only seems to grip Nico harder, who turns red and gasps for air.

"Lenny, stop, you're killing him! Please, stop!"

"That's kinda the point."

Lenny's body is rigid, and I know he's in a rage. I know this because when faced with bloodshed, my body responds the same way. This is why Lenny and I are bad for one another.

But regardless of this, we would kill for the other.

"He shouldn't put his fucking hands on you!" Lenny screams.

Nico is losing consciousness, his eyes fluttering, the fight in him dying.

"Please, please stop," I beg, hugging Lenny tight.

Our altercation soon turns into an embrace, and it seems we both realize how badly we craved each other's touch.

Lenny loosens his grip on Nico's throat and lets him go.

Nico gulps in mouthfuls of air, rubbing his red neck.

"I'm sorry," I say to Nico, still clinging to Lenny's back.

Nico looks at me, finally, how I deserve—he looks at me with disgust.

He doesn't say a word as he storms out the back door, his bike tearing down the driveway a moment later.

I doubt I'll ever see him again.

As always, Lenny and I seem to destroy everything we touch—us included.

But regardless of this, it feels so good.

I hold on tight, pressing my cheek into Lenny's back. We're silent, surrounded by chaos. We are the calm to one another's storms.

"What are you doing here?" I whisper, eyes closed. I am suddenly so tired.

"I protect what's mine...even if you don't want me to."

Tears wet his black T-shirt because that's the most beautiful thing he's ever said. But as I look around at the mayhem surrounding us, I remember the promise I made to myself.

Lenny and I are toxic together.

We haven't seen one another for weeks, and look at how our reunion went. How can I bring a child into that environment?

I can't.

"Come home," he says, interlacing our fingers.

"You know that I can't."

"We will fight Gianna together."

Once upon a time, I would have opposed, but now, that sounds like heaven.

But I can't be around Lenny. It's not safe.

For any of us—our baby included.

Look at what he did to Nico.

He has a darkness within that matches mine, and together, we're no good.

I want to be good.

I want to try.

And being with Lenny doesn't allow it.

So I must let him go…and for good this time.

I don't know where I'll go, but what I do know is that I can't be anywhere near Lenny.

He can never know about Lettie.

No one can know that she is our daughter because she will be hunted by my enemies.

She will be hunted by his.

"I won't leave Italy."

"So you'll leave me?" He backs me up, placing me onto the

counter.

He turns to face me, the anguish clear on his beautiful face.

"We don't work together, Lenny. You know that as well as I do."

"That's fucking bullshit!"

"Too much has happened. Resentment from both of us. I can forgive, but I can never forget. And I'm certain you feel the same way. I know you feel as though I betrayed you."

"Because you fucking did! You left, remember? You chose a side, and it wasn't mine!"

"And that's exactly what I'm talking about. This will always be a rift between us, one which I don't think either of us will ever get over."

He inhales slowly, releasing the breath just as slow. "I have proof. I wanted to show you later, but it can't wait. Once you see this, everything will change. I wanted to tell you sooner, but I needed to make sure I had all the evidence I needed."

He walks to the black backpack he dumped by the door and opens it, pulling out a laptop. He places it on the counter and waits for it to power up. Once it does, he scrolls through files, and I wonder what he's about to show me.

Proof of what? What does he have that he's so adamant can change my mind?

After a couple of minutes of searching, it's apparent that whatever he wanted to show me isn't there.

The hue from the screen lights up his face, and I commit it to memory because this has to be the last time. Unless he can reveal some grand epiphany, we can no longer see one another.

He made it clear that he hunts me if we're not on the same side.

And we never will be.

"I don't understand," he mumbles under his breath as he frantically searches through file after file.

"What is it?" I ask as his agitated state reveals that whatever he wanted to show me, he believed would change everything.

"Fuck!" He slams the laptop shut.

I wait for him to explain what is going on.

He runs both hands through his hair, yanking at the strands. "You just have to trust me. Come back to America, and I will show you the proof."

"Just how you were going to show me the magical file on the laptop? Do you think I'm stupid?"

"I most certainly do not," he replies, offended.

"You expect me to just trust you after everything that's happened?"

"I did actually, but clearly, I was mistaken."

"Do you remember our parting words?"

He doesn't reply.

"Shall I remind you then? They were 'love can't save us from what's fated in the stars. Run far away because when I find you…I'll never let you go.' Well, you found me, so what do you plan on doing?"

He's furious, but he knows I'm right.

However, he thinks I remain here because of my loyalty to Gianna. Once upon a time, that was the case, but now, I stay here because it's the only haven I can provide for Lettie.

This is why I can't tell Lenny about her because the truth is, I don't trust him. Although I love him with every inch of my heart, I know we aren't good for each other.

"Trust me. Please," he begs, placing his hands onto my knees.

I ignore the goose bumps and shake my head. "I can't. Too much has happened, and you and I, we just don't work."

I say what I must to hurt him because although the pain is unbearable, I know that it's for the best. Our past is paved with nothing but sorrow and carnage.

I no longer want that life.

"Tell me you don't love me, and you'll never see me again. I promise," he says, sashaying his finger back and forth over my knee.

His touch is intoxicating, but I measure my breathing. "Love can't save us from what's fated in the stars," I recite his words back to him. "Our love blinds us to the truth. You're no good for me. And I'm no good for you. If you do love me, I ask that you leave and never return."

As much as this hurts, I mean it.

His hurt is reflected all over his handsome face because one of us had to end this, and he didn't have the strength to.

How lucky I am to be loved so passionately. I'll never forget this almost obsessive love because it's a once-in-a-lifetime kind of love.

"Valentina…" he says, but it appears we've both run out of words.

I place my finger over his lips. "Just kiss me."

It feels like he stares straight through to my soul as he grips my wrist and rubs his mouth back and forth over my pointer. I allow him full control. This is my final gift to him because, although I'm breaking up with him, so to speak, I don't want him to think it's because I love someone else.

One of us must surrender to the other…but neither of us will.

So this is the only way.

Breaking up is such a juvenile term because this is so much more. This feels as if I've lost a piece of myself and it will never be found. Now, I must deal with the aftermath and try my best to survive without the man who I'll love with my last dying breath.

But love has never been enough for us. It's because of our destructive love that we continue this cycle, but it has to end.

I slip my finger into his mouth and exhale shakily when

he sucks it, never breaking eye contact. Once my finger is wet, he guides it under my dress and into my underwear where he slowly sinks it into my pussy. I hiss the moment he starts fucking me with my own finger.

I open my legs wider as the urge to come blinds me to anything else. My body has been in a heightened state all day, so this is almost too much.

Lenny controls the speed, and when he slows down, I groan in frustration. "More," I plead, but Lenny will make me work for it.

He withdraws my finger, only to draw it to his lips and suck away my taste. The sight is beyond erotic and turns me on even more than I already am.

But I want more.

And Lenny knows it.

"No matter the distance between us, or the time which will lapse, you and I will always be connected—in one way or another."

He doesn't realize how accurate that statement is.

He grips my neck and arches my head backward. "You can fool yourself into thinking that you can live without me"—he squeezes my throat, drawing us nose to nose—"but sooner or later, in the dead of night, the darkness will come calling your name, and when it does...you'll remember who you belong to."

I hate him.

I really do, and that's because…he's right.

"Fuck you," I spit, unable to conceal my hatred for him because the line between love and hate has always blurred between us.

"There she is," he mocks with a smirk.

"I hate you, Lennon." And at this moment, I really fucking do.

"And I hate you, Valentina."

As much as it hurts, I need to let him go.

So if this is the last time, then let it be just us, the only way we know.

Lenny grips my chin and slams his mouth to mine. He allows me no reprieve as he kisses me hard, biting my bottom lip and sucking my tongue.

He slides me forward, coaxing me to wrap my legs around his waist. His hard cock presses into me, sending my body into sensory overload. I almost come at the simple touch, and that's because I know what's coming.

I want him in me.

All over me.

I can never get close enough.

Our kisses are almost violent, and when I bite his lip, tasting blood, I know we've crossed the line of no return. He pulls away, and without hesitation, he rips the front of my dress. The buttons are scattered all over the floor.

His aggression only fuels the fire within me.

He helps me strip off my ruined dress. I am sitting before him in only a bra and underwear. The way he looks at me, anyone would mistake his desire for me adorned in lace and silk. But my simple lingerie is anything but.

Regardless, Lenny takes a step back, running a hand over his mouth as he consumes me from head to toe. My body responds as it always does when I'm with him—I want more.

We don't speak.

No words are needed.

I reach around and unhook my bra.

My breasts feel heavy.

Lenny steps forward, and I reach for the hem of his T-shirt, taking it off. A moan slips past my lips when I see his bare chest.

The dark hair on his pecs, trickling down his stomach and into his low-slung jeans, turns me on so much. It's all man. His abs look to be carved from granite, and the urge to run my tongue over each hardened bump has me rubbing my legs together to stop the burn between my thighs.

His jeans sit low, exposing his V-muscle that I like oh, so very much.

His messy hair, heavy growth, and hungry-as-fuck eyes will be the death of me.

And he knows it.

He runs his palms down the tops of my thighs. He stops

when he reaches my knees.

Our eyes lock.

I hold my breath.

In one swift move, Lenny flips me over so my chest is splayed out on the counter with my ass poised high in the air. He yanks down my underwear, and without a word, he spanks me.

I jolt at the force because he is far from gentle, which is exactly what I want.

The sting burns, and when he brings his hand down a second time, it radiates all the way to my pussy.

He spreads my legs, drops to his knees, and eats me out from behind. He grips my thighs, holding me prisoner. I grasp the edge of the counter and arch my back, granting him deeper access to every part of me.

He spreads my ass, opening me up wide, and buries his face between my cheeks. He uses his tongue in ways that have me screaming at the top of my lungs.

He doesn't allow me a reprieve. My cries only spur him on further.

He scoops a hand under my belly and coaxes my hips backward so I'm riding his face as he's eating my ass. My clit is throbbing. I desperately need a release.

Reaching down, I begin playing with myself while Lenny teases my back entrance with his tongue by using a circular motion before slowly tunneling into me.

I open to him like a flower in bloom.

Something which some may see as taboo is nothing but carnal hunger between Lenny and me. The fact we can engage in something so depraved and for it to feel so good only heightens everything I'm feeling.

He suddenly shoots up and flips me over so my back now rests on the counter.

I don't stop pleasuring myself.

Lenny watches in utter desire and soon joins me as he unfastens his jeans. His cock is hard and glistening from the pre-cum that coats his thick head. He strokes his shaft, his eyes fixated on my sex.

Lifting my shoulders from the counter, I watch Lenny jerk himself off.

The sight is utterly erotic.

He strokes himself leisurely, the sound of his rhythm intensifying everything tenfold.

I drop my head back to the counter and squeeze my eyes shut, listening to the impassioned low moans slipping past Lenny's lips as well as his hand stroking his cock.

I spread my legs wider and dig my heels into the counter as I increase the speed of my fingers.

My clit throbs, and my nipples are erect. My pussy is so wet. The familiar burn begins to burn low in my belly. I finger myself harder and faster, desperate to come, and I almost do, but the air is ripped from my lungs when I'm yanked down the counter only to be thrust back up it. My brain doesn't have time to catch up because my body wins the race when Lenny sinks his thick, hard dick into me.

He doesn't move.

He allows me to adjust to his girth.

He bends and takes my right nipple into his mouth. He knows this drives me wild.

I squirm, wishing for him to move.

My body is begging for a release.

Opening my eyes, I peer up at Lenny.

The dim light behind his broad shoulders illuminates him in a way that is almost angelic. But when he seizes my hips and fucks me with ferocity, that ethereal glow fades and I am in the strong arms of the devil.

The force of his strokes is so wild, they propel me up the counter. I am lax and take everything he gives because the harder he fucks, the closer I am to coming all over his throbbing cock. His punishing grasp on my hips is sure to leave bruises, and the thought has me mewling for more.

He releases my hips, only to loop his hands behind my knees, using them as anchors so I can bounce on his cock. He hits me hard and deep, so deep that each time he sinks into me, he robs me of air. His thrusts are impassioned, as well as hate-filled.

We love to hate one another.

And we hate the way we love one another.

He fucks me like an animal, not holding back.

I can't stand it.

It's too much.

The sight.

The smell.

The feel of him.

The veins in his thick neck are taut. The muscles in his shoulders and arms bulge from the intensity of his strokes.

He hits me in just the right way, and my hypersensitive body doesn't stand a chance.

I come loudly.

Starlight flashes behind my eyes, which are squeezed shut. My body undulates in pure ecstasy. My heart threatens to burst from my chest. I can't get air fast enough, but Lenny doesn't care.

He pulls out, drops to his knees, and eats my delicate pussy.

I scream, tugging at his hair in pleasure and a lick of pain. But he doesn't stop. He sucks my clit, flicking his tongue over it. I squirm, unsure if I can take any more.

He spreads my legs wide open, licking my labia up and down and side to side, before driving his tongue deep into my sex. He suckles my clit, before using two fingers to rub over it.

I try to shift away, but Lenny holds me in place, and before long, I'm turned on again.

I want more.

And more he gives.

He hooks his arms under my knees and yanks them wide open. He places a kiss over my sex before trailing kisses along my inner thigh and across my knee, where he then licks a path down my calf. He takes hold of my ankle and peers up at me while he sucks my big toe into his mouth and twirls his tongue around it.

I lean up on my elbows and watch him closely.

I am nothing but worshipped.

Every inch of my heated flesh jolts and spasms with each touch.

He moves over to the other leg, kissing my ankle, before licking all the way upward. I cup his handsome face as he's still on his knees before me, a gesture of surrender. The sight touches me, and nostalgia overwhelms me, right in the pit of my stomach where our miracle is.

I grapple with the moral decision. *Do I tell him?*

I know it would change things.

"What's the matter?" he asks, still on his knees.

"Let's run away together. Forget who we are and what we've done and start over."

Lenny's eyes soften. "That sounds like a nice dream. But

that's all it'll ever be."

"Why can't we?"

"You know why," he replies, saddened.

"I know, but can't we forget?"

"I wish we could."

And there is the answer I always knew to be true.

This is why I can never tell Lenny.

This is really it.

"*Ti amo.*"

"*Ti amo anch'io. Per sempre.*"

He said he'll love me forever, but our forever comes with an expiration date.

I drag him up and smash my mouth over his. He kisses me back with passion and love, but also an undertone of sadness.

I don't know why, but Lenny and I just don't work. I wish we did, but we never can.

Coming to a stand, I pull back and closely examine his beautiful face. I run a finger across his furrowed brow, down his strong nose, which no longer has a nose ring in it, and last, over his lips. My heart is melancholy. To love someone this much only to let them go seems like a waste because this sort of love is a once-in-a-lifetime kind of love. Perhaps we will meet again in another lifetime, where things will be simple.

But for now…it's goodbye.

So…if that's the case, then let it be a farewell we will never forget.

I drop to my knees and take his cock into my mouth.

He threads his fingers through my hair and uses it as reins as he controls the speed and how deeply I take him in. He coaxes me to take as much as I can before gagging. I try to pull away, but he keeps my head down, groaning when he hits the back of my throat.

He releases me, and I pull away, gasping for air.

As I peer up at him from under my lashes, he slaps my cheek.

Not hard.

But with enough force to feel it.

I like it.

I also like when he grips the front of my throat and forces me back down onto his cock.

This is all consensual. The rougher the play, the more aroused I become. Lenny understands my needs because they are parallel to his.

Placing my hands on his upper thighs to support myself, I deep throat him. Saliva dribbles from the corners of my mouth.

It's so primitive.

He thrusts his hips, fucking my face while talking dirty to me in Italian. He pushes the back of my head down on his cock, then draws it back off so I can gasp in air. When I do, he drives me back down.

I am so wet by his passion.

His cock is hard and heavy in my mouth. Every time he throbs against my tongue, I suck harder and deeper. I want him to come, but he makes it apparent that when he does, it won't be in my mouth.

He yanks me up from under the arms and kisses me passionately. We bite, lick, suck, and scratch at the other, desperate to eat one another alive.

He bites over my racing pulse at the side of my neck.

I score my fingernails down his back.

He bends me over the counter, swiping a glass fruit bowl off it and smashing it to the ground. Apples and oranges roll all over the floor. The mess we're making is reflective of us—a silent chaos.

Lenny places his thumb against my back entrance, slowly wedging his way in.

I squirm, but he leans against my back and whispers, "If this is it, then I want to own every part of you."

I understand his possession, so I relax as best I can, but it's a tight fit.

The organic honey-scented body lotion I bought from the market sits within reach. Lenny reaches for it and unscrews the lid. He scoops out a blob on his fingers, and I gulp when he places it where his thumb was.

The feeling is neither unpleasant nor particularly pleasing.

My muscles give way, and Lenny inserts a finger.

I gasp and grip the counter tightly.

"Sei bella."

He knows his Italian calms me, so I close my eyes and lose myself to his words, as well as the feeling of being owned by the man I will forever love.

"Sarai sempre mia. Saremo sempre una cosa sola."

Hearing Lenny say I will always be his and we will always be one is my undoing. I arch my back, encouraging him to replace his fingers with his cock.

He presses the tip against me, and when I inhale, he slowly inches into me. Only on my exhale does he slide all the way in.

A cry leaves me because I feel so full. It hurts, but it hurts so good.

He grips my hips, and slowly, he begins to move.

It burns, and I am scared something is wrong because it feels so tight, but when Lenny reaches around and begins playing with my clit, I loosen up, and it feels good.

He encourages me to bounce back and meet him thrust for thrust. We go slow at first, until I find my rhythm. We speed it up, but Lenny ensures he isn't too rough.

"Feel good?" he asks, kissing my neck and shoulder.

"Yes."

"Good, *tesoro mio*. You feel fucking incredible. This is mine." And he slaps my ass cheek.

I grunt as it's sure to leave a handprint.

"This is mine." He slaps over my pussy.

I jolt at the force.

He commences fucking me harder.

I let go and surrender to everything because we will never be this way again.

Tears trickle down my cheeks at the thought.

I'm not dead inside after all.

"And this is mine." He places his hand over my heart.

He fucks me without remorse, rubbing my clit with as much passion.

It's too much.

I explode with a sob, crying tears of joy and sadness.

Lenny pumps into me wildly, and before long, he follows suit and comes with a roar inside me.

I collapse onto the counter with him cradling my back, and it's here that we stay, breathless and sated, knowing this was our final goodbye.

And for good this time.

CHAPTER 6

VALENTINA
ONE MONTH LATER

Italy is utterly magical.

It's modern, yet still true to its ancient roots.

It's rich in history wherever one looks. It's no wonder people come here and fall in love—with the food, the people, and the country itself.

It does feel as if magic is present, and tonight is one of those nights.

If this were any other woman, she would feel like a princess in her golden ball gown. A sweetheart neckline, which puffs out in layers of tulle, and a stunning emerald necklace with matching drop earrings complete the outfit.

But this is merely a uniform, a disguise to lure in my prey, and that is Enzo Cattaneo.

Vince texted me earlier today, informing me of a ball I must attend, as anyone who is anyone will be in attendance. I was told to buy a pretty dress. It was to be suggestive but still conservative.

Now older, I see what Gianna did the night Lenny and I attended that ball, the ball where I made my first kill.

I was nothing but a pretty pawn to do her dirty work while she watched on.

And tonight is no different.

She wants me to do the same thing to Enzo that I did to that disgusting pig. The only difference is that Enzo hasn't done anything to me. He's Gianna's rival, not mine, and I'm suddenly grappling with the morality of taking a man's life who I don't even know.

It feels almost cowardly.

What of Enzo's family?

How will they explain to his kids and his grandkids that their beloved father and grandfather is dead?

I peer at myself in the bathroom mirror, gripping the edge of the marble basin, knowing this is so fucking wrong.

I don't know why I give a damn. But I do.

However, if I don't do this, then I will never be free.

As I am soon to be a mother, I can understand why my mother did what she did, to some extent. She thought she was protecting me against Aldo. However, it was a cowardly, selfish act. I suppose my mother and I are not made of the same girth.

I will do anything to protect Lettie, but I would never abandon her as my mother did to me. Regardless of this, I wonder if her coming to Sicily is merely a fantasy that will never come to fruition.

I wrestle with these endless thoughts because I'm trying to justify what Gianna wants me to do.

The bathroom door opens, reminding me that this isn't the time or place to suddenly have a guilty conscience.

If I do this, I am free.

But deep down, will I ever really be free?

My hands tremble as I open my gold clutch to retrieve my red lipstick. I apply it to my lips not to rouse suspicion. The woman who entered does the same two basins over. Our lipsticks don't need touching up, but it appears we both need a breather from the vile men and women who fill this spectacular venue.

Once a castle, it has been transformed into a hideaway for the rich to be themselves as they check their coats and morals at the door. I have no idea what the occasion is, but it seems anyone with wealth and power is here.

I have yet to see Enzo, though.

Vince sent me a photo of him, and the resemblance between him and Aldo is apparent.

Thoughts of Aldo have me getting back in the game.

Enough of this pity party for one.

I gently wipe any excess lipstick from the corners of my mouth and exhale slowly.

I look how I should, and that is bait.

I disassociate from what I am about to do and think of the bigger picture. To achieve this, I must detach myself from emotion, something I was once very good at doing. But I now realize that isn't entirely true. If it were, I would have no qualms about killing Enzo and making it home in time to binge *Baywatch* reruns.

The woman I pass on the way out appears to be wrestling with her own personal demons. It seems that even in the most beautiful of settings, we're still prisoners to our pasts.

A string quartet plays classical music, and servers in tuxedos serve drinks and canapés from silver trays. People mingle, chatting animatedly as most Italians do.

I snag a glass of orange juice from a server who, no doubt, has been instructed to blend in. He doesn't speak. He doesn't make eye contact because he knows what happens if he sees or hears too much.

I try my best to fit in as I don't want to draw any attention to myself. Vince is adamant that no one knows who I am. But once tonight is over, that will soon change.

A loving couple to my right has a pang hit me low.

I haven't seen Lenny since the night we said goodbye. I woke the following morning, and he was gone.

No note.

No nothing.

No sign that I hadn't dreamed the entire thing.

I knew I hadn't because I was enveloped in his scent, and my body ached for days.

It still does.

But it aches for a different reason this time.

I didn't think missing someone could physically cause pain. But I'm living proof that it can. My heart is empty and missing an integral part.

I know I will see him again, but our reunion will be filled with violence and bloodshed as we fight on opposing teams.

The quicker I finish tonight, the faster I can attempt to live some sense of normalcy.

The thought has me snickering to myself because, who am I kidding?

But I can at least try.

I realize what I probably look like. Laughing to myself, I'm probably not the most appealing sight, which is why at that precise moment, I meet the gray eyes of Enzo Cattaneo.

It's that meet-cute moment you read about, but my narrative isn't a romance story.

It is far from it.

I can see from the get-go that he's interested.

Some men are such simple creatures—like a crow, mesmerized by shiny things.

He's about to meet something shiny, and that is the blade of the knife I have stowed away in my purse.

My instruction was to seduce Enzo and learn his secrets, only to then betray him. But there is one not-so-tiny problem with that scenario—soon, my already growing belly won't be easily concealed. Unless Enzo has a mommy fetish, this plan won't work, which is why I plan on killing him tonight and dealing with the consequences later.

Gianna won't be happy.

But she can do her own bidding if she isn't pleased with my tactics.

It feels almost sacrilegious to disobey her this way.

Enzo looks rather sharp in a navy suit with a crisp white shirt. He's opted for no tie, but instead wears his shirt unbuttoned with a gold crucifix chain on display.

He reeks of power and money.

Different from Aldo, who, although dressed well, was never flashy like Enzo appears to be.

I shyly avert my eyes, playing the game as I was taught by

the best.

A moment later, a man is by my side. "Mr. Cattaneo wishes to speak with you."

I nervously curl a loose strand of hair behind my ear. "Who is he?"

"Best you do not keep him waiting," he says in a strong accent, ignoring my question. "He wants to talk to you in private."

Nodding, I follow the man as he leads me through the unsuspecting crowd.

This place is like a maze, but I ensure I keep count of the turns. The man stops and opens the library door.

Enzo stands with his back turned to the door, perusing a shelf.

The man gestures for me to enter, and when I do, the door closes behind me.

Is this how these men woo women? They believe barking a possessive order makes us women putty in their hands?

I suppose money talks, as there is no mistaking that Enzo is extremely wealthy.

The gold Rolex speaks for itself.

I don't speak.

I wait for him to address me as a good little lamb is expected to.

He retrieves a book from the shelf and opens it, appearing

to read over it. It seems like a rather strange time to engage in some light reading, but to each their own.

"*Ciao,*" he finally says, placing the book back.

"Hello, I don't know a lot of Italian. I'm sorry." I scare myself by how easily I can slip into this damsel-in-distress role.

Enzo turns with a smile. "Ah, American. I knew something was different about you. Who do you belong to?"

His comment has me biting the inside of my cheek to stop from telling him to go fuck himself. I *do not* belong to anyone.

My heart, however, does.

But my mind and who I am as a person—I belong to myself.

Swallowing down my profanity, I reply as Vince instructed, "I am here with Elio Barone. He's my uncle."

Elio is no doubt on Gianna's payroll and will vouch for my story. But I don't need anyone to be my alibi because Enzo is minutes away from taking his last breath.

"How long are you here?"

"I don't know yet. I came here to study history."

Enzo doesn't care why I'm here. I could tell him I was interested in flying to the moon, and it wouldn't make a difference because I'm good for only one thing in his eyes.

Killing him suddenly becomes a whole lot easier.

He walks toward me, but I stand my ground regardless of how he towers over me. He doesn't hide his appraisal of me. And when his eyes linger on my breasts, it's evident he likes what he sees.

He cups my cheek.

I try not to flinch at his cold touch.

"Allow me to show you the most beautiful history in all of Sicily, then."

I chew my bottom lip, faking playing coy, before nodding. "I would like that."

"I would too." He leans down and plants a chaste kiss on my lips.

I slyly unfasten the clasp on my purse, and as my fingers pass over my knife, Enzo throws a curveball I was not expecting.

"But first, tell me who the *fuck* you really are."

It appears *I* was the one being played all along.

Before I have a chance to retaliate, Enzo snatches my purse out of my hands, and when he sees my knife, he grins.

"A girl can never be too careful," I quip, refusing to back down.

"Somehow I doubt you're just a girl."

I search for a weapon, just as Gianna taught, and see them in the form of books.

Lunging for the shelf to my right, I grab a hardcover and throw it in Enzo's face. The moment he swipes it away, I punch him in the stomach, winding him.

I don't give him time to recover before I yank up my ballooned skirt and kick him in the ribs.

He staggers back three steps, gripping his side.

But the bastard is smiling. "Finally, I have my revenge for my brother."

He has worked out that Gianna has sent me.

He doesn't know the details, but he doesn't care because we're both out for blood.

Tossing book after book at him, I move around the room, seeking out something heavy and preferably pointy. But Enzo reads me like a book—pun intended—when he uses a Bible as a Frisbee and clips me in the throat.

I cough, needing air, but soon regain my momentum when he tosses my knife at me, and it embeds into the front of my shoulder.

Immediately, I yank it out because I got my weapon.

Enzo laughs merrily. "Maybe I should keep you alive. You're fun."

His words enrage me, but I keep a level head. "You probably shouldn't make the same mistake Aldo did. He underestimated me, and look what happened to him."

Enzo's happiness soon dies, and utter hate overcomes him, which was my intention all along. An emotional fighter is a distracted one.

Emotions make us weak…the first lesson Gianna taught me.

Enzo charges for me, but I duck low and plunge my knife

into his back, stabbing him in the kidney.

His white shirt soon stains red.

And just like that, my bloodlust raises her sleepy head.

I want more…

I quickly withdraw my blade and am about to stab Enzo again, but he elbows me in the nose.

Blood pours from it.

This wasn't part of the plan.

It was supposed to be a surprise attack, and Lettie and I would leave here semi-unscathed. But when Enzo punches me in the stomach, and I feel my underwear growing wet, I realize how wrong I was.

Blood trickles down my legs.

It gushes from my nose.

I need to finish this.

But I can't.

Once again, it seems Gianna was right because emotions do make you weak, which is why instead of fighting, I do the complete opposite—I run for the balcony doors and kick them open. I don't hesitate as I dive over the balustrade and drop three stories into prickly blackberry bushes.

I pick myself up without looking behind me and hobble as fast as I can. I have cuts all over and a sprained ankle, but that's the least of my concerns.

I see an unattended Mercedes with the keys in the ignition.

I start it up and take off into the night, cursing myself and cursing Gianna.

I fucked up.

I fucked up big time.

But all I can think about is Lettie.

I can't go to the hospital.

There is only one place I can go.

The bleeding has lessened by the time I arrive at Nico's.

I leave the car running as I stagger to his front door. The porch light flickers on before he sleepily opens the front door. When he sees me, his sleepiness is replaced with urgency when he runs to catch me as I collapse into his arms.

"Valentina! *Quello che è successo?*"

"I-I…I'm sorry."

After that…I don't remember.

I wake to unknown, muted female voices.

I don't understand a word they're saying.

But I don't think they mean any harm.

"Oh, grazie a Dio."

That voice, I do recognize.

And I soon remember the last conscious thought I had was that I owe Nico.

When I open my eyes, everything is blurry, and that's because of the flickering candlelight. But through the dimness, I can see, bright and clear, the enormous wooden crucifix pinned to the wall in front of me.

Shrieking, I jolt up and scamper backward, knees toward my chest.

Where the fuck am I?

Childhood memories soon become a reality when I see three sisters in habits sitting by my bedside with rosary beads and Bibles in their laps. They're praying for my soul, it appears. Looks like they missed the memo.

Nico takes my hand. "You safe," he says kindly, but anywhere is safer than here.

"Why am I here?" I ask, peering down and blanching when I see the white nightgown I wear.

Ripping my hand from Nico's, I brush my fingers through my hair, a sigh of relief expelling from my lungs when I feel my hair isn't in two braids.

This is too much.

My mind and body slip back into a past I will forever be running from. But that can wait, when I pass my hand over my belly.

One of the sisters smiles. "Your baby is all right."

How does she know that?

Unless I underwent an ultrasound when unconscious, then

no one can know that, and I refuse to accept their knowledge as God telling them so.

"Doctor come," Nico says, reading my disbelief.

There is no judgment in his tone.

Nor does he look at me with disgust.

He knows my secret, well, one of them, and he still wants to be here. He doesn't ask what happened or why he had to bring me to this safe place. I don't know what I did to deserve him, and if I believed in God, perhaps this is divine intervention.

Whatever the reason, I am thankful.

I hate that this place of worship provides me with a sanctuary. In the past, it was my hell. So the irony isn't lost on me how the tables have turned.

Peering around at this holy place, I realize how smart Nico was for taking me here. This is probably the safest place for me to be, considering I started a war with the Sicilian Mafia boss.

I don't know what to do.

If it were only my well-being I had to think about, I would fight.

But there's so much more at stake now.

My purse is back at the castle. No doubt Enzo has studied it in hopes of finding out something about me. But there is nothing.

However, I'm not naive.

He will find me.

Sooner or later.

Peering at the crucifix, I wonder if this was destined for me all along.

Jesus's faith was tested by His Father to see if He was worthy.

Is *my* faith being tested?

The sisters get up and give Nico and me some privacy. When they're gone, he shifts his chair closer to my bedside.

He types on his phone, and the robotic voice asks the inevitable. "The father is the man who was here?"

There's no point in lying.

I nod.

Nico doesn't hide his disgust, and I don't blame him.

This would be the time Nico gets up and leaves. He has every right to. I have brought him nothing but trouble. The last time I saw him, my ex-boyfriend almost killed him. And then I turn up on his doorstep in the middle of the night, bloody and beaten, passing out, where he then had to take the initiative and bring me here.

This friendship is definitely one-sided.

Nico is quiet. But it's apparent it's anything but in his head.

Whatever he says next, I am ready for.

His fingers work frantically as he types what seems like a very long spiel.

"You are not safe at home, and I don't think I can protect you. You must stay here and have the baby. I will look after you.

And the baby. I will raise her like my own."

And clearly, I am *not* ready for anything because that is the last thing I *ever* imagined him saying.

I stare in bewilderment, wondering if perhaps the app has a glitch and is spitting out an incorrect translation. There's no way Nico would just offer to help me raise my baby.

But when he nods, there is no glitch. Only a man who is the most selfless human being I have ever met.

"No." I shake my head. "I can't ask that of you."

Besides, I can't stay here.

I have a duty to serve Gianna.

I can't stay here for the remainder of my pregnancy.

But Nico is right.

It's not safe.

There's no way for me to get in contact with Gianna.

After tonight, however, I fear she will penalize me for my rebellion and either turn her back on me or I will no longer be the hunter.

I will be the prey.

Nico takes my hand and slowly says, "Marry me. We will make a happy life."

I stare at him, open-mouthed.

Funny, the first thing that comes to mind is that his English is improving, and I'm touched that he's learning it for me. The proposal comes after. That's how my messed-up brain processes it.

"But you don't love me. And I don't love you," I reply, shaking my head. "That isn't fair to you."

He passes me the phone so I can type out my reply, which I do.

He quickly responds, typing frantically. "Love grows. But for now, this is what is important for you and the child."

This is the plot twist no one saw coming, not even me, the narrator of my own story.

I mull over his words, his suggestion.

With the crucifix bearing down at me, I lower my head and clasp my hands and whisper, "Forgive me."

Who I'm asking clemency from, I do not know.

I have wronged many.

Can I repent for my sins?

Time will only tell…

CHAPTER 7

LENNY
PRESENT DAY

"I'm so-sorry..."

I peer down at my Rolex, disgusted at this grown man slobbering all over himself.

Donkey looks just as bored. "I'm going to ask you again, where is she?"

"I-I can't—"

"Kill him," I cut him off, done with this conversation about ten minutes ago.

Donkey does as I order and shoots one of Gianna's minions

in the forehead.

He collapses on his side, blood trickling from the wound.

"Take out the trash."

Donkey nods and gets to work while I walk toward my black SUV, desensitized to this entire event. That's because this is just another day for me. The faces of the men I've killed are a blur. Their names? I couldn't even tell you one.

They're all nameless, faceless pests who stand in my way.

Over the past five years, my empire has grown. At the beginning, my leadership was tested by some, but when they and their families were made an example of, the men bowed to me.

I am ruthless.

And I don't give a fuck.

That's because I have nothing left to lose.

Everything I ever cared for is gone, myself included, because I am a stranger in familiar skin.

Lewis is now Gianna's most loyal lapdog. He jumped ship when she promised him every drug in the world, and in return, he was to be her inside man. Because what better way to reach the drug users than by a junkie himself?

The only reason he isn't dead is because Gianna keeps him safe, saving him for a rainy day, so to speak. But his day will come. And when it does, I will have no qualms about shooting him, just as I have done to the hundreds before him.

Blood or not, he is nothing to me.

Although Bria is my wife, our love is transactional.

It made sense to marry her.

We fight on the same side.

And I trust her.

I don't trust many, but Bria, for the most part, is someone I do.

And she trusts me because she loves me.

She had hoped that when we got married, we would be the perfect Mafia king and queen and live happily ever after.

But she was wrong.

I love her, but am I in love with her?

No, I am not.

And that leaves me with the only woman I have ever loved.

Valentina.

I lost her the minute I left Italy.

I knew it.

She knew it.

I thought that perhaps over the years, things might change. But with money comes power and respect, and both things were ingrained into us from childhood. It's hard to change a life lesson when it's the only thing that brings you joy.

I have seen Valentina over the years, us fighting to conquer the other. But when push comes to shove, neither of us seems to be able to be the one to "do it."

End it—once and for all.

Gianna got what she wanted—Valentina and I on opposing sides.

My hunt for Gianna has never stopped, but Valentina and I have come to an unspoken truce.

She keeps to her side.

And I keep to mine.

Gianna attempts to challenge me every so often. And I remind her that she cannot win by slaying every single man she sends my way.

I don't know what happened between her and Valentina.

It was radio silence for over a year, and then one day, it was war.

Valentina sent man after man, under the orders of Gianna, but she never succeeded. My men are loyal as I have proven to be a fruitful leader, and our empire is strong, stronger than Aldo's.

But it's because of him that I am the leader I am today.

Then Gianna backed down, as she knew she couldn't win against me.

Things were quiet—for a while.

But I knew it was the calm before the storm, and Valentina's arrival three days ago confirms this.

"I am here because I need you to give up. Gianna is planning a takedown so large, Lennon, you will not survive it."

She's lying. This has nothing to do with Gianna. Something bigger is on the horizon. Valentina is simply using Gianna as an excuse. She is pretending to do Gianna's bidding to get to me for a reason, and that reason has nothing to do with Gianna.

The question now is, what does she want?

I have no doubt Gianna has asked Valentina to come here, but something else is going on.

My phone ringing over my car Bluetooth snaps me back to reality.

"Hello, darling."

"Hi, babe. Don't forget to pick up a bottle of red on your way home."

"I didn't forget." I totally did, but Bria doesn't need to know that.

As I said, I do trust Bria, for the most part.

I trust that her love for me is real, so real that she's the reason Aldo's computer was wiped clear of any evidence that he had gathered on Valentina. I went to Italy armed with the truth to show Valentina who Gianna really is.

But when I arrived in Italy, the evidence was gone, thanks to Bria, who deleted every single file.

I had nothing to show. Therefore, I knew Valentina would never believe me.

I came back to America, ready to rip off Bria's head. But what I came home to was Bria taking control and defending her father's legacy to the death.

While I was away being a lovesick fool, she was here protecting her name and ensuring our kingdom didn't crumble.

She showed resilience and strength.

When I confronted her about what I suspected, she owned up and didn't hold back. She told me to grow up and stop chasing someone who doesn't want to be caught. She gave me an ultimatum—Valentina or her father's legacy.

At first, I was enraged and told her that I won't be forced or blackmailed into making a choice. She replied she was doing neither.

I was either all in.

Or I wasn't.

This wasn't a game.

She wouldn't allow her father's death to be in vain. She would get her revenge with or without me.

And deleting the evidence from Aldo's computer was the first step in her destruction of Valentina. Valentina didn't deserve happiness. She didn't deserve to know the truth because she was the enemy. It was because of Valentina's actions that her father was dead.

So again, she told me to choose.

My goal was to destroy Gianna, not Valentina. But Valentina was so far gone, I chose option number three—I chose myself.

I gave up the notion of saving Valentina because Bria was

right. Valentina didn't want to be saved, and I was naive to think I could change her mind.

I had really fucking tried. So I gave up and focused on something I could change—and that was Gianna's power.

I lived and breathed to ruin her and her empire, and succeeded. I overthrew her. I stole her men. But she always remained two steps ahead, where I could never catch her. Somehow, she always knew I was coming.

Eventually, she faded away, but I knew she was laying low and licking her wounds and waiting for me to fuck up.

She sent Valentina in hopes I would crumble.

But we were both different people.

Time had passed, and we had grown.

Her loyalty hadn't shifted from Gianna, but her motives had changed. It seemed she fought because she had to, not because she wanted to.

If we wanted each other dead, we would be. But instead, we've played this game of cat and mouse for years. I thought nostalgia held us back.

But I was wrong.

And this is why what's-his-face was shot in the head because he made the fatal mistake of mentioning Valentina's name, claiming he knew where she was because Gianna had told him. I called bullshit, but thought I'd give him the benefit of the doubt.

But as always, I can only rely on myself.

I pick up Bria's favorite bottle of red on the way home. Apparently, we're having a business meeting with a new investor. This is Bria's project, so I'm interested to see who has sparked her interest since she usually is a little more cautious than this.

But if she believes this person to be beneficial to us, then I am happy to hear their pitch.

I pull in front of our steel gates, nodding at Rodney, our gate guard. "Evening, Mr. Shepherd."

After the gates open, I drive up the winding driveway, and when my home comes into view, a sense of fulfillment overwhelms me because I built this from the ground up. This is on the back of the sacrifices I made.

But something is always missing…just how it always is.

The white mansion displays wealth, but is tasteful. The many arched windows give it a *Gone with the Wind* feel. The upper level, which houses Bria's and my bedroom, features beautiful ornate doors that open to a wraparound balcony.

The Roman pillars supporting the peaked roof of the balcony only add to the rustic charm.

The gardens are manicured, but I've ensured there are no places for an intruder to conceal themselves. So everything is kept short.

My home is exquisite, but as I have learned over the years, beauty is nothing if there is ugliness within. And regardless of this beauty, horror resides because of the darkness within me, which only grows every single day.

I pull into the large garage and park the car among the many others I have.

I don't forget the wine and enter the house through the garage door. I hear Bria chuckling. It seems our guests have arrived.

They're in the kitchen, and who I see sitting at the counter has me stopping dead in my tracks because he looks familiar—I just don't know how.

"Darling," Bria says, rushing over and kissing my cheek.

I stand frozen, eyeing the distinguished older gentleman. "Who are you?"

"Lenny," Bria gently warns, reading my apprehension immediately. "This is Francesco, an old friend of my father's."

And that is why he looks familiar—Aldo suspected him to be Valentina's father.

Bria read the files. Has she connected the dots that this is potentially Valentina's kin?

Instantly, I retrieve the gun from the small of my back and point it at Francesco. "You have three seconds to tell me why you're really here."

"Lenny!" Bria exclaims, attempting to lower my arm. It seems she's forgotten her father's findings.

But I don't budge.

Francesco isn't troubled by a gun in his face as he stands slowly. "It's all right, Bria."

Bria looks between us, confused.

"Leave us," I order, never taking my eyes or gun off Francesco.

"I will no—"

"Don't make me ask you twice."

I don't have time for Bria's antics.

She hesitates, then storms off with a huff, taking the bottle of red with her.

"Talk," I say when Bria is gone.

"It appears you know who I am."

"Enough with the bullshit. Why the fuck are you here?"

"The rumors are true," he says with a smile. "Lennon Shepherd is the ruthless killer after all."

"Nice chat," I quip. "Now answer the fucking question."

"You know who I am. That is why you are pointing a gun at me, no?" His thick Italian accent reminds me of Aldo's.

Perhaps they knew one another. Aldo always had his suspicions, but he could never prove them. So why is Francesco willingly divulging this information to me now?

When I neither confirm nor deny his claims, he continues. "I *am* Valentina's father. Aldo knew it all along, but it was never spoken of. We arrived from Italy together as we grew up in the same village. I was the one who introduced Gianna into this world."

"You wanted to double-cross Aldo, but Gianna double-crossed you, didn't she?"

He nods.

It doesn't take a genius to figure it out, because I know Gianna. The moment Francesco introduced Gianna to Aldo, he was always going to be the runner-up to Aldo, as Gianna saw his power and what she could steal from him.

"Aldo turned his back on me for 'love.' My fault for trusting either of them."

"Did you know about Valentina?"

He shakes his head.

"She had left me by the time she was heavily pregnant. She kept hidden, even from Aldo, as she didn't want anyone to know about her pregnancy."

Of course, she didn't. It was her plan to exploit Valentina all along.

"Aldo protected her. God bless him for falling in love with *il diavolo*. It cost him, and now, Gianna is after me. She wants to tie up 'loose ends' as she is coming for you, Lenny. She is merely biding her time and compiling an army that is stronger and smarter than yours.

"I come to you, asking for protection. I once worked for Aldo, so now, I offer my services to you. All I ask for is sanctuary in return."

"How can I trust you? For all I know, Gianna sent you."

"Over time, I can only earn your trust. But as a good gesture, I will give you what you want."

"And what is that?"

Francesco stares me dead in the eyes, revealing he knew he would always win. "Valentina."

I cock the trigger on my gun. But Francesco doesn't waver.

"I will tell Valentina the truth about who her mother and father really are."

I lower my piece because Francesco is the missing piece I need.

I gave up after all these years because with the evidence gone and Sister Margarette's mysterious death—which I know was Gianna's doing—I couldn't prove to Valentina who she really was.

But now, I can.

"How do you know about Valentina?" I doubt Gianna told him they had a daughter. If she did, then why does he want her to know the truth now?

"Rumors are circulating about Valentina. There is a mole among us who wants to harm Valentina. They know too much. It's not Gianna, since that would make her vulnerable, and she doesn't want anyone knowing about her secret weapon.

"One look at Valentina and I knew she was my daughter. She's in danger, Lenny. We must protect her."

Is that why Valentina is here?

Nothing makes any sense.

Putting my gun away, I open the freezer and retrieve the bottle of vodka. I pour two glasses and offer one to Francesco. We both take a much-needed drink.

Truth be told, I don't trust Francesco. This entire ploy smells of Gianna.

But what if it's legit?

I know what my answer is. Regardless of good sense, I know I will give Francesco what he wants because he's the only one to give me what I truly want—and that is Valentina.

He places the crystal glass on the counter. "I'll see myself out. Bria has my number. The ball is in your court."

He leaves, and I take a moment to digest everything.

If Francesco is a mole, then I'm about to welcome the enemy into my domain. I'll take my chances because if Valentina is in danger, then it's only a matter of time before she is another fatality in a war we never wanted.

I walk up the staircase, and when I enter my bedroom, I duck to miss the flying bottle of wine that Bria's aimed at my head.

It smashes against the wall, staining the paint red.

I close the door, sighing because I'm not in the mood for what's about to transpire.

"Please explain to me what's going on because, correct me

if I'm mistaken, but we're supposed to be partners in all things, are we not?"

"Stop with the sarcasm. It's most unbecoming."

"You know what's unbecoming?" she screams. "You giving me bits and pieces of yourself. I don't know what more I can do."

"Stopping screaming would be a good start." I kick off my boots.

Bria doesn't appreciate my suggestion and storms over, attempting to slap me.

I grip her wrist and arch a brow. "Careful."

"Or what?" she challenges, her chest heaving in anger.

I don't reply.

"This has to do with that *cagna*, doesn't it?"

I clench my jaw.

"I am *your* wife, Lenny! Not her. She left you. She has done nothing but be a major pain in our asses for years, and here you are, pining after her like a fucking pathetic dog! You should be embarrassed. I am embarrassed for you.

"She is the reason my father is dead! She is the reason we can't live in fucking peace!"

"Wake up, Bria! There is no peace in our world. This is the life we've chosen!"

"Well, maybe I don't want it anymore."

"That's your choice then," I counter, letting her go.

"I fucked Alex," she reveals, gloating.

Honestly, I have no idea who Alex is, which really isn't the moral of the story.

"He wanted me, unlike my husband!"

I won't do this with her. I don't have time for childish games.

I turn my back and walk toward the en suite. "I'm taking a shower."

"I tell you I fucked another man, and that's your response?"

I've run out of words because I honestly don't care.

After I strip off my shirt, I turn on the faucets and wait for the water to warm. I take off my pants and step into the double shower. The hot water feels amazing against my aching body. The bliss is short-lived, however, because Bria charges into the shower and stabs me in the shoulder blade.

Placing my forehead against the tiles, I inhale slowly because a man can't even take a shower in peace.

Reaching around, I withdraw the blade. It's only a flesh wound, but regardless, it'll need stitches.

Turning around, Bria stands in the shower, fully clothed and soaking wet.

She goes to slap me again, but this time, I grab her by the throat and shove her back against the wall. She fights to free herself, but I tighten my hold.

I am fucking pissed off…which is exactly what she wants.

"I fucked him in our bed," she gasps as I squeeze her throat.

"He fucks like a real man."

"Not sure what that even means, but kudos to him."

Her eyes narrow, angered I'm not taking the bait. "No wonder she left you…you're a miserable sack of shit who can't fuck! She's probably found a real man who fucks her—"

Bria never finishes her sentence because I spin her around and slam her front to the tiles. I yank up the hem of her dress and slap her bare ass.

She jolts up the wall with the force, groaning in delight.

Reaching around, I grip her throat and arch her head back where I fuck the shit out of her mouth with my tongue. We kiss like we hate one another, and that's because we do.

But with hate comes love, and I am suddenly hard.

Bria rubs her ass against my cock, and I give her what we both want as I thrust into her. A guttural cry leaves her as she takes everything I give, bouncing back on my cock. I yank her arms above her head and capture her wrists in one hand, restraining her.

She surrenders like always since this is the only sex we have—rough and animalistic.

I think it's because we hate each other more than we love. But despite this, we have a connection, no matter how messed up it may be.

I fuck her hard, punishing her.

She feels like heaven on my cock, but it's always been a

substitute for who I really crave. Thoughts of Valentina have me fucking Bria faster and deeper. I withdraw only to shove my cock into her so hard, driving her up the wall.

"I love you!" she screams, arching her back.

And I know that she does.

There are parts about her I love, but I can never say it back and mean it the way she wants.

"I love you…even if you don't love me back. But you will," she pants, before coming loudly.

I have no idea what that means, but it sounds like an ominous warning of things to come.

But what's fucking new.

CHAPTER 8

VALENTINA

"*Papa, ti amo.*"

"*I love you too, cara mia.*"

It's Lettie's fifth birthday, and Nico insisted our little principessa *gets spoiled, not that that's any different.*

It's a warm summer day.

The afternoon is filled with happiness and fun. A three-tiered pink ballerina birthday cake sits in the middle of the table. My little Lettie, in her tutu and tiara, claps her hands in excitement as we sing "Happy Birthday." She patiently waits her turn to blow out her five candles.

Nico is taking photos, smiling proudly.

I stand aside, wishing to take it all in because this is what we live for—moments in time.

"Make a wish," I say, nodding at Lettie.

She chews her bottom lip, deep in thought, before she leans forward and blows out her candles.

We cheer.

Our glasses are raised.

Cake is eaten.

Coffee is drunk.

Night falls, and Nico takes the broom from my hands and escorts me to the bathroom, where we make love in the shower.

He's such a wonderful man.

How he's changed my life.

I wish I could say I've changed his for the better, but I know that I haven't.

He stuck true to his word and raised Lettie like his own.

I had my baby in secret.

The convent was my home.

I forgot who I was and focused on repenting for my sins.

My labor was hard.

I believed it was punishment for all that I had done. But the moment I heard Lettie's screams, it was worth it.

I kissed her ten fingers.

I counted her ten toes.

I was in love.

There is no other word for it. For the first time in my life, I felt perpetual love and knew I would die for my daughter.

I didn't know what to expect when I left the convent. I had just disappeared. Gianna would surely be hunting me.

But I was surprised when things remained calm—for a little while anyway.

Lettie was six months when I received a package on my doorstep.

A box and inside, a phone.

Within minutes, I was sent a text with an address.

The peace within soon vanished, and I was thrown back into a world I did not want to be in.

I met Vince at a farmhouse.

He made it clear that I was seen as a traitor, and I should feel privileged that Gianna gave me another chance.

I killed Enzo that night.

And since then, I've killed many sons and daughters in hopes that I will be one step closer to saving mine.

I thought with Enzo's death, I would be free.

I thought wrong. Because his death gave Gianna the power she wanted.

But she needed someone to run her empire in Italy.

I never understood why she didn't just come here and do it herself. It's what she wanted for so long. But instead, order after order came, and I carried out each one. Numb to it all.

Her instruction led me back to America, which made me believe she couldn't come to Italy, as her empire in America was crumbling, thanks to Lenny.

I fought him, and although both of us could overthrow the other, we never did.

I couldn't kill Lettie's father.

I couldn't kill the love of my life.

The feelings were still just as strong.

Instead of fighting, we would just end up fucking.

And then, like always, one of us would disappear come morning, leaving the other wondering if it was all just a dream.

And that was how life was for a little while.

Gianna's demands lessened, and I was able to live a relatively quiet life.

But I knew it was only a matter of time.

Over the years, I grew to understand Gianna and learned her habits. She never gave up. If she was quiet, it was because she was conspiring to succeed.

I would get instructions when she believed she could win, only for her plans to fail.

Someone was always two steps ahead of Gianna.

The question was, who?

I searched high and low but to no avail.

I thought it was Lenny, but when he swore it wasn't him, I believed him.

Gianna had another enemy, and that enemy was now mine because I was no longer Gianna's hidden secret weapon.

Just as I knew it eventually would, my identity was uncovered, which made me, and by extension, my family, a sitting duck.

"Nico!" I scream, my home in disarray as I frantically go from room to room.

Please, God, no. I chant this over and over, but when I burst through the back door and see Nico lying in the middle of the garden, bloody and beaten, I realize I was foolish to ever believe God was real.

My sandals are left behind in haste as I run toward Nico, dropping to my knees and gripping his head in my hands.

There's so much blood.

"Nico!" I sob, tears blinding me, drowning memories of my once perfect life. "Where's Lettie?"

He remains unconscious.

"Nico!" I scream his name over and over, to no avail.

I sit with him for what feels like hours, until he stirs.

Stroking his hair, I peer into the heavens and wish hard, just as Lettie did on her birthday. I wish that she would be brought back to me.

But as Nico groans, I know that wishes don't come true.

"Where is Lettie?"

He wheezes, his eyes swollen shut.

I lower my ear to his mouth, and my world crumbles when he whispers, "She's gone."

I jolt upright, my body covered in perspiration.

Another nightmare.

However, this is real.

My daughter has been kidnapped without a word.

No ransom.

I have no idea what I need to do to get her back.

This is why I'm back here in America.

I need Lenny's help.

With Lettie gone, we are both at risk because she is the greatest collateral one can have. I would rather he hear it from me than from whoever has her.

I know the consequences of withholding this from him will most likely bring down our kingdoms. Lenny will destroy anything and anyone once he knows the truth.

But I accept whatever response he has.

I will do anything to get Lettie back.

Nico is in the hospital.

Whomever attacked him ensured to beat him within an inch of his life as a message to me.

The thing is, I don't know who would do this because I've

made so many enemies over the years. It could be anyone, and that's what scares me.

But what I do know is that Lenny is on my side—for once. I know he would never take our daughter if he somehow found out about her. But I've been so careful.

The clock on the bedside table in this shithole motel reads just after six a.m. I kick off the blanket and take a shower. Once dressed, I decide to go see Lenny. Hopefully, it won't end up the way it did the last time I saw him.

First and foremost, I'm here to tell him about our daughter. But I also want to warn him that Gianna is done waiting in the shadows. Vince let slip that she has something planned, something that will guarantee Lenny's demise—once and for all.

I don't know what, but I don't think she's bluffing.

A small part of me wonders if perhaps she has Lettie, holding her for ransom, with the intent of using her when she needs to. I've kept Lettie hidden as best I could, but I knew sooner or later, Gianna would find out about her.

I don't want to believe this as truth because I've done everything Gianna has asked. But if what Vince says is true, then she knows Lenny is my Achilles' heel and that I'll need some encouragement, like kidnapping my daughter, to do what she wants.

If I find out that this is the case, Lenny will have to fight me to kill Gianna because she's mine. I will ensure she suffers in unimaginable ways before I kill her.

I must tell him today.

Grabbing my backpack, I lock the door and make my way down the stairs. The parking lot is poorly lit, and the flickering motel sign creates a strobing effect that hinders my vision.

I hear it before I feel being unexpectedly hit by an unfamiliar black car, which blindsides me.

Thankfully, my training kicks in, and I roll under an SUV, shielding myself from the car, which comes to a screeching halt before reversing, intent on finishing the job.

I peer out from under the SUV, hands splayed to the asphalt, my breathing labored as the car comes to a stop and the door opens.

Fuck…

I watch as black boots crunch the gravel, the owner resolved to finding me. The boots are big, so I assume my assailant is male.

He gets closer and closer until he is feet away from the SUV. I try my best to reach around and unzip my backpack to grab my gun, but I have limited space and can't maneuver myself properly.

I have no weapon with a bastard hot on my ass.

He gets closer and closer, and just as he bends, I hear someone shout out.

"Hey, man, whatcha think you're doing? That's my truck."

My attacker quickly retreats, returning to his car, which speeds off out of the parking lot.

With a sigh of relief, I roll out from under the SUV and bend low, using the other cars as coverage so I can limp off, undetected.

I've been hit on my left hip and leg, but nothing feels broken.

Once I'm on the road, I hail a cab and go to the only place I can. Suddenly, being hit by a car doesn't seem so bad.

The security guard at the gates looks at me with interest when I approach his booth. "I'm here to see Lenny. Tell him Valentina is here."

Lenny clearly doesn't get random women appearing at his house after seven o'clock in the morning because the guard continues to look at me like I'm about to tell him a joke.

But when I arch a brow, indicating he's wasting my time, he quickly picks up the phone.

He nods, never taking his eyes off me.

Once he hangs up, he exits his booth and walks over to a golf buggy. "I'll drive you to the house."

Usually, I would argue, but my leg feels like a balloon, so I doubt I could walk up the incline. I get into the buggy without complaint. We drive in silence toward the mansion.

Lenny has done remarkably well for himself. This home is rich in possessions, but we both know money doesn't buy happiness.

The guard drops me off at the door, which opens. Lenny stands in the doorway in gray sweats and nothing else. I've interrupted his training as he's like me and barely sleeps four hours a night, which means we're up before the crack of dawn.

I hobble out of the buggy, trying my best not to draw attention to the earlier mishap.

But it's hard to miss.

Lenny walks down the stairs, and my heart does a tiny flip-flop because I instantly feel a sense of peace in his presence.

That's soon to change, no doubt.

He leads us away from the house. I forgot about Bria. Thoughts of her have me wanting to punch something.

We walk toward a small building at the back of the house. We enter, and I see it's a training room. It's equipped with everything we grew up with. Seems fitting I'm about to divulge what I am in a room full of weapons.

"What happened?"

"Someone hit me with their car. Fucking rude if you ask me."

His lips twitch. "Did you see who?"

"No, but it was a man, I think, judging from his shoe size."

"Stupid question, but any idea who wants you dead?"

I scoff in humor. "Could be anyone."

He takes a step closer. My mouth instantly waters because he is fucking delicious, and I want to climb him like a tree. "Anyone but me?"

I fold my arms, arching a brow.

"Well, you wouldn't be here if you thought it was me."

"Lenny, if we wanted the other dead, it would have happened long ago."

He nods, running a hand over his heavy growth. That's when I see scratch marks on the side of his neck. I also notice white gauze over the back of his shoulder.

Love taps, perhaps?

My blood boils.

My need to punch something returns.

Kicking off my shoes, I take down a pair of nunchucks from the wall and twirl them, needing to distract myself from punching Lenny.

I have no right to be jealous.

But the thought of him with Bria makes me want to vomit or scream. Maybe both.

"Let's fight."

It seems we both need to do something with our hands other than throttle each other. Or worst still, tug at one another's hair as we fuck the shit out of each other.

Lenny gets into a fighting stance as I move the nunchucks in a sequence. He watches me closely, and when I strike, he blocks me with the back of his wrist.

He grins. Sparring has always been a favorite pastime of his.

"I need to talk to you," he says as we circle each other.

"About?" My interest is piqued.

Does he know about Lettie?

"About…you."

"What about me?"

He pauses, which costs him as I strike him in the knee. I don't hold back, and he jumps back, flinching. But he doesn't back down.

"I…your—" Lenny is at a loss for words? I don't know what to think.

"Spit it out."

"It's not something you can just spit out."

"That's never stopped you in the past."

"This is different."

"Why?"

This banter just riles me up even more, and I attempt to hit him again. He disarms me this time.

We stand staring at each other, the mat beneath our bare feet, our chests rising and falling.

I don't know what's happening, but it doesn't seem good.

"Lenny, you're scaring me."

"I'm sorry, I just…this is something that will change everything. I just need you to trust me. Please listen and—"

"Hello, Valentina."

I turn over my shoulder and see a man standing in the doorway. I don't know who he is. I've never seen him before.

"Who's this?" I ask Lenny.

"I'm your father."

Lenny flinches, and that's because what this stranger says is true.

Lenny wouldn't have brought him here if he didn't believe him or didn't have the evidence to prove it.

"Lenny?" I question, my quivering voice betraying me.

He nods slowly, confirming this man's claims.

"I…don't…how?" Constructing a coherent sentence is clearly not feasible.

Lenny attempts to comfort me, but I shrug away. "Start talking."

"My name is Francesco, and I was married to your mother."

"That's impossible!" I scoff, shaking my head. "My mother was a nun. I don't need to listen to this. More ploys from you, Lenny? I'm disappointed by your predictability."

I turn to leave.

Lenny sighs, rubbing his forehead. "Please listen. It'll all make sense. I promise."

I don't know why, but I stay because deep down, I feel this may be the answer to finding Lettie. Someone is after me, and I don't know who. So perhaps, this may give insight into something I am unaware of.

"Your mother isn't Sister Margarette," Lenny says gently, his hands raised in surrender. "Your mother is…your mother is… fuck!"

He runs his fingers through his hair. "Your mother is… Gianna."

"*What*? Have you gone mad?" I cry, unbelieving he would even suggest such a thing.

"It's true, *bella*."

"Don't you fucking *bella* me!" I scream at this strange man who is my apparent father.

Lenny tips his head toward the ceiling, blowing out a frustrated breath.

"I know this is hard for you to believe, but here." Francesco retrieves a photo from his pocket and offers it to me.

I see it's a photograph of him and Gianna. Although young, it's definitely her.

"I fell deeply in love with your mother. But Gianna is incapable of love. Look at what she's done to you, her own daughter. She has lied to you since the moment she left you on the doorstep of that orphanage."

"No." I shake my head, stepping backward, needing an

escape.

"I was the one who introduced her to Aldo. It was the worst mistake I ever made. She saw his power and respect. And she wanted it.

"She hid when pregnant with you. I didn't even know you existed, Valentina. I swear it. If I did, I would have never allowed you to grow up without me."

"Shut up," I mumble, a fire starting at my feet and working its way up.

But he does not.

"Gianna knew you would always be the ace up her sleeve, which is why she hid you from the world, only to play martyr and come 'save you.'

"But in reality, she was merely waiting for you to become useful—young enough to brainwash but old enough to learn the ways of her world. It's the only reason she kept you. If I'm lying, why wouldn't she raise you? Instead, she locked you away and made you someone else's problem. It wasn't because she had a change of heart. It was because she doesn't have one."

"Shut up…shut up." I place my hands over my ears, needing to shut out the noise.

How can this be true? If that's the case, then Gianna is the biggest monster of them all.

If this is true, then Gianna is to blame…for everything.

If this is true, then I will fucking kill her.

"Valentina—"

"Enough. She's had enough. Get out."

I faintly hear Lenny's voice because the white noise is deafening.

I drop to my knees, covering my ears, rocking back and forth, my head bowed. "No...no...no," I repeat, panic overcoming me, and I can't breathe.

The harder I try to catch my breath, the harder it becomes to breathe.

My heart is pounding. It feels as if I'm underwater.

I want to give up, but I can't. Lettie needs me.

Everything is upside down.

Side to side.

The faces of every life I've taken flash before me, their mouths twisted wide open, screaming for help.

This is hell.

This is where I belong.

"Come back to me, *tesoro mio.*"

But I can't.

Gianna's blood runs through me.

And it runs through Lettie's veins.

What does that mean?

Have I created a monster, for I am a monster?

I am the spawn of the devil.

I thought nothing was worse than being the daughter of a

serial killer and a nun.

This, however, is so much worse.

"Lettie? Who's Lettie?"

Her name brings me back to the now, and I'm refusing to slip away because I can't. I must fight. It's a mother's job to protect her child.

I won't be my…mother.

I won't.

Now, it's my job to be the mother Gianna was not.

The noise softens, and I focus on Lettie's innocent smile. Her trusting eyes. I focus on the feeling of being her mom.

Peering up at Lenny, I release the guilt and anger and whisper, "She's your daughter."

And now, it's Lenny's turn to question everything he thought he knew.

"My da-daughter? What? *What*? No. I don't…understand."

Tears stream down my cheeks because the truth is supposed to set one free. Yet all it's done is confirm that I'll forever be repenting for my sins.

He doesn't speak.

I hear his determined footsteps pace back and forth. I need time to compose myself before I look at him.

He mumbles incoherently.

It seems we've both been delivered a bombshell.

I can't comprehend any of this.

It seems so far-fetched. How could Gianna do this? If what my "father" says is true, I've been siding with the person I've been hunting my whole life.

That's the reality check I need to measure my breaths and calm the fuck down.

In and out.

I take my time to focus on the only thing that matters, and that's our daughter.

"For the first time in our lives...we fight for the same thing," I say, slowly brushing the hair from my eyes as I look at Lenny.

He stops pacing and interlaces his hands behind his head. I understand this is hard. There was no easy way of breaking this kind of news.

And I soon realize that this is the secret Lenny has wanted to tell me for years. He knew Gianna was my...I can't even say the word without wanting to break something. But he knew that without proof, I wouldn't believe him.

He came to Italy with the proof he needed. I too had the proof to reveal to him that he was going to be a father.

But it seems the universe had other plans for us both.

We possibly needed time to grow. Or maybe there were more life lessons to learn. Whatever the reason, it does not matter because it feels as if we've come full circle.

Perhaps Gianna trained us for this precise moment in time.

"How could you keep this from me?"

"To protect our daughter." There's no hesitation in my response.

"Protect her from me?" His voice is trembling in anger.

"Protect her from us both. How long have you known about Gianna?"

Lenny is now the one to feel guilt. "It was Aldo's last words. He was the one who told me she was your mother."

I feel betrayed by so many. It appears everyone knew the truth except me.

"I guess in that regard, the same question applies to you."

"Would you have believed me without any proof?"

I shake my head.

I barely believe it now.

"I came to Italy with Aldo's computer, with the evidence I needed, but Bria wiped it clean without my knowledge."

I come to a slow stand. "It appears we both had secrets, then."

"So why the sudden change of heart? You've kept my daughter from me for this long, what's another few years?" He's livid and lashes out, punching a bag so hard that it swings high and almost comes loose.

"Our daughter, Lettie…she's been kidnapped."

Lenny pales and wavers on his feet. He holds the punching bag for support. "Lettie?" he whispers, touched by her name choice as it's so close to her father's.

I give him time to digest this.

"How old is she?"

"She's just turned five."

He does the math in his head and realizes she was conceived that fateful night.

"I'm a father?"

I nod, quashing down a new tsunami of tears.

He stares off into the distance, likely replaying everything I just shared.

My brain refuses to process the revelation about Gianna. Deep down, I hope that this is all a bad dream, but I know Lenny would never lie about this.

He's been fighting for me for so many years. He never gave up on me when he had every right to.

He retrieves a folded piece of paper from his pocket, offering it to me. "Francesco gave me this before he left."

I accept, and when I unfold it and see that's my birth certificate, in some macabre way, I finally am free.

Free of the shackles of my past.

Free of whether something was wrong with me, because what mother abandons their child on the steps of an orphanage?

And free of the guilt which has forever plagued me that I was to blame for any of this.

This is my mother's fault; Gianna Ricci whose name I read before my eyes.

She *is* my mother.

And she is really fucking dead.

A thought hits me and I gasp, covering my mouth.

"What if…what if Gianna has her?"

Lenny's jaw clenches. "She knows about her?"

I shake my head.

But this possibility makes sense. Perhaps Gianna has her to ensure I don't betray her. She did the same thing to me, didn't she?

"We have to find her."

"Gianna aside, who else could have her? Who else knows about her?"

"I don't know," I reply, unable to process any of this. "I've gone over this a million times. I've kept Lettie out of sight for this exact reason. Nico has—"

The moment I say his name, Lenny closes his eyes and exhales slowly. "That fucker has been raising my daughter?"

"Lenny."

"Answer the fucking question, Valentina!"

"Yes," I reply, full of defeat.

Something in Lenny snaps, and he goes into a rage, tearing the gym apart.

I stand aside, watching in horror at the pain I've caused, making me hate Gianna even more than I do.

"How could you?" he pants, dropping to his knees in

front of me, tears in his beautiful eyes. "You robbed me of my daughter."

I can't hold back my tears and sob. "I did what was right. I did everything to protect her. She doesn't belong in either of our worlds."

"You don't get to decide that! I'm her father!"

"We're fucking criminals, Lenny! We kill people like it's nothing! I didn't want our daughter to see both her parents as the bad guys."

"We *are* the bad guys, Valentina, and shielding her from the truth would never change that! Instead, you took a choice away from me which you had no right to do! If I knew, I would have—"

"You would have what?" I cry, spreading my arms out wide. "This is your life!"

"As it is yours."

"I did what I had to do to protect our daughter."

His anger soon turns to sorrow. "And I would have done the same thing."

I could stab back and point out that he too sat on a secret. But he's right in thinking I wouldn't believe him.

I knew this wouldn't be easy, and I accept whatever decision he makes. I would be angry with me too. But anger aside, he will soon realize why I did what I did.

But I failed because Lettie is gone.

"I have so many questions, but for the first time in my life, I've run out of words."

I've broken him, that much is clear.

I am riddled with so many emotions, but at the forefront is that we need to put our differences aside. Lettie is depending on us.

"I won't insult you by apologizing."

"Thank you." He nods in gratitude. "You need to tell me everything, from start to finish, because that's the only way we're going to find her. But get this clear, Valentina."

He steps forward, towering over me, his anger suffocating. "I am only doing this for a daughter I didn't even know I had. When we find her, and we *will* find her, this won't end in a happy family reunion. I intend on getting back the years I missed out on."

I stand my ground even though I'm trembling on the inside.

"I didn't think you could hurt me more than you already have. But I was wrong. This is the ultimate betrayal. We find Lettie. And…we kill Gianna—together.

"What happens after that is that you go the fuck back to Italy because you are dead to me."

Lenny and I have fought countless times, but this is different.

There's no coming back from this.

He'll never forgive me.

But I never expected anything less.

"If you think I'm leaving my daughter here, you're sorely mistaken," I state very clearly.

Lenny laughs, and the sound has my entire body breaking out into goose bumps. "You need me, Valentina. You wouldn't be here if you didn't. So be very careful that you don't end up missing too."

I smack his cheek, fury animating me. "Threaten me again, and you'll never see her. I promise you."

I'll make a deal with the devil himself, and that devil is Gianna even though I know the truth. I'll put my revenge aside if it means Gianna will help me find my daughter.

And Lenny knows that.

It seems we're finally on the same side…fighting for the same thing.

But this doesn't mean we're united.

If anything, this means war, and our feud is so much worse than any before it.

Let the best man, or rather, *woman* win because I won't lose.

CHAPTER 9

LENNY

"**A**re you fucking insane!"

The honest answer to that is that I am questioning my sanity daily.

"Bria. Enough," I groan with my back turned as I'm cleaning out a spare cupboard of clothes we barely use.

Bria yanks on my arm, spinning me around to face her. "She's not staying here! She killed my father! Have you forgotten?"

I knew this would go down like a bag of dicks, but there's no way I'm letting Valentina out of my sight. I'm not sure what she thought would happen by coming here, but a happy reunion is definitely off the cards.

I don't plan on telling Bria about Lettie because the fewer people who know about her, the better. Until I have some clue about what's going on, I will behave like Lettie doesn't exist.

Valentina did as I asked and told me everything.

Someone is hunting her, and I'll bet my entire fortune that it's Gianna.

I have no doubt that Gianna knows about Lettie, and when Valentina told me about the bogus Madam Gazella, I suspected she knew more than she was letting on.

And I was right.

The internet is every stalker's best friend because after twenty minutes, I was able to confirm what I suspected— Madam Bullshit is Gianna's mother.

So it seems even Valentina's grandmother is an evil bitch who is about to pay dearly for her lies. I figure if she's a clairvoyant and all, she should be able to see me coming.

If she doesn't, then that just proves she's all smoke and mirrors.

She's the only link I have to Gianna.

She's collateral, so I need her alive.

Valentina is concerned for Nico's safety and asked if he could come here.

As much as I would rather cut off my arm and beat myself to death with it, I agreed because as far as I'm concerned, everyone's a suspect.

Nico may have staged this entire thing.

I need to keep my friends close and my enemies even closer.

Even Valentina.

For all I know, this whole daughter facade is just a big ploy by Gianna to tug on my heartstrings, and Valentina will strike the moment I let my guard down. Valentina is the one who warned me that Gianna is up to something so big that I won't survive it.

And this is pretty fucking big.

So it seems we're all about to be one big happy family.

"This house is big enough that you never have to see her. It's only for a short while."

"That's beside the point! Her being here is disrespecting my father and putting our lives in danger. You're literally inviting the enemy into our home! After everything she's done, you still trust her! You're pathetic!"

There will be no bargaining with Bria.

Turning around, I hate to see her in turmoil this way, but this is happening. "You've always wanted to explore the Greek islands, how about you go on—"

"You're just shipping me off? Un-fucking-believable! There's no way I'm going anywhere."

This is one argument I'll never win.

"Over my dead body will she step foot inside this house,

and if she does, I will fucking slit her throat."

I wish she was merely being melodramatic, but she's not.

I understand her anger. I would react the same way. However, if she stands in my way, I *will* send her away, kicking and screaming if I must.

"What does she have over you?" Bria asks, her eyes heavy with tears. "You won't even tell me what's going on. This isn't a marriage, Lenny. I didn't sign up for this."

"Then fucking go!" I scream, pointing at the door. "No one is holding you prisoner."

"Is that what you want?"

"I'm not playing these childish games with you."

"Then choose. Me or her."

Leveling her with utter gravity, I state, "I don't do good with ultimatums, you know that. But I choose neither. If you want to leave, then that's your choice. I'm telling you what's happening. You either accept it or you don't.

"I'm sorry this is upsetting you. I understand why it is. But please, understand me—this is happening with or without your blessing."

Harsh, but true.

My daughter is the only thing I care about right now, and Bria's tantrum is just wasting my time.

I turn back around, which probably isn't wise because the last time my back was turned, Bria stabbed me. But I guess we're now even because I am doing the same thing to her—figuratively speaking.

Bria sniffs but is too strong to cry.

She leaves, and I honestly don't know if she'll return.

I finish clearing some space for Valentina, not that she deserves it.

We may be fighting for the same thing, but we're not on the same team.

My cell chimes, and it's a text from Donkey, reminding me about inventory tonight at the shop.

This is the last thing I want to be doing, but at the end of each month, I do a count on what we have. Then we place an order with our suppliers. I keep a close eye on my product because I don't want anyone stealing from me, like Bria did to Aldo.

This is the only way I can ensure my men are loyal and not stealing from me or undercutting me in any way.

"Hi."

I clench the cell in my hand because her voice soothes and angers me in the same breath.

Valentina was waiting for me while I spoke to Bria, not that I accomplished anything. She would have heard the whole thing.

At least she knows to stay out of Bria's way.

But Valentina isn't here to rekindle old flames. She's here

because something bigger is at play, and if Gianna is the mastermind, then who better to take her down than the kids she shaped into killers?

I have no idea when Nico will arrive. If I don't see him, we won't have a problem. It's a laughable notion that we're all to coexist under the same roof because one of us *will* snap.

Living together like one big happy family is the most absurd idea.

"I'm happy to stay in a motel," Valentina says for the tenth time.

"It's safer to stay here."

She arches a brow because that's not entirely true. Not with Bria on a warpath.

"I understand why she's upset, and I don't want to encroach on her home. I'm not here to cause any trouble. You're her husband, and I get it. Your virtue is safe, trust me."

"Ditto, sweetheart."

We both hate one another, so any secret rendezvous is out of the question.

"This is your room. I have a meeting I must attend."

She dumps her backpack near the dresser. "Okay, let's go."

"Pardon me? That wasn't an invite."

"I really don't care. I'm here because you don't trust me. You want to keep an eye on me in case this is one of Gianna's ploys to infiltrate your home. But guess what? I don't trust you either.

So where you go, I go."

She has every right to think this.

"Suit yourself."

She gestures for me to lead the way.

Bria has thankfully made herself scarce as we make our way to the garage. Valentina doesn't say a word when she sees my collection of cars. I decide to take the pickup as I have a dollhouse for Donkey's daughter. It's her birthday this weekend, but I won't be attending. So I'll give it to him tonight.

We drive in silence, the radio's background noise filling the quiet. My thoughts are with my daughter. I don't even know what she looks like. However, seeing a photograph of her makes this entire thing real.

And it makes me despise Valentina more than I already do.

I park the car in the private parking lot at the back of the store. I notice Valentina looking at the shop closely. I suppose this brings back memories of Aldo.

She now knows he wanted to adopt her to keep her safe. Or at the very least, use her against Gianna. The lesser of two evils, I suppose.

I take in our surroundings, ensuring nothing feels out of sorts. Donkey isn't here yet because I'm early. We get out, and I'm on edge as I walk toward the back door. I keep looking over my shoulder. Something doesn't feel right.

I retrieve my gun from the small of my back and unlock

the door. Entering cautiously, I switch on the light. Everything looks the same.

"Stay here," I softly instruct Valentina.

She nods, and I am not surprised when she produces her own gun.

She occupies the front as I do a quick sweep of the store, but I know this place like the back of my hand. There is no place to hide, other than the storeroom, which I have torn apart to no avail. All my stones are where I left them, and I can't see anything out of place.

All the hippie shit is still emanating its mumbo jumbo.

My safe and the money, jewels, and drugs inside are untouched.

Perhaps I'm just on edge.

I walk back out to Valentina, who looks at me. But I shake my head.

We hear a car pull up out back, and both of us are on guard as we peer out. It's dark out as the moon has gone into hiding. But the taillights belong to Donkey's sedan.

Valentina and I walk outside to meet him, and when he sees her, he soon works out who she is. He knows better than to ask questions. He instead looks at the pink monstrosity in the back of my pickup.

"For Amelia," I clarify. "Every six-year-old likes pink, right?"

Valentina's demeanor instantly softens.

Donkey's lips twitch. "Yes, she'll love it. But you're not coming to her birthday party?"

I shake my head.

"Do you need me?"

"I appreciate the offer, but it's your daughter's birthday. Celebrate with your family. Nothing is more important than that."

Valentina busies herself by studying her nails since I've clearly hit a nerve.

"But you can't fit it in that thing," I mock, looking at Donkey's sedan. "Take my truck and drop it off at home. Come back when you're done."

"I'll be back soon."

I toss Donkey my keys, which he catches. "Thank you, Lennon. Under your asshole exterior lays only half an asshole."

Valentina muffles her laughter behind her hand.

My cell rings, but the caller is unknown. "Saved by the bell," I tease, giving Donkey a wave as I enter the store to take the call.

Valentina stays outside.

"Hello." However, it's silent. "Hello?" I repeat in case it's a bad line.

I hear Donkey talk to Valentina.

"Hello?" I say one last time.

Suddenly, I hear a nursery rhyme over the phone. *Ring*

around the rosie…

I don't have a chance to speak because the caller says one word. "Boom."

Dropping my cell, I run faster than my feet can keep up and scream, "No! Don't start the—"

But it's too late.

I feel the heat on my face before the sound erupts, and my eardrums vibrate with the destructive *BOOM*! I'm knocked back into the store from the explosion, everything shaky, and my ears are ringing loudly.

The red hue from the blazing fireball hurts my eyes, but I shield them with my forearm as I run back outside, screaming, "Valentina!"

The flames from my truck are licking the heavens. The roar is deafening.

It's too late for Donkey.

With my heart in my throat, I frantically search for Valentina.

The ringing in my ears has me swaying from side to side, throwing off my balance, and the smell of burning rubber and fuel burns my eyes and nostrils, but I push past it and continue my search.

"Valentina!" I bellow, ignoring the rumble coming from my burning car.

A relieved breath escapes me when I see her slumped

against a dumpster.

"Valentina!" I run to where she is and drop to my knees, cupping her face in my palms.

She's unconscious, but thankfully breathing.

Looking over my shoulder at the inferno, I know I have mere seconds to drag her to safety. I pick her up and toss her over my shoulder, then run down the street. The moment I enter an alleyway, an earsplitting eruption rocks the entire neighborhood.

The fire ignited the fuel tank, causing an explosion that shatters the windows of adjacent buildings. The sound wakes Valentina.

She groans.

I sigh in utter relief.

Gently placing her on the ground, I lean her back up against the bluestone wall. "It's okay, you're safe. Can you open your eyes?"

She opens and closes her mouth, but no words come out.

Her face is black with smoke, and her forehead is bleeding from where I assume she hit her head when she fell. But apart from that, I can't see any open wounds.

No matter my anger, I'm thankful she's all right.

Brushing the hair from her brow, I cup her cheek. "*Tesoro mio,* can you hear me?"

She wets her lips with her tongue. "Le-Lettie."

And it's at this moment that I know Valentina isn't lying.

Lettie is real.

"We'll find her. I promise. But for now, I need you to open your eyes."

Her eyelids flutter, appearing to be stuck together, but eventually, I see those incredible blue eyes. They slay me just like always.

My heart returns to a semi-normal pace.

It takes her a moment, but she realizes what happened. "A bomb?" she asks, her voice hoarse.

I nod. "Meant for us."

She pales. "Who called you?"

"I don't know, but I heard a nursery rhyme before he said the word, boom."

"What nursery rhyme?" Her voice quivers, and the answer may be the key.

"'Ring Around the Rosie.'"

Tears fill her eyes, and I know it has nothing to do with us almost being blown to smithereens.

"Explain why this is important."

I see her slipping away to a past she's tried so hard to escape.

But I won't let her because this time, she's not alone. We'll face her demons together, and I'll slay each one.

"It's just you and me," I whisper, lowering my face to meet her downcast eyes. "I'll keep you safe. He can't hurt you ever again."

A tear falls down her cheek.

"Father Merry…it's what he used to sing when he—"

But she shakes her head, eyes squeezed shut.

She doesn't need to explain.

I understand.

I understand why she did what she did to that motherfucker.

She crawls into my arms, wrapping herself around me while I cradle her tight.

Sirens sound in the distance, but she never lets me go.

Nor do I.

Father Merry is dead.

But someone knew of his despicable ways and is now trying to torment Valentina from the grave. The question is, who?

I can think of only one person—Gianna.

The bomb was in my car, but was it a coincidence that Donkey decided to drive his wife's car tonight?

The phone call was a warning.

We're not safe anywhere.

Our attacker is two steps ahead. They knew we would be here tonight.

So the question is, who wants us dead?

Chuckling under my breath, I hold Valentina tighter because the better question is, who doesn't?

Bria isn't around when we arrive home after midnight. As much as this makes me a bastard, I'm glad for the fact, as I can't deal with any more drama.

Thankfully, I have the right cops on my payroll who wrote off tonight's incident as a freak accident. My insurance company will take care of it.

As for the store, nothing but some broken windows and a few other minor damages. The crystals were working their magic, it seems.

Valentina is sitting on the balcony, peering into the starless night sky.

I almost lost her tonight.

It certainly brings home some hard truths that if she died…I would have too. I don't know what that means because I am still furious that she kept Lettie away from me.

Everything is just a fucking mess.

"Do you know where Gianna is?"

She shakes her head.

I rack my brain.

Suddenly, the answer stares me straight in the face.

"Did she send you any text messages?"

She meets my eyes, the confusion apparent. "Yes."

"Give me your phone."

She doesn't question my request and hands it to me.

I lost my cell in the explosion, but I have a burner phone.

Quickly dialing Gonzo, one of my men who is a tech whiz, I order he gets his ass over here immediately.

He arrives in ten minutes in his blue striped pajamas, his blond hair a mess.

I toss him the phone. "I need you to pinpoint the location from which this text message was sent. Go into my office and don't come out until you have an answer."

He makes it clear that I'm asking the near impossible, but nods nonetheless. He opens his briefcase and retrieves a fancy-looking laptop. He plugs the phone into it and frantically types away. Two minutes later, he passes me the phone.

I'm assuming he has copied the data from Valentina's phone onto his laptop.

He retreats inside.

Valentina is beyond exhausted.

This could take a while, so I say, "Go to sleep. I'll take care of it."

"I can't sleep," she confesses, drawing her knees toward her chest. "I keep hearing that nursery rhyme. What if…what if he's not dead?"

Crouching before her, I place my hands on her knees. "Father Merry is dead because you killed him."

"Then who is it?"

"I wish I knew, but we're going to find them."

She works her bottom lip, deep in thought. "I'm fearful for our daughter."

To hear her refer to Lettie as ours tugs at my heartstrings.

She taps her phone and scrolls through it. When her eyes soften, I know she's looking at our child.

"This is Lettie, the day she was born." She offers me her cell.

I cradle the phone, unable to take my eyes off the screen.

I'm hit with so many emotions. It almost feels surreal to look at the baby on the screen and be told she's mine.

She's the most beautiful thing I've ever seen.

Her hair is dark, and her eyes are blue.

"You can scroll across. There are thousands of pictures of her."

I take a seat beside Valentina and get lost in a life I never experienced, but now, I can live it through these photos.

Each one takes my breath away.

Seeing my daughter grow before my eyes is poignant, and a warmth I've never felt before fills me. I don't know what this feeling is.

It's beyond love.

"She's perfect," I whisper, running my finger over the screen, caressing her face.

I'll never tire of looking at her.

Through Valentina's happy snaps, I'm able to see my daughter grow. From birth until her fifth birthday. I'm an outsider, looking in on a life I wished I had lived.

And now, I get it.

I understand why Valentina did what she did.

Do I agree with it?

No.

But I understand why she wanted to keep Lettie hidden.

It's a parent's job to protect their child, and Valentina did what she had to do to keep our child safe. I assume she used her childhood as a blueprint on how *not* to raise a child. We both were dealt a shitty hand when it came to our parents. Valentina was doing what was best for Lettie.

I don't realize the time, but over an hour has passed.

Valentina sat silently as I caught up, so to speak.

I peer up from the phone and look at her. She is plagued and broken. Harm done to us, we can accept. But to our daughter? It's a different sort of pain.

"What happens if we don't find her?" she whispers, her lower lip trembling.

"We will." I will search high and low until she's found. "I promise."

Gonzo knocks on the balcony door before coming out to greet us.

I arch a brow.

He nods.

Jumping up, I slap him on the shoulder happily.

He pushes his thick black glasses up his nose. "Here. All the messages were sent from this address."

"Congratulations. You just earned yourself a pay raise," I say, reading over the address in his scribbled handwriting.

"I tried to trace the call made to you before the explosion. No luck."

I pat him on the back. "It's all right. Thank you."

The new lease on life animates Valentina. I see the fire in her eyes.

She's ready.

"Where is she?"

She reads my face instantly because Gianna is where the ghosts of Valentina's past dwell.

"You don't have—"

"Yes, I do," she interrupts. "We're doing this, and we're doing it now."

This place is a haven for the depraved. So it makes sense that Gianna is hiding out at Saint Maria's Orphanage.

What better place for a fugitive to hide?

I have no doubt she's putting on a holier-than-thou act.

If anyone came looking for her, she would say she found her calling helping the less fortunate.

No one questions someone who is doing "good" or someone who is repenting for their sins.

She has connections with the sisters. So they are providing her sanctuary.

Most would not start a war in the house of the Lord.

But we're not most.

We're sitting in the car, taking in this Gothic-style orphanage that was once our home. Far from welcoming, the outside reflects the gloom within.

Valentina is silent, but she's wrangling a personal battle because this place holds memories that won't let go.

"Father Merry often told me I looked just like my mother. Sister Margarette. That she was to blame for my suffering, for she knew what she was doing when she left me on this doorstep. But she wasn't my mother. So why did Father Merry think she was?"

We both know the answer to that.

Gianna appears to manipulate every person she meets, crafting a story to support her claims. "I suspect Gianna is a benefactor to the orphanage. This was the only one where she could keep an eye on you. Because of her friendship with Sister Margarette, she could fabricate a story and tarnish her name. And Sister Margarette couldn't defend herself because Gianna had her committed, but not before cutting out her tongue."

"I was really, really mean to her," Valentina confesses with remorse. "I was just so angry. Gianna had told me so many lies. So when I went to see her, I exploded. I wish I could take it back. What happened to her?"

"She's dead. A heart attack, apparently. But I believe Gianna just finished the job."

Valentina shakes her head, her fury evident. "I need to hear it from Gianna."

"You'll never get the truth from her."

"Do we have a plan?"

I do…but she's not going to like it.

Here goes nothing.

"The urge to torture her will be unbearable, but until we find out if she is involved with Lettie's disappearance, we need to play her at her own game."

Valentina exhales slowly. "Do we tell her I know the truth about…everything?"

"No," I reply without pause. "She cannot know. As far as she's concerned, you're still on her side."

Her mouth falls open. *"What?"*

And this was the plot twist no one saw coming.

"The plan is we pretend you're going to overthrow me and my empire, and I will surrender."

"She'll never believe that."

"Yes, she will. She'll believe it because you're going to tell her about Lettie."

"Lennon…have you gone fucking mad?" Valentina's eyes are wide as she attempts to decipher what's going on.

"Madam Gazella, the old *strega* you told me about. She's Gianna's mother, and the fact she's your grandmother, a minor detail she didn't deem fit to share with you, has me believing she's just as evil as her daughter.

"Gianna knows about Lettie because her mother told her."

Valentina simply stares at me. I know it's a lot, but I don't have time to divulge all this over scones and tea.

"Gianna was the one who told me where you were in Italy. I always wondered why she would do that. And I now know the reason is because she knew you were pregnant and that you wouldn't leave because of the baby. She wanted me to believe that you were lost to me.

"And I did. But now, I know the reason."

Valentina clenches her hands into fists atop her thighs. "It makes sense."

"So the plan is you go into the orphanage on the ruse that you believe I have Lettie and you need Gianna's help in finding her. You've tried on your own, but failed.

"You're going to beg for forgiveness for lying to her, and you'll do anything to earn back her trust. Play on the fact that you never knew your mother, so you wanted to provide a stable, safe environment for Lettie. You wanted to be the mother you never had."

"This will not work!" she exclaims, her cheeks reddening. From anger or fear, I'm not sure.

"It will. Gianna knows you'll do anything for Lettie, even betray her. So tell her you'll give her what she's wanted all these years…"

"And what's that?" she asks in a small voice, knowing the answer.

"My head."

I am ninety-nine percent certain Gianna has Lettie. She knew Lettie would always be Valentina's Achilles' heel. Gianna is sick of waiting. She is sick of Valentina and me playing this game of cat and mouse. Gianna would have killed me herself if she could.

But I'm smarter since she raised me. I know her.

However, having Lettie is the ace up her sleeve—just as she used Valentina—and it ensures her victory. And my throne.

"This is insanity! She'll see straight through this."

I'm certain this will work for the mere fact that…" In her eyes, you betrayed me once before. You must do it again. And she will believe it because there's so much more at stake for you now. You cannot let on that you suspect she is the one who has Lettie.

"You must say that you believe I want revenge for keeping

my daughter a secret. You believe I have kidnapped her, waiting for you to come begging because I know you can't win against me. Your men cannot match mine. But you'd rather die than surrender to me. Therefore, you need Gianna's help to find Lettie. And in return, you'll kill me, and my kingdom will be hers."

Valentina sighs, turning in her seat to look at me. "She'll believe it because that's what I deserve."

I stop myself from reaching out and touching her, reminding myself that I'm still furious at her. However, it's becoming increasingly difficult to remember that.

"It's going to be really, *really* hard to pretend I don't know the truth. Just saying her name makes me want to—" She doesn't continue because no words could ever sum up what we both want to do to Gianna.

"I know, but we don't have a choice. You said Gianna is planning a takeover so big that I won't survive. We could fight her, but I won't risk our daughter's life that way."

"Gianna's contact in Italy let it slip that she is planning something big. I don't know what, but he was confident she would win. And I believe him. That's why I think she has Lettie. She is the only thing we would both die for. It's why I came here. I needed to tell you the truth."

"And if none of this happened, would you still make the same choice?"

Her silence speaks volumes, which has my anger returning tenfold.

Any sentiment I feel for Valentina dissipates. I remind myself I'm here because she needs me. I shouldn't mistake this as her desire to be one big happy family once this is done and dusted. She has that in Italy, with Nico.

The urge to punch the windshield is debilitating.

But I quash down my need for violence and focus on what's important.

"Gianna won't let me out of her sight once I go in there."

"I know. Whatever she asks, you must do."

"So this was your plan all along? That we fight on opposing sides once again?"

"We'll never be on the same team, Valentina."

She flinches.

Harsh, but true.

She has Nico.

And I'm married to Bria.

Valentina and I will never just be friends.

We can't.

We will learn to coexist because of Lettie, but that's all it'll ever be.

Loving Valentina hurts.

It's destructive and appears to only cause pain.

A part of me is disappointed when she nods. I suppose I

had hoped she would defy me, as she always does, and fight for what I want but can't have.

"Goodbye, Lenny. I'll be in touch when I can." She opens the door, and I watch as she walks away from me…again.

CHAPTER 10

VALENTINA

I allow a single tear to fall as Lenny drives away.

He's right.

We'll never just be friends.

But hearing what I know is true still breaks my heart.

I focus on what's important, and that's putting on the best performance of my life. Gianna needs to believe that I'm coming back to her with my tail between my legs. This plan isn't foolproof, but it's the best plan we have.

We could fight Gianna, but if we overthrow her, she'll never tell me where Lettie is.

And I won't risk that.

If she doesn't have Lettie, then all this would have been for nothing, and Lettie will likely be gone forever. So I have to work fast because my daughter's life depends on it.

It's nostalgia as I sneak in the same way I did when I killed Father Merry. This place, a place I hate with every morsel of my being, is home.

I grew up here, and even though no fond memories will ever be associated with this hell on earth, it's still so familiar. Gianna could be anywhere, which is why, unlike with Father Merry, I make my presence known.

I knock on the glass door.

The gates around the property prohibit any late-night visitors. Or allowing babies to be dumped at the doorstep. Perhaps these high gates were erected because of me.

A young sister I don't know comes to the door, clearly stunned to see me.

I don't bother with formalities. "I need to see Gianna Ricci. Tell her Valentina is here."

The sister doesn't know what to do, but when I make it clear I'm not going anywhere, she soon retreats.

Gianna knows I'm here. She's watching me right now. So I purposely look at the camera mounted in the corner and wave.

The door buzzes open a second later.

There's no hurry to my steps as I walk down the long white

hallway. I mopped these floors many times as punishment for merely existing.

The place still smells the same—sterile and full of despair.

Heels echo in the distance. I know it's Gianna without seeing her. She appears at the end of the hallway, awaiting my arrival.

A ghost in the shadows.

A monster in my dreams.

My heart begins to race.

My palms are sweaty.

My mouth is dry.

And the urge to choke the life from Gianna is suffocating.

But when I approach her, I go against every moral standing and kiss both her cheeks. A sign of respect.

She stands unmoved. "Look what the cat dragged in."

I bite the inside of my cheek to silence myself.

She doesn't speak further and instead leads me down the hallway where I'm expected to follow the devil in Louboutin pumps.

This place hasn't changed.

I pass the same painting of Christ on the cross, bleeding, with His face twisted in agony. Hardly an inviting image to a terrified orphan. But Catholicism seems okay with instilling the fear of God into its faithful followers. With fear comes power and control.

Perhaps that's why Gianna finds solace behind these walls, for she too exercises these practices.

It doesn't surprise me when she pushes the doors to the chapel open. She knows what took place here. She knows how I was defiled over and over. It was because of her that Father Merry took his sick perversions out on me.

But I also had my revenge here.

I peer up at the large golden crucifix behind the altar and remember the one which once stood before it, the one I hung Father Merry from.

I'm unable to wipe the smile clean as it's one of my favorite memories of all.

"Why are you here?" Gianna asks, breaking my tranquility.

Looking at her, I see the real Gianna for the first time. I see a selfish coward who I am going to thoroughly enjoy torturing endlessly until death seems a mercy.

Her attire is her standard black jumpsuit and flashy jewels, with not a hair out of place. Her makeup is flawless even at this time of the night.

But it's all for show.

I can't believe she's my mother. The woman I have pledged my loyalty to for all these years is the monster I was hunting all along.

"I'm here because I need your help."

Gianna folds her arms across her chest, indicating she's

listening.

"I don't deserve your forgiveness. You've done nothing but care for me since I left this godforsaken place. And in return, I know I let you down. But there's a reason.

"When I arrived in Italy, I was…I was pregnant. I didn't know. But I had the child in secret. It's the reason I vanished for so long. You had every right to throw me out and disown me, but you didn't. And for that, I am eternally thankful."

"The child is Lennon's?" she asks, pretending she doesn't know.

I nod. "It's the reason I didn't want anyone knowing about her. I kept her hidden as best I could, even from you. I'm sorry for that."

Gianna has the nerve to appear hurt by my actions. "I would have supported you…just how I always have."

"I know, but I couldn't allow my child to suffer the same childhood I did. So I vowed to be the best mother I could be. To be the mother my mother was not." My words are filled with emotion and meaning because they are directed to Gianna.

"I still carried out your orders, but the reason I couldn't harm Lenny was because he is the father of my daughter."

Gianna remains unmoved, confirming what a heartless bitch she truly is.

But I am past being hurt.

"You allowed your emotions to get in the way once again.

Have I not taught you anything?" She scolds me like I'm a naughty child who disobeyed a simple order.

But there's nothing simple about this.

I take her reprimanding me and cast my eyes downward. "I know. It won't happen again."

"How can I trust you? It's because of your weakness that I struggle. Lenny has been nothing but a thorn in my side since the moment I adopted you both, and after I have given you everything, this is how you show me gratitude."

Her gaslighting techniques won't work anymore. Quite frankly, they're making this so much easier.

"Please forgive me. I'll do anything."

"What's different this time?"

Here goes…

"Because my daughter is missing…and I suspect Lenny is the one who has her as revenge for keeping her a secret from him. I need your help and the help of your men in taking him down. I can't do it on my own. I've tried.

"If you help me…I promise you, you'll get his kingdom… as well as his head."

Gianna weighs my proposition. "You have disappointed me, Valentina. And honestly, I should have you killed for what you've done. But perhaps I too have failed at my own teachings."

She reaches out and caresses my cheek.

Bile rises, but I swallow it back down.

"Are you certain he has your daughter?"

I shake my head. "I am not. But who else would take her? I've been careful, here and in Italy."

Gianna is the perfect actress. She deserves a fucking Oscar. "Yes, this is true, as I was not aware of her. But we both know how persistent Lenny can be. We also know how charming he can be when it comes to getting what he wants. I'm ashamed to say I have fallen victim to those charms."

She's baiting me, but I simply nod.

"Okay, I'll help you."

"Thank you, Gianna."

But things aren't that easy. I know a sacrifice will have to be made to regain her trust.

"I've lost everything. Calling this place my home confirms this. I was once a queen, now merely a peasant, watching Lenny steal everything that is rightfully mine, all because he's a man. Those men couldn't bear a woman as their leader."

Wrong...those men couldn't bear *her* as their leader because she isn't fit or deserving of the title.

"How did we end up at the bottom of the food chain? Perhaps my sympathy for you both is the reason."

Once again, Gianna is playing martyr. At least this time, I'm privy to her manipulations.

"I understand being here may evoke unpleasant memories."

"On the contrary, it's because of this place I am who I am

today."

"*Brava.* Let us get to work, then. Not a minute to spare." She claps her hands, and the person who enters the chapel has me almost tripping over my own feet.

It's Lewis.

Lenny failed to mention that his brother is now Gianna's gofer boy.

This is a test.

Gianna watches me closely.

I remain aloof.

"Lewis, Valentina will be staying with us. Will you show her to her old room? The attic, correct?"

That fucking…bitch.

I envision grabbing her by that long hair and using her face to wipe the altar clear of the religious relics. That heavy gold candelabrum would be the perfect object to smash her face with, knocking out her perfect straight teeth.

I push aside these thoughts and nod.

"Wonderful. Rest now, for tomorrow is a big day."

Lewis is still a junkie. The scabs on his scrawny arms and pale, gaunt face cement that some people just don't want to be saved. No matter what Lenny did, it would never be good enough because Lewis chose this life.

Lenny sacrificed so much for his brother, and this is the thanks he gets.

Lewis doesn't speak.

He turns, about to lead the way, when Gianna purses her mouth before smacking her lips together. The pop echoes loudly.

"You said you'd do anything," she ponders while I remain still. "You'd do anything to prove your loyalty to me, and that I can trust you."

"Yes."

"All right then, shall we put that theory to the test?"

This is her show, so I wait.

She looks at Lewis, and I see her disgust. He's merely a pawn like we all are. She knew he'd come in handy one day.

"Prove your loyalty to me, then. You've had ample opportunity to kill Lenny, but failed. So to make amends…I want you to kill Lewis." Her order is like she's discussing the weather, not taking someone's life.

In her mind, I guess it's one and the same.

She knows if I kill Lewis, this will destroy Lenny. The woman he loves would be responsible for his brother's death.

But if I don't do this, then Gianna will guess this is a ruse, and we're all dead.

At first, Lewis believes Gianna is joking, but when neither of us laughs, he soon realizes his life means nothing to her.

Or to me.

I reach for my gun in the small of my back and point it at

Lewis.

He instantly interlaces his hands, begging. "Please, no. I haven't done anything wrong."

"Well, that's not entirely true," I rebuke. "You betrayed your brother."

Gianna watches her plan unfold with a smile on her face.

"I made a mistake!" Lewis says, his panic rising. "Lenny wants me to be him! But all I see is disappointment when he looks at me. I'm nothing but a failure in his eyes."

All I hear are excuses. Lewis is weak and nothing like his brother.

To think Lenny sacrificed so much for him makes pointing a gun at him easy. But I know Lenny doesn't want him dead.

Gianna, however, does. "I know you like it messy," she says, placing a large hunting knife on the altar.

The silver blade catches the flickering candlelight.

Lewis screams and runs for the door.

This is a test I can't fail. It's either me or him.

I fail, and Lettie suffers.

I am Gianna's perfect killing machine because I'll do anything to save my daughter.

Reaching for the knife, I throw it with precision. It embeds into Lewis's back between his shoulder blades. He drops to the floor.

Gianna arches a brow, indicating we're not done.

I switch off any emotion and walk to where Lewis crawls toward the door. It's merely a flesh wound, but he's weak because of the shit he injects daily into his body to survive.

I yank out the blade from his back and use my foot to turn him over. Tears stream down his cheeks as he begs me to stop.

But I can't.

"I'm sorry," I whisper before straddling him and stabbing him in the chest and throat. I stab him over and over again, and end up covered in his blood.

The blade is slippery, and I cut my own hand during stab twenty-two.

I hit bones, arteries, and organs.

He coughs up blood, his eyes pleading I show mercy. I can't stand the look he gives me, so I stab him in the eyeballs. The only mercy I can show him is when I grip him by the hair and run my blade across his throat.

Blood oozes from the incision, bleeding out Lewis's life, and with one final breath, he perishes by my hand.

He collapses onto the hard floor with a heavy thud.

My hands tremble as I come to a slow stand.

What a mess I have made. What a mess indeed.

Usually, this kind of scene would leave me wired for days. But now, I want to be sick looking at my handiwork. I took an innocent man's life. Regardless of his weakness, he didn't deserve this fate. I killed Lettie's uncle.

I killed family.

I have done some awful things in my life, but this is unforgivable.

"I had my doubts, Valentina. But you've proved me wrong. There's one last thing I need you to do."

Of course there is because nothing is ever enough for Gianna.

"Bring me Bria and do to her what you just did to Lewis, and only then will I believe you. You forget, I raised you, *piccola*. You are shrewd and cunning because I taught you well. Sweet dreams."

She leaves me alone with the mess I made, knowing this is just the start of things to come.

I barely sleep.

Being in my old "room" doesn't bring back happy memories. It just fortifies my hatred for Gianna.

Lewis's blood is still under my fingernails, no matter how hard I scrubbed.

How am I going to tell Lenny what I did?

I shower and dress in an outfit that Gianna left out for me, which reminds me that I left my things at Lenny's.

I don't know what comes next.

I've done as Lenny said. But the jury is still out on whether Gianna believes me.

Once dressed, I hear the joyous laughter of children from the dining hall. I decide to go check it out. When I enter, the smell of greasy breakfast turns my stomach.

Sisters peer up at me, but don't say anything as they tend to the children.

Kids of all ages sit at the tables, poking their food and laughing with friends. Not much eating is occurring, not that I can blame them. I wouldn't feed this slop to a dog.

I look at the table I was sitting at when I drove my spoon into Hugo's eyeball. It was a proud moment for me. I finally stood up to the bully. And Lenny took the blame for it.

He's been my savior since the very beginning.

I notice a young girl with messy blonde pigtails sitting at a table at the back of the room. She clutches a rag doll close to her chest, her wide eyes taking everything in. She looks about eight years old.

My heart bleeds for her because with her tattered clothes and eyes too big for her emaciated face, I can't help but see me in her.

I grab a glass of milk and an apple from the breakfast selection and walk to where she sits by herself. The moment she sees me approaching, she shrinks in on herself, wishing to disappear.

"Can I sit?" I ask with a gentle smile.

The girl won't look at me, but she nods.

I put the glass of milk in front of her and casually cut the apple into quarters. "My name is Valentina. What's your dolly's name?"

The girl's tiny fingers grip the doll tighter.

"Is her name…Sally?"

The girl shakes her head, her pigtails wobbling with the movement.

"Hmm, Gracie?"

Again, she shakes her head.

"I know," I say, taking a bite of the apple. "Her name is Robert."

The girl peers up at me and giggles. "Robert is a boy's name."

"It is?" I ask, faking shock. "Well, what's your name, then?"

The girl looks at the apple, licking her lips in hunger.

"Would you like to share my apple with me?"

She nods.

I offer her a quarter.

She takes a small bite, which pleases me immensely to see her eating. "My name is Elena. And my dolly is just Dolly."

"You know, I once had a cat called Cat." I wonder if he's still alive.

The girl's eyes widen. "Really?"

"Yes, really." I subtly push the plastic cup of milk toward

her, hoping she'll drink it.

"Everyone thinks I'm stupid for calling her Dolly. They say Dolly isn't a name."

"Dolly is a name. A very famous singer is called Dolly." I begin to hum "9 to 5" by Dolly Parton. "So next time someone calls you stupid, you can correct them."

She smiles happily, and with Dolly under one arm, she reaches for the cup of milk and drinks it.

Once she gulps it down in one mouthful, she wipes her lips with the back of her hand. "Will you read to me?"

"I would love that," I reply with a smile.

Elena leads me to the library, her small hand in mine. We read her favorite fairy tales while she sits on my lap, listening intently.

The book is worn; the pages tattered and torn. The library hasn't changed since I was here, which gives me an idea.

I kill bad men.

They have a lot of money.

Perhaps by giving to the disadvantaged, my conscience may lighten.

When I think of the sins I've committed behind these walls, I know my conscience will be tarnished forever.

"There you are."

The moment I hear Gianna's voice, the urge to protect Elena is overpowering.

"I'll finish the story later. Okay?"

Elena nods, sensing the sudden shift in my demeanor. She quickly jumps off my lap and disappears before Gianna pokes her head around the corner.

I smile, attempting to act nonchalant.

Gianna's red dress matches her devilish charm perfectly.

"I've made some calls. I hope to have news of your daughter very soon."

My daughter is *her* granddaughter. The way she speaks so flippantly about her own kin angers me profusely.

"Have you given much thought to…Bria?"

Truth be told, I have.

I have no idea how I'm going to do this. It's a choice I don't wish for Lenny to make—his wife. Or his daughter.

But in the end, that's what it comes down to.

I think of the state of the orphanage and wonder if perhaps I could kill two birds, so to speak.

"What if we threw a charity ball? Here, at the orphanage."

Gianna hints that she's listening. "We invite anyone who is anyone and raise money for the orphanage in the process. Lenny wouldn't miss this for the world. And where Lenny goes, Bria goes. We have home ground advantage. We can't go to them, so we make them come to us."

"How did you know I was here?" she questions.

Thinking quick on my feet, I reply, "I traced the text

messages you sent me. You taught me some very valuable life lessons, Gianna."

She nods, thankfully believing my bullshit.

"I'll have to be more careful in the future. But this is a good idea. We bring them to us. Lenny won't start a war here, not with the lives of the children at stake. He knows he'll lose. It's only a matter of time."

Vince's warning plays over in my head. But I know better than to ask her what she has planned. This will merely rouse suspicion.

"Well, I do love a good party. And what better way to display my power to my peers than by taking down the enemy in a private yet public affair. I'll find your daughter, I promise you that."

I nod in what appears to be gratitude.

"It looks like I have a party to plan. In the meantime, I need to send a message to Lenny. He's made a fool of me long enough.

"Drop the body of his brother on his doorstep."

I cannot show emotion, but this is the most horrible thing to do. He was the one who said whatever she asks, I must do. But this will destroy Lenny.

However, what choice do I have?

"I'll send one of my men with you," Gianna says, a sure sign that she still doesn't trust me.

I don't want to do this, but what would Lenny expect of me

in this circumstance?

He would expect that I do as Gianna says.

"Am I to make myself seen?"

Gianna smirks. "Oh, of course. You can do the honors in telling him that you are the one responsible for his brother's death. An eye for an eye." She snickers as if remembering a fond memory. "Well, that seems rather obsolete, seeing as Lewis has none."

I can't believe I once respected this woman.

What a fool I was.

"No time to waste, then." I stand, wanting this to be over ASAP.

Gianna is happy with my enthusiasm to destroy Lenny. She sends a text to my minder, no doubt. "Danny will meet you around the back."

I don't ask any questions because I know better.

Walking through the orphanage on autopilot, I wonder if I should send a text to Lenny. It's too risky. Gianna is the one who taught us never to assume no one is looking, because that's usually when someone is.

I can't help but see the irony that once again, I am a prisoner behind these walls.

This ground is forever cursed, for it has been housing nothing but horror and pain. If I make it out of this alive, I plan to change that.

No child deserves to be frightened, abused, or neglected. And that is all this place seems to offer. But I vow to protect children like Elena who don't have a voice. I'll be their voice because I'll ensure vile people like Father Merry and Gianna will listen.

I didn't have a voice when locked away in here, abandoned and forgotten.

But I have one now.

It surprises me to see a security guard stationed at the back door. This is new and, no doubt, under the orders of Gianna.

She's worried about someone breaking in.

But when the guard eyes me closely, I realize it's not about someone breaking in; it's about someone breaking out. And that someone is me.

I'm under no false pretenses. I'm a prisoner here.

I do what Gianna says. When she says. And if I don't, if I dare disobey her again, then those I love will suffer the consequences.

If only it was as easy as killing her. But until Lettie is safe, I am her slave.

The guard covers the keypad when he punches in the door code. Next time, I'll ensure I make note of what the code is.

I step outside, and it's pouring rain. The sky is black. The wind is bitter cold. A perfect reflection of the predicament I find myself in. A white van has pulled up by the ramp. I sprint to it and open the passenger door.

Danny doesn't bother saying hello.

I peer over my shoulder into the back. I see a blanket covering something. Or rather, *someone*. This is how I'm to deliver Lewis to Lenny—in a floral blanket.

We commence our journey in silence.

The wipers grate my nerves, and soon, their sequence is in time with the thumping of my heart. The louder they swipe, the more anxious I become. I grip the leather seat and measure my breaths as I feel a panic attack approaching.

I focus on Lettie and how happy she was on her birthday. That calms me down because if I don't keep it together, she'll forever be five because she won't live to see another birthday.

The car ride feels like ten hours, but when we pull up to the familiar gates, I wish I had more time to prepare. But nothing can prepare anyone for what's about to unfold.

The guard at the gates is the same man who let me in yesterday. Or was it the day before? Time just seems to be one excruciating loop. He peers into the windshield and reads my expression immediately. He places his hand over his gun holster, but I subtly shake my head.

He's debating what to do.

Thankfully, he chooses to go back into the gatehouse and picks up the phone.

Danny's attention bounces between the guard and me. He

trusts neither, and he shouldn't.

After a minute or so, the gates open, and Danny sarcastically gives the guard a thumbs-up. He drives toward the house. Three men stand guard on the porch, their large guns in hand.

Danny cracks his neck from side to side, clearly ready for a fight.

I detach myself from any emotion when Danny parks the car and turns it off. I slowly get out of the van, hands raised in surrender. The heavy downpour has now turned to a drizzle. The men instantly point their guns at me, their fingers on the triggers as I slide open the side door.

The floral blanket is an insult to Lewis. I wish I could have wrapped him in something a little more dignified. But I step away from the van, suggesting to the men that I have something for them to see. They descend the front steps with caution, one man's gun trained on Danny, and the other two on me.

The man with ginger in his goatee steps forward and carefully pulls back the blanket. "Motherfucker..." he curses under his breath, before pressing a button connected to his earpiece. "Sir, please come outside."

I'm shivering, but not from the cold.

The front door opens.

I hold my breath.

Lenny appears, stone-faced, ignoring me, ensuring not to make eye contact.

Raindrops stick to my lashes, curbing my vision. But I don't need to see, for I know how the next thirty seconds are about to pan out.

Lenny slowly takes the stairs and walks to the van. His men step aside in a sign of respect. Or perhaps they don't want to be close when he sees what's in the back. He pulls back the blanket, and suddenly, it feels as if the world stands still.

He doesn't move a muscle.

He simply stares at Lewis's corpse.

The rain begins to pick up once again.

"Sir—"

"Shut the fuck up!" Lenny roars, never taking his eyes off Lewis.

He needs time to process this as real. I understand. When something so traumatic occurs, it's your body's natural response to go into self-preservation mode. It wants to protect your mind and your heart.

I was the same when I walked into my home and was greeted with smears of blood. And when I saw Nico, beaten and bloody, I didn't want to believe this nightmare was real.

But as your mind processes what's happening, a flood of emotion hits you, and that's when you spiral.

I'm drenched, but don't seek shelter.

I stand with Lenny, mourning his brother.

He turns over his shoulder, finally meeting my eyes.

His beautiful blue-gray eyes are now swarming with black.

I want to console him.

I want to beg for forgiveness.

But I can't.

I am nothing but akin to a cat, bringing their beloved a dead bird as a gift. "Take my family...and I take yours."

Lenny's mask slips for a nanosecond. He understands loud and clear that I was the one who killed Lewis. I see hatred, real hatred, and this is what Gianna wanted.

Danny watches on, no doubt eager to recount all the horror to Gianna. At least we've provided a stellar performance.

But this isn't fiction.

This is real.

We both knew sacrifices would be made, but when will this stop? How far will we go, selling our souls to the devil before it's enough?

"You won't win, Lenny. Your brother's blood is on your hands. Give me back what's mine, and all this will stop. Until then...I'm coming for you and won't stop."

Lenny tongues his cheek before he pulls out his gun and points it at me. "I can stop you. Here. Right now."

"Go on then," I challenge, casually walking toward him. "Do it."

The rain soaks through my tennis shoes.

And my wet hair sticks to my face.

I look a mess, but I exude power.

Lenny's gun never wavers from me as I stop only when the muzzle is pressed into my chest. This moment is where only he and I exist.

The rain encompasses us in our bubble, shutting out the real world and the atrocities it brings.

The pain in his eyes stabs at my heart.

I want to say so much.

But I'm a prisoner to silence.

However, with a simple nod, he sets me free.

"You're about to lose everything you love," he warns loudly over the punishing rain.

"Too late."

Here we stand—together, but divided.

I want this to be over.

I don't want this life anymore.

I know I need to fight, but this is a battle that I am fearful both Lenny and I will lose.

"I—"

My sentence dies in my throat. Just how I would have if not for Lenny shoving me to the ground to avoid the bullet fired from a gun that wasn't his.

"I'm going to fucking kill you!" The gun it was fired from was Bria's.

"Run!" Lenny mouths to me, offering me his hand.

Our eyes are frantically speaking where our mouths cannot.

I pick myself up from the gravel, yank out Lewis's body, and dive into the back of the van.

Lenny orders his men to stand down when they raise their guns. Bria careens down the stairs, and as Danny madly reverses away, she aims and shoots, shattering the windshield.

We both duck for cover.

Bria continues shooting until the van spins around frantically, and Danny speeds away to safety.

I'm half expecting Bria to give chase like in *The Terminator*. But we're in the clear.

Resting my head back against the cool metal door, I close my eyes and wish I were anywhere but here.

CHAPTER 11

LENNY

'm sitting in the basement, with Lewis's body laid out on a table in front of me.

The only thought I have is, *where did this table come from*? I don't remember seeing it down here. Or in the house. Is it real marble? I wonder how much it cost, as it looks expensive.

In times of crisis, the mind does what it can to survive.

And this right here is a perfect example.

Regardless of his choices, Lewis doesn't deserve this.

The multiple stab wounds, missing eyeballs, and the gash to his throat are not the way I wanted my brother to die. I can't help but feel responsible for this. If only I'd let him be, he'd still be alive—a junkie, but likely still alive.

I just wanted what I thought was best for him. But this isn't what's best.

His face isn't peaceful as they portray it in the movies. His last few minutes on this earth were excruciating. He suffered, suffered because of Valentina.

I did instruct her to do whatever it took to convince Gianna.

I cradle my face in my palms, bowing my head.

What a fucking mess.

"I'm sorry about Lewis."

Bria sounds genuine, but she's angry with me for pushing Valentina out of the firing line. She has every right to be mad. Bria is my wife, and I'm disrespecting her with my loyalty to Valentina. My loyalty is with my daughter too—but this is something Bria can't know about.

For now, anyway.

She sits beside me, gently placing her hand on my leg. "She needs to die, Lenny. Now. Look at what she did."

I remain quiet. So she tries another tactic.

"If the roles were reversed, what would you expect me to do?"

She's right. This is a double standard. I know that it is.

But I don't have a choice.

She doesn't understand because I haven't told her the truth, and I don't think I ever can.

"I think it's best if we have some time apart. I'm not making you happy. And I don't blame you for being angry with me. But please understand, there's a reason for all of this."

"Look at me," she pleads.

The hurt in her voice has me lifting my weary head.

"I love you. So much. Why are you doing this? What does she have over you? There has to be a reason."

I don't deserve Bria's love. Most wives would have left by now, but Bria has been loyal from the very beginning.

"It's complicated."

Such a cop-out.

Bria holds her composure like the Mafia princess she was born to be.

She stands, her eyes filled with pity. "You know something, she won't destroy you…you'll end up destroying yourself."

And she leaves me alone with the corpse of my brother.

Reaching out, I stroke his cold forehead. "I'm sorry."

Taking one last look at him, I cover him with the black sheet and make a call to one of my men. He won't have a funeral. I mean, what would I write on his headstone? And who would mourn him?

I certainly won't.

And neither will Gianna.

She would have promised him the world. And he fell for

her smoke and mirrors. Or more like, he was lured in by the copious amounts of drugs she supplied him.

Every action has a consequence, and this was Lewis's.

My cell rings, and I see it's Taylor, calling me from the gatehouse.

"What now?" I groan to myself before answering.

"Sorry to disturb you, sir, but there's a man at the gates. He doesn't speak a word of English."

And the day just keeps on giving.

"Send him up."

Taylor doesn't argue.

I forgot I agreed to allow Nico to stay here.

But how the fuck did he get here so quickly? According to Valentina, he was beaten within an inch of his life. Alarm bells begin to sound. If this were true, then how is he standing, let alone able to fly halfway across the world?

Valentina's attacker was a man. Could it be closer to home than we thought?

Quite frankly, everyone is a suspect. And I intend on treating him like one.

I go upstairs and decide to check emails while I wait for my guest. I sit at my desk, but when I see one hundred seven emails waiting for me, I slam my laptop shut.

Roberto knocks at my study door.

"What?" I snap, my elbows propped on my desk as I rub

my temples.

"Sorry to intrude, but Nico is waiting for you in the foyer. Shall I escort him in?"

My temper is already boiling over, and seeing this asshole will just make it worse. This meeting will not go well. But this day is already a disaster, so what's one more dilemma to add to the shit pile?

My leather seat rolls and hits the wall as I stand abruptly. "No, it's fine."

Roberto quickly moves out of my way as I storm past him. Nico's back is turned, but he quickly spins when he hears my boots pound on the polished floors. His face is badly bruised, and he has tape across the bridge of his broken nose.

His hair is snarled.

His face unshaved.

His shirt crinkled.

Overall, he looks like hell, and when he throws a punch, connecting with my jaw, I realize why he got here so fast.

He's here to find his—*my* daughter.

Regardless of his injuries, he traveled in the state he's in for his family.

Valentina got up and left.

Lettie is missing.

He's doing what any man should do when his family is at stake.

"Cazzo di bastardu!"

I may not understand Sicilian, but I'm pretty sure he just called me a fucking bastard.

Rubbing my jaw, I grin, impressed 'cause his little delicate hands can surprisingly throw a punch. If I didn't hate the dude, I would respect him for being here and standing his ground.

But I'm not that kind of a forgiving guy.

Nico has memories of my daughter that should be mine. He protected my family when I should have. Valentina calls him darling. And my daughter calls him Daddy.

I'm envious of him because I may be rich in possessions, but I would give all of them up for the life he lived. To me, he is the wealthiest man in the whole world.

So now, I get it.

I get why Valentina loves the guy.

He's honorable, protective, and puts his family first—he's everything I'm not.

He raises his voice, asking me something, using his hands as all Italians do. Unlike Valentina, I don't have the patience for a translator, so I call out to Roberto, who isn't far away.

My men know to be on hand in case shit hits the fan, which is often.

"You're Sicilian, correct?"

He nods.

"Good. From now on, you're my translator. Tell me what

this motherfucker is saying."

I gesture to Nico that the floor is his and for him to speak his piece, and fuck me dead, does he speak. But it's far from peaceful.

His monologue goes on for what seems like minutes.

His voice gets louder and louder.

His cheeks redder and redder.

Roberto nods, appearing to take it all in.

When Nico finally shuts up, I look at Roberto, who opens but soon closes his mouth. He rubs the back of his head, clearly attempting to sum up what Nico just spewed.

"He said…he said he'd rather not stay here."

I look at Roberto for a full ten seconds before bursting into hysterical laughter. Both he and Nico look at me like I've lost my mind. And I probably have.

Once I'm done cackling like a schoolgirl, I say, "I think he said a little more than that."

Roberto adjusts the thick gold crucifix around his throat. "He wants to know where his daughter and Valentina are. That America is an ugly place with terrible food."

"And?" I prompt, as there is more.

"And that you're a fucking asshole, and when he gets better, he's going to kill you." Roberto takes a subtle step backward while I cock my head to the side, impressed once again with Nico's balls.

"Anything else?"

"Nope," Robert replies, popping the P. "I think that sums it up."

Nico can insult me all he wants. Nothing can hurt me more than the fact that he raised my daughter as his own and that he has Valentina's heart. If it wasn't for this, he would be dead by now. But I can't do that out of respect.

But if he hits me again, I won't be so understanding.

He looks me dead in the eye and snarls, "Where is Valentina?"

It seems love is the universal language because I understood him loud and clear.

My cell rings, and I wish it was a case of saved by the bell, but it's Romeo, my bodyguard. When he calls, it usually isn't with good news.

"For the love of God, what has happened now?"

"Sorry, boss, but you might wanna come down to Mario's Deli." Romeo's thick Brooklyn accent is what you expect to hear out of every gangster movie.

I hang up and walk back to my office. I pull the infamous oil painting of *The Last Supper* aside, revealing the hidden wall safe beneath. I punch in the code and retrieve some guns and cash. I don't know what I'm walking into, but weapons and money always seem to help in one way or another.

Once everything is packed into a duffel, I charge out the

door and bump straight into Nico. He makes clear he's not done. His tenancy is about to get him a black, or rather, a blacker eye.

"I don't have time for this shit." Without warning, I knock Nico out cold.

I leave him on the floor. One of my men will ensure he is detained until my return. And then I'll decide what to do with him.

Jumping into my Mercedes, I make the forty-five-minute drive downtown. I keep to the speed limit. I don't run any red lights. Even though a lot of cops are on my payroll, I don't want to draw any attention my way. After the day I've had, odds are I'll end up getting pulled over.

It's hard not to think that even with the power I wield and the people I know, I can't find my daughter. It seems it's one shit show after the other, with no hint of things getting better.

And when I pull up at the deli, I just add this establishment to the shit pile.

I put money into this place when it was on the brink of bankruptcy. Mario makes the best meatball subs in town. Too bad his gambling problem saw him flushing his profits down the toilet. He sold to me for cheap. I said he could stay on the proviso that he turned a blind eye to the unlawful dealings that took place.

I needed a legal business to throw my illegal money into. And what better place than a business that actually makes money? This shop is just a front for me. The more property I own, the fewer questions I get asked by the IRS.

There isn't a whole lot of money in selling crystals.

But who doesn't love a hoagie?

No cops out front. Maybe my luck is changing.

However, when I enter the deli and see Romeo standing off to the side, turning all shades of green, I know I've spoken too soon.

I make the sign of the cross because, what in the ever-living fuck have I walked into?

Hell, that's what.

The polished white floors are now smeared with bright red. The immaculate silver counter is blotted with puddles of red.

Drip.

Drip.

Drip.

This only adds to the puddles.

Peering upward, I see Mario hanging from the silver, cured meat rack above the sandwich bar. He's been strung up by his feet like a slaughtered pig. His throat is cut, and he's disemboweled.

His innards are neatly stacked in the silver containers behind the glass. Where customers once chose their fillings for their sandwiches, now they have a selection of eyeballs, teeth, organs, and hearts; everything one would expect to find in an all-you-can-eat human buffet.

Hanging beside Mario are seven of my most loyal men. They've all suffered the same fate.

"A message from Gianna?" asks Romeo, unable to look at the macabre scene before us.

"Yes, this is war."

However, I remember the way Valentina sliced open one of my men in that hotel room. This smells of her handiwork. I understand we agreed she was to do what Gianna ordered, but this is the work of a very sick and twisted individual.

I suppose we would do anything for our daughter, but this attack seems personal. Whoever did this wanted to leave a message.

And that message is…we're coming for you.

Valentina and I were waiting for the right time, but there will never be a right time.

Gianna must die…and she must die now.

She's stronger than I thought, and Francesco is right—there is a mole among us.

Gianna is taking out my most loyal men, leaving behind the cowards who will sell out their own mother if it means saving their own skin. My empire is crumbling. It won't be long until she conquers me.

"Burn the place down. Inform their families and make sure they're taken care of financially," I blankly say to Romeo, unable to take my eyes off the gruesome scene before me. "Trust no one, Romeo. Everyone is the enemy."

"Yes, boss."

The bell above the door dings as I exit. The night is cool, and for the first time in my life, I feel cold. I feel it all the way to my bones. It has nothing to do with the weather. It has to do with the fact that my empire is being destroyed, and I don't think I'll survive it this time.

Gianna only grows stronger thanks to whoever betrays me. Soon, she'll have all the ammo she needs to overthrow me. But I must get to her first.

I get into my car just as the first licks of fire can be seen from the storefront window.

I drive into the darkness, wishing I could slip away and just start over. But that's an ending for quitters. And when my phone rings over my car Bluetooth, and the caller is Bria, I know that will never be on the cards for us.

Bria's hatred toward Valentina only grows, and only one of them will survive.

"Hey."

She immediately senses something is wrong.

"What happened now?"

"Mario and seven of my men were murdered tonight. Strung up like a piece of meat."

I can hear her intake of air. "Lenny, this has to stop. This all started when she came back. Do what's right. Do what you promised you would do."

I did promise Bria, while we stood over the corpse of her father, that she would have her revenge. But so much is different. I made that promise before I was a father.

The safety of my daughter takes precedence over anything and anyone. Which is the reason Bria can never know about Lettie.

I don't trust Bria when it comes to Lettie because she knows that Lettie is the only thing I would sacrifice anything, even myself, for.

When I don't say a word, she sighs. "Valentina's beau is tied to a chair in the basement. I'm assuming he's to be used as collateral? That's the reason he's still breathing, right?"

"Brains and beauty, how did I get so lucky?"

She ignores my attempts to deflect the topic at hand. "We got a hand-delivered invite."

"From?"

"Gianna Ricci."

It seems tonight wasn't enough of an insult.

"She's holding a charity ball to raise funds for Saint Maria's Orphanage."

"You've got to be shitting me. That woman doesn't have a charitable bone in her body."

"Gives us an excuse to dress up and fuck shit up."

"Since when do we need an excuse?"

She chuckles lightly.

No matter how angry we are at one another, carnage always lightens the mood.

"Lucky we have Valentina's lover as collateral because this ball is merely a ruse to lure us in like prey. She has home ground advantage. But we have the manpower, and now, we have something that's precious to Valentina."

I flinch at her choice of words; words she chose with intent to remind me that Valentina belongs to another now. Little does Bria know, Valentina doesn't belong to anyone…and she never has.

So, it appears that D-Day has finally arrived.

The final showdown lingers, and honestly, I don't know who will win.

CHAPTER 12

VALENTINA
ONE WEEK LATER

"Will I find a mommy and daddy?" Elena asks as I tie the elastic around the end of her pigtail.

She's in a light blue pleated dress. Her white socks are pulled high. Her black shoes polished bright. She looks like a cherub you'd see on any chapel ceiling. Although she looks adorable, it sickens me that Gianna has chosen the "pretty ones" to support her bogus sham when she's not doing this for anyone other than herself.

Ten children are dressed in their Sunday best. Gianna plans on showcasing them off to her guests in hopes they believe her bullshit and give her their money. They believe this money will go toward the orphanage, but it'll be pocketed by Gianna.

She grows more powerful each day. I assume the new faces I see are men who have jumped ship, getting wind of Gianna's flourishing reign. These men were once loyal to Lenny, but in this world, loyalty is a thing of the past.

Only greed remains.

"Valentina?" Elena prompts, alerting me to the fact that I need to get my head back in the game.

Tonight, Gianna dies.

As does Bria.

I have a plan, one which Lenny will not like.

But it seems easy enough—I hand over Bria. I get Lettie back.

I'm giving Gianna the benefit of the doubt, not that she deserves it. If I'm wrong, then I'll wear it. But I don't think I am, and the reason is that she loves playing the martyr. She sees a good deed as just another thing to hold against me, and why I should be at her beck and call.

Lettie is the ultimate thing to hold over my head if I ever dared question her authority.

But she has misjudged me if she believes I'm going to roll over and be her little bitch a second longer. The moment I have

Lettie, I'm going to slaughter Gianna in front of her peers, but not before revealing what a monster she truly is.

And I have Francesco to back me up.

He has come through for me in more ways than one. I'll never call him Father, but he's all the family I have. God forbid if something ever happened to us, he's all the family Lettie has.

This may seem like a family spat, but when I reveal the Riccis' dirty little secrets, killing Gianna will be a mercy.

But I don't intend to show any compassion toward someone who does not deserve a lick of it. Instead, I will deliver back to her every ounce of pain I suffered because of her.

The thought of slaying the real dragon in my story is liberating, and perhaps that new life I have dreamed of may be within reach. With Lettie's return, anything is possible.

My future with Lenny is still unknown.

But after everything I've done, and will do, I doubt we'll go sailing off into the sunset together. That's a risk I'm willing to take, though.

"Will you be my mommy?" Elena says, her big blue eyes slaying me where I stand.

Dropping to a squat, I gently stroke her cheek. "I promise that whatever happens, I will keep you safe."

Her lower lip trembles before she throws herself into my arms, wrapping her tiny arms around my neck. She holds on tightly, afraid that I'll disappear. I know the feeling too well because once upon a time, I was Elena.

I was every orphan in this place.

I'll ensure the money raised tonight goes to the orphanage and that no child will suffer the fate I did. I feel responsible for each one.

As a tear rolls down my cheek, I finally realize that I am not bad.

I always thought I was.

But I was made to believe that I was beyond salvation, that feelings made you weak. But Gianna is wrong. It's because of my feelings that I will happily destroy her and won't feel a thing.

The door opens, and I quickly wipe my face, not wishing Gianna to see me crying.

I come to a stand, and Elena runs behind me. Children seem able to sense evil more readily than adults.

Gianna looks stunning in a peacock-colored sequin dress. The plunging neckline complements the mermaid silhouette with a sweeping train. It hugs her slender form, leaving nothing to the imagination. But it's tasteful.

She wears pearl earrings and a large sapphire ring. Her hair is twisted into an elegant chignon and fastened with a diamond clip. Her makeup is light. But she wears her trademark red lips with pride.

"You're not dressed yet," she says, her annoyance clear.

"It doesn't take me long," I reply smoothly, an intentional

stab since she's been getting ready all day.

She looks down her nose at me, her lips tight. She's looking for any signs of deceit.

She can look all day because she won't see a thing. I'm the master of hiding my emotions, thanks to her teachings. Everything she drilled into me has been life lessons I have used against her.

And I cannot wait to rub the fact into her face. Not before I smash her head through a mirror, of course, wishing for her to see the ugliness she truly carries within herself.

I take Elena's hand, but Gianna shakes her head. "Leave the girl. I must speak with her. I have something special planned for her. You'd like that, wouldn't you, sweetie?"

Elena squeezes my hand, begging me to take her with me. "She'll help Sister Gina in the cloakroom. I thought a beautiful face is what you wished the guests to be greeted by."

Gianna smiles. "Yes, you're right. That's very smart. Let's tug at their heartstrings so they open their wallets and donate vastly."

I don't dally and lead Elena from the room.

When we're far away, I whisper, "Never trust that woman. Promise me."

"I promise," she whispers back.

When we arrive at the kitchen, Sister Ursula, who I trust, takes Elena's hand. Elena looks over her shoulder, apprehension plaguing her, but I nod with a smile.

She eventually follows Sister Ursula.

This entire affair makes me sick, and when I enter the private bathroom and see a red ball gown hanging from the towel rack, that sickness threatens to choke me. I cough past the bitterness lodged in my throat and quickly shower.

Once I am clean, I wipe down the mirror and stare at my pale complexion.

I remind myself that this is almost over. Just a few more hours.

Gianna has left everything I need on the vanity. Even as a grown woman, she still thinks she has a say over how I dress. God forbid I think for myself. But in the past, this is what I have done. She has controlled me, which I stupidly mistook for love.

So I apply my makeup one last time.

I style my hair in a low bun, fastening it with a jeweled clip.

And I dress in the sequin ball gown with the intention of never wearing another like it again. It's a beautiful dress, featuring embroidered patterned sequins over a red underlay. The dress is a tight-fitting halter neck with crisscross straps at the back that hold it together as the dress plunges all the way to my waist. The thigh-high side split complements the flare shape and sweeping train.

This is the last time I'll ever wear something chosen by anyone but me.

Gianna has controlled every aspect of my life.

And tonight, it stops.

For she will cease…to breathe.

The thought of sullying this perfect dress with her blood has my skin prickling with goose bumps.

I step into a pair of heels as it seems Gianna wishes for us to be stiletto twins. She knows my tactics well, for she taught me. Usually, I wouldn't opt for a dress with a split because where am I supposed to hide my weapons?

This means she anticipates we're at an advantage.

I need this to be over with.

The bell in the clock tower chimes six times—it's showtime.

Tipping my face to the heavens, I inhale deeply, before an exhale slowly leaves me.

It's time to put my game face on.

I force myself to smile, practicing my peopling until I look convincing. There's no room for error. Lettie's life depends on it.

Gathering my dress with both hands, I saunter out of the bathroom and down the hallway toward the ballroom. My heels stab at the linoleum, in sync with Gianna's customary trot.

This place was once opulent and thriving, until Father Merry and his predecessors desecrated something beautiful with their depravity.

However, Gianna has managed to transform this ballroom in just one week into a vision from the past, as I envision it once looked.

The crystal chandelier is something you'd expect to see in any Disney Princess movie. It adds elegance and wealth. Servers wear white and black, carrying silver trays topped with flutes of champagne.

A quartet plays classical music in the corner of the room.

Men and women in suits, furs, and jewels mingle around the room, laughing and engaging in small talk. They look to be having a grand time.

But I see the way the men's eyes follow other men's wives. Or the wives' ogling the young, handsome servers.

This charade is all for show.

There isn't a single shred of decency here. All I see is greed. All I smell is depravity.

And when ten children are ushered into the room and sit on the small stage, it confirms that every person here is a predator, waiting to catch their prey.

Elena catches my eye, and I nod subtly.

She sits tall, sniffling back her tears.

I snatch a glass of champagne from a passing tray, needing to blend in. Also needing to do something with my hands other than choke the life from these perverted snakes.

Soon, the ballroom is filled. Gianna couldn't throw a party without it being the biggest this town has seen. It reminds me of the one we attended when I was a child. When Gianna knew of the man who I met as a child was in attendance.

The need to hurt her only grows stronger.

When the crowd gushes and carries on dramatically, I know our host has made a grand entrance. Gianna does stand out from the rest. But her beauty was never questioned. It was her heart that was.

But it was soon realized by many that she does not have one.

Everyone rushes over to Gianna, wanting a piece of the ice queen. She laps up the attention, for she knows she's now top dog. I don't know how she's done it, but she's respected how she once was. Lenny is now the underdog.

I gulp down my champagne before placing the empty glass on a passing tray.

Gianna works the room while I subtly keep an eye out for Lenny. I also ensure Elena and the children are okay. They're sitting quietly and obediently. Anger rolls over me because I too was as submissive as these innocent children.

I know what it feels like to be afraid all the fucking time of the adults who are meant to protect you.

Suddenly, the hair at the back of my neck stands on end.

A distinguished-looking man with immaculate black hair and a three-piece suit is slyly slithering closer to the stage. He is making small talk, but it's a ruse for what his true intentions are.

I know that look.

I can smell the depravity seeping from his pores.

On the outside, he appears notable, but on the inside, he is a cesspool of filth. And his attention is riveted on Elena.

A server offers him a sandwich from his silver tray. The man graciously takes two napkins and places a sandwich on each. He then walks over to the stage.

He gestures to Elena, who instantly makes eye contact with me.

I frantically shake my head, a word of warning to stay put. I'm about to charge over, but Gianna and a woman with a ridiculous wide-brimmed hat step in front of me.

"Mary-Lou, this is Valentina."

"Oh, you were right. She is beautiful," Mary-Lou says in a thick Southern accent. "It's so nice to meet you."

I'm not really paying attention because I'm trying to see over Mary-Lou's fucking hat. She is in direct line of Elena, prohibiting my view. Gianna notices my distraction immediately.

She's about to turn to see what has captured my interest, but I step forward and quickly hug Mary-Lou. "The pleasure is all mine."

Gianna smiles, and I am off the hook for now.

"Gianna told me she adopted you from this very orphanage. Imagine that."

"Imagine that," I quip, but she doesn't read between the

lines.

"Gianna's kindness knows no bounds."

I choke on air, but soon recover. "It was so nice meeting you, Mary-Lou, but if you'll excuse me."

Mary-Lou appears stunned I would want to flee such a pleasant encounter. What a moron.

I make a break for it, but Gianna grips my bicep, digging in her fingernails. I peer down at her fingers, arching a brow. My poker face has slipped, but Elena is in danger, and I made her a promise. I can't be like every other adult who has disappointed her in the past.

"Is everything all right?" she whispers.

"I think I saw Bria," I fabricate as this is the only excuse that'll fly.

It works.

She instantly releases me. "Go, do what you must."

What I must means detain her until Gianna can do whatever the hell she wants to her.

That can wait because as I finally am free, I see that Elena is gone, as is the pervert who was hovering.

As gracefully as I can, I make my way over to the stage. "Where did the little girl go?" I ask a boy, pointing at Elena's empty chair.

He chews his lip, not making eye contact. These fragile souls are wounded and damaged beyond repair. Is there not a kind person within these walls? If I cannot save these children, then I will burn this place to the fucking ground and take them with me.

"It's okay, sweetheart. I am Elena's friend."

The boy lifts his chin, sorrow laden in his green eyes. He points over his shoulder to a door that leads outside.

I don't hesitate.

I push aside anyone who stands in my way and burst out that door. It's pitch black, and the noise from inside interferes with me hearing anything that may hint to where Elena is. She hasn't been gone long. I doubt the asshole would take her toward the house, so I rip off my heels and turn right. I run down the hill to where the shrubbery is thick and no one is in sight.

It's the perfect place to remain hidden while destroying an innocent child's life.

With my heart in my throat, I beg whoever may be looking over me that I'm not too late. But when I hear a pained scream, I know that I am.

I see a small, abandoned cottage a few yards away, and even in the darkness, the silhouette I see brings back memories which only enrage me further.

I can see Elena's front pressed to the wall of the cottage, her attacker behind her, ripping off her pretty blue dress. She is screaming, her tiny arms fighting back, but he punches her in the back of the head. Her screams soon fade as she goes limp.

That doesn't stop him, however, as he tosses her to the muddy ground. Her blue dress, the one she was so proud to wear, is now ruined.

Just as he unzips his trousers, I come up behind him and ram my stiletto into the back of his skull. He wavers on his feet, unsure what just happened.

I'm about to show him.

Grabbing his upper arm, I spin him around to face me. He is confused by the commotion, but soon regains his composure.

"The little girl, she was like that when I—" He stops mid-sentence, raising his arm and touching the high heel that is still embedded into his skull. "What is happening?"

"What is happening is…well…I'm about to fucking kill you."

His attention drops to the other shoe in my hand, and he soon realizes, like Cinderella, I'm missing a shoe. But this is no fairy tale.

This is a horror movie.

I drive the other heel into his groin.

I never miss.

It takes him all of three seconds before the pain kicks in— no pun intended.

He howls like a little bitch, his eyes wide as he cannot believe the sight of a shoe sticking out of his groin. He attempts to take it out, but I kick him straight between the legs, the heel embedding deeper into his groin.

He drops to his knees, and this sight would be fucking comical as he has a heel embedded into the back of his head and one between the legs. But there's nothing funny about what this asshole was about to do.

Looking at Elena, her form is replaced with mine.

I see myself begging Father Merry to stop.

I see the men in that filthy basement, licking their lips like starved beasts.

So yanking the shoe out from the back of this motherfucker's head, I jam it into the side of his throat.

I do this for the old me.

I do this for every child who fell victim to obscene deviants who could never save themselves.

Blood gushes from his neck wound as I struck him straight in the jugular. His hands are coated in blood as he attempts to remove the shoe. But I punch him in the face, breaking his nose.

He falls backward, groaning and writhing, and all I can think is, *shut the fuck up and die.*

I've wasted enough time on this asshole, so I pull out the shoe from his groin and ram it into his temple.

His moans cease.

He twitches for a few seconds and then...there is silence.

It's comforting.

I yank him up and remove his shirt, curling my lip in disgust. I shove him back to the ground and retrieve my shoes. I use his trousers as a rag to wipe away his blood.

Gently lifting Elena, I wrap her in the shirt and cuddle her into my arms as I walk her up the hill.

She stirs, but I softly shush her. "Go back to sleep, princess. It's all a dream."

She nuzzles closer into me, falling back asleep, and I can only hope that when she awakens, she will believe that it was just a dream.

I sneak in through the side door and place Elena into bed. I put on her Disney pajamas and tuck her in. I stay with her for a little while, but then I have to go.

I press a soft kiss to her forehead and stand, but she breaks my heart before I leave when she whispers in the darkness, "You kept your promise."

The promise I made to keep her safe.

Her soft breaths indicate she's asleep.

I brush away my tears as I enter the hallway, needing to compose myself before I enter the shark tank. My heels are shiny, one wouldn't imagine where they were moments ago.

I measure my breaths and brush down my gown.

Let's do this…

As I step into the foyer, I bump straight into a solid wall of muscle, a familiar wall that silences the voices within.

My cover slips as I look up at Lennon from under my lashes because his eyes soften. He realizes something is wrong.

God, he is beautiful.

His simple tuxedo accentuates his broad frame and height. The longer strands of hair are styled, giving him the look that he just rolled out of bed. The pinkness of his full lips only appears more succulent thanks to his heavy growth.

His eyes smolder as he takes me in from head to toe.

But we both remember the roles we're meant to play and slip back into rival mode. We quickly detangle ourselves from one another.

"Look what the cat dragged in," Bria snarls, her arm looped tightly through Lenny's.

She looks stunning in a royal-blue gown. But akin to Gianna, the ugliness within cancels out any beauty.

I deadpan her, not in the mood for her bullshit. Truth be told, handing her over to Gianna doesn't bother me in the slightest. It's what it'll do to Lenny that I have the issue with.

"Oh, how lovely to see you two. Thank you for attending." Gianna appears by my side.

Lenny tightens his grip around Bria to stop her from causing a scene.

"Your time will come," Bria sneers with nothing but hatred.

"Let's hope it's after the canapes. The shrimp is to die for."

Gianna grips my elbow, escorting me away.

And here we are—one big happy family.

We're rivals and have attempted to destroy each other for years, but for the sake of pretense, we're pretending to play nice.

I know what I'm supposed to do.

Gianna doesn't need to remind me.

She wants Bria.

So Bria will be hers.

There is no elaborate plan.

No double-crossing.

We brought them here for a reason, and that reason is to capture Bria. What fate will befall Lenny, I don't know. I suspect it'll be for Gianna to humiliate him before taking his throne.

But Lenny won't go down without a fight.

I can only hope we get Lettie back before that happens.

"I don't want to give them an opportunity to blindside us," Gianna softly says, smiling at guests like everything is kosher. "During my speech, I want you to subdue them both."

I don't even bother asking how she expects me to do that in a room full of people.

One of her rules is don't ask stupid questions.

That's why I don't bother asking if she has Lettie.

"It's do or die…don't let me down." And with that, she struts off, mingling with her adorning devotees.

I didn't think I could hate her any more than I do, but her

arrogance has her believing she's untouchable. And that's why I know she has Lettie.

One way or another, I *will* get her back tonight.

The quartet finishes, and Gianna strolls to the stage like she's the queen of England. This is where she believes she belongs—at the top, with her minions fawning over her beauty and power.

I close my eyes for a moment, composing myself because it's not much longer.

"Friends," Gianna commences with. "Thank you for coming this evening to support such a great cause. Children have a special place in my heart, especially those who call Saint Maria's their home."

Guests nod with smiles on their gullible faces while I try not to gag on this syrupy bullshit Gianna feeds them.

"Saint Maria's needs your help. Without your generosity, children like the ones behind me cannot be fed, they cannot learn. Your donations help better these little darlings' lives."

I place a fist in front of my mouth to stop the vomit.

"I wish for you to see how your donations help them. So, come tomorrow, these children will be available for you to get to know them. I don't mean adoption, but day trips, or taking them to the movies. Anything you wish.

"And perhaps the more time spent with them, some may open your hearts and homes and make them a permanent part of your lives."

I look around, expecting to see horror. But instead, I see admiration for Gianna. And I also see the perverse faces of some because what Gianna is proposing puts the children in the hands of potential predators.

This is unethical and unheard of. Some sisters cover their mouths, their eyes wide as they too see the wrongdoing of Gianna's scheme.

I'm about to voice my horror, but am drowned out by thunderous applause. These people are monsters.

Gianna puts on a meek front, but she is anything but. All she sees is money by venturing into new territory—pimping out orphans.

I'm so triggered.

My body threatens to shut down, just as it once did when I was a child. Every face in here is the enemy, and the urge to flee is suffocating.

This is against Gianna's protocol, but if I don't get out of here, I'll lose Lettie forever.

I push my way through the crowd, which only seems to cave in on me. Someone reaches out, asking if I'm okay. On instinct, I shove them aside. The woman gasps, seeking refuge in her snooty husband, who looks down his nose at me, protecting his wife from the unhinged person.

But I feel like the only sane person in this room.

I finally break free and take slow, calming breaths as I stand in the hallway. People are looking at me, so I quickly make my way to the bathroom near the chapel, which is far enough away from anyone to see or hear me. Once inside, I lock the cubicle door and commence dry retching into the toilet.

My empty stomach has nothing to purge, but it's the sickness I feel I wish to expel.

I don't know how long I stay this way, but I feel a bit better after a while. I flush the toilet and come to a shaky stand. I peer at myself in the oval-shaped mirror as I wash my hands. I feel a hundred years old.

Tossing the paper towel into the waste bin, I open the door and bump straight into the last person I want to see right now.

Bria opens her mouth, but I am done with this game. This needs to end now. I am toeing the line between stability and psychosis, and I'm fearful I'll slip and be lost for good. So, without thought, I punch Bria in the face.

She staggers back, caught off guard.

I don't give her time to recover before I punch her again.

"Valentina!" Lenny hisses, his polished shoes skidding on the linoleum as he races toward me. "What the fuck!"

I don't have time to sugarcoat anything. "We give her to Gianna, we get Lettie back."

Bria wavers on her feet, fingers brushing over her bloody lip. Her eyes are flickering as she fights to stay afloat.

"Choose," I say, prepared for anything.

Lenny wrestles with what's right and what's wrong. But in the end, his choice proves that no matter what, he'll always choose me.

"Lenny, no," Bria slurs.

But it's too late.

"Forgive me," he states with utter remorse, before knocking her out cold.

She collapses to the floor like a rag doll.

Lenny is broken. He peers at Bria with sadness and guilt as he grips his hair in both hands. "What have I done? I'm so sorry."

Regret swarms me because I hate he's been put in a predicament such as this. I would feel the same way if faced with the choice, which reminds me of Nico.

I had forgotten that he was arriving in America.

That speaks volumes.

I wonder if he's here. If so, he would be at Lenny's.

This shit show just won't end.

"What now?" Lenny asks, never taking his eyes off Bria.

Again, there is no method to my madness.

Peering around for options, I refuse to think this is divine intervention, but the chapel is the closest thing we have.

Taking off my heels, I open the door without a word.

Lenny sighs before picking Bria up and tossing her over

his shoulder. This place has a chokehold over me, but I ignore the imminent panic in the pit of my stomach because we need something to restrain Bria with.

Lenny produces zip ties from his inner jacket pocket.

I arch a brow.

"I thought they'd come in handy."

And this is our life because he's right.

We quickly tie Bria to a chair. Guilt hinders me from looking Lenny in the eye. This is so wrong.

Once she's tied, I look down at my clean dress and then at Lenny, who doesn't have a scratch on him. I then peer at an unconscious Bria.

Lenny understands my concerns. He takes off his jacket and bow tie, tossing them onto the altar. "Hit me."

I flinch at his suggestion, but we're running out of time.

So I punch him in the jaw.

His head snaps back with an awful crack. But he turns his cheek, a sinister grin tugging at his luscious lips. "Is that the best you can do?"

It's the motivation I need as I punch him again, busting open his lip this time.

He wipes away the blood with the back of his hand. "There's my girl."

His hoarse voice and blood dripping down his chin turn me on. A fire begins to burn. The room closes in on us, and our frustrations explode. We charge for the other at the same time. I throw another punch, which he blocks.

A quick succession of punches and kicks is also blocked. Now, we're fighting for real.

Just as Gianna trained us, we fight like the skilled warriors we are. He allows me to connect at times that are conflicting. I know we both need to look like we've just had the fight of our lives, but I've hurt him enough.

He needs to give as good as he gets.

He shoves me into the wall but never strikes me. That won't work, however.

"This will be a lot more believable if we're both bleeding."

"I won't hit you."

We circle the other, eyes locked. He stands firm on his stance, so it seems I have to do the dirty work myself. I reach for a Bible from a pew and whack myself in the face with it. Instantly, blood pours from my nose.

Not broken, but effective enough.

Gripping the thin halter strap of my dress, I tear it with ease. It unravels, and Lenny's eyes darken when the tops of my breasts are exposed. My now ruined dress is only held together by the straps at the back.

"Choke me."

That order is one he doesn't object to.

He grips my throat in one hand and walks me backward.

My back slams into the scratchy wall. He holds me in place and yanks out the clip in my hair. My long hair tumbles free. He pulls my hair and tugs my head to the right.

Bending down, he bites over my pulse.

Gripping the collar of his shirt, I yank it apart, the buttons scattering all over the floor. He smells fucking delicious, like blood and sex.

We bite and tear at each other, intent on eating the other alive.

I can't stand it a second longer.

I need to taste him.

Licking across his mouth in one slow sweep, I lick away the blood I spilled. I then work my way down the side of his throat, over his Adam's apple, then down the front of his chest. I have always been a sucker for the soft dark hair that paints his chest.

I rub my face in it, inhaling deeply because he smells like home. Even in the direst of circumstances, his scent calms me.

A low growl vibrates in his chest.

He drags me up by my hair to meet his lips, where we kiss passionately, like we're each other's lifeline.

It's a kiss of desperation.

A kiss of hope.

This may be the beginning...of the end.

"I love you," he whispers against my mouth.

After everything I've done, to hear those words...I feel

undeserving.

So all I can do is love Lennon Shepherd back for the rest of my life. "I love you too."

We press our foreheads together, savoring this moment of peace because the next few moments will be anything but.

Eventually, we break apart, but not before I slap his cheek— just for old times' sake.

He rubs his cheek, smirking.

Pulling up a chair beside Bria, he sits down and places his hands behind his back.

With regret, I fasten the zip ties around his wrists, ensuring they're done up tight.

Stepping back, I take in the scene. We're all battered and bloody, but Gianna won't believe I was able to subdue Lenny without him submitting. He's stronger than I am, and although it looks like I put up one hell of a fight, she'll know something is off.

"You submitted because of Bria," I instruct Lenny. "She won't believe us otherwise."

"What's the story?"

"We fought, but I'm stronger. You surrendered because I threatened to kill Bria. It's hardly credible, but Gianna won't care because she has you both where she wants you."

"You trust her?"

"No. I'll most likely be sitting next to you soon."

"Weapons?"

He reads my face as that would be a negative.

"Backup?" I ask him.

He nods. "They're far enough away that they won't be detected, but close enough to come if needed. But I can't trust them."

"What happened?"

His face pales slightly. "So it wasn't you?"

I have no idea what he's talking about. "Gianna has been busy planning this bullshit gala all week. I've barely seen her."

Lenny mulls over my revelation. "Seven of my men and a work colleague were hung up like pigs, their insides on the outside. I thought it was Gianna. But perhaps I'm wrong. We both know Gianna doesn't like getting her hands dirty. Could she have someone else working for her?"

"It's very probable. This might very well turn to shit, which is why I have done something I hope won't be necessary. But if anything were to happen to either of us, or to Nico, then I won't leave Lettie to the state. No way will she be dumped in this hellhole like we were.

"Francesco, as her grandfather, is to have custody of her. I really hope it doesn't pan out that way, but I had to be sure."

Lenny's cheeks billow as he exhales slowly. "Smart. Speaking of Nico...he's safe, tied in my basement. Nothing will happen to him."

"Was leaving him in the basement really necessary?"

"He has a TV," Lenny replies as if that's any consolation.

Lenny was smart not to bring him here. I don't want him to see me this way. This is who I really am, and that's someone not many can love.

If we live through this, then I'll tell Nico it's over. It isn't fair to him. He was always the runner-up. I don't regret the life we lived. We have some beautiful memories. But I don't want to live my life a second longer without Lenny.

Bria is still out cold. But I imagine when she wakes, she won't be too pleased about my admission.

"So what happens now?"

"We wait."

"So typical."

I do wonder what she expects me to do. There's a house full of people, and I don't see the night wrapping up anytime soon.

But that's what gives Gianna the control she craves, knowing that she can engage in illegal dealings under the noses of so many and no one would do a thing about it because they fear her.

And when I hear her trademark walk echo off the hallway walls, my theory is merely confirmed. She is going to do whatever she wishes and return to the party like normal.

Lenny hears her heels stab at the floor and shifts in his seat.

This will change everything, and the terrifying thing is that we don't have a backup plan. We don't even have a plan. Until I know she has Lettie, we are at her mercy.

And when she pushes open the chapel door, she knows it.

I remain perfectly still, while Lenny cannot hide his contempt.

"You proved me wrong, Valentina," Gianna says, the train on her dress now looking more like a tail dragging behind her. "But I knew you wouldn't fail me. Too much is at stake."

"Oh, for fuck's sake. Kill me already and be done with it. Death is preferable over having to listen to you for one more second."

Gianna doesn't flinch at Lenny's words because she's won.

"So what now?" I ask calmly.

Gianna walks over to Bria, grips her chin, and arches her head backward.

"Get your hands off!" Lenny roars, rocking in his chair.

I know this isn't an act. He is concerned for Bria's safety.

"You show compassion for your wife, but feel nothing for your daughter?"

Low blow, but Lenny plays along. "I didn't even know I *had* a daughter until a few weeks ago. This daddy gig is still fresh. Not that I expect you to understand."

Lenny can give as good as he gets.

Gianna's top lip twitches. It's small, but he's hit a nerve.

Gianna ignores him. "You kept to your word, and I reward

those who obey me."

Surrounded by religious relics, I pray that luck is on my side this time. And when the sacristy door opens, it's apparent that…I will forever be a sinner in the eyes of the Lord.

Everything feels like it's moving in slow motion.

I watch as Francesco leads Lettie into the chapel, her tiny hand in his. She wears a beautiful white dress. Her hair is in pigtails. Too reminiscent of what I was once dressed in to appease Father Merry's sick perversions.

Tears instantly roll down my cheeks.

How she's grown. It's only been a few weeks. But those are weeks I'll never get back, thanks to Gianna.

Oh, how she's about to suffer…

"*Cara mia*," I cry, gesturing with my hands that she's to come to her mother.

But Francesco doesn't let her go. "Forgive me," he says, guilt-ridden.

I don't understand what's happening right now.

Who has double-crossed who?

"You're not *that* good of an actress, *piccola*. You disappoint me," Gianna says, ambling over to me. "You continue to lead with your heart, and where does that get you? A failure, that's what."

"Call me all the names you want, but give me back my daughter, and you'll never see us again."

Gianna's attention turns to Lenny. "Lost for words? That's a first. You too disappoint me. *Bella*, you see that man over there? Well, I hate to tell you, but he's your father. Don't ever be like him."

I charge forward, ready to rip off her head, but Francesco places a knife to Lettie's throat.

"Careful," Gianna warns.

Lenny is surprisingly quiet. And when I see the look on his face, I understand why.

This is the first time he's seeing his daughter. Talking about her and actually seeing her are two totally different things. And Gianna was the one to take away his rite of passage of telling Lettie he's her father.

Peering at my parents, I vow here, and now, that come morning, they'll both be dead. I don't care that Francesco appears as if he was coerced into doing Gianna's bidding. For all I know, he isn't even my father.

The only person I trust is Lennon.

We both knew this outcome was likely, but I was right—Gianna did have Lettie all along. And regardless of whether we were deceived, we've won because I got what I came here for.

My daughter.

Now, I just need to get us out of this alive.

"Enough with the dramatics, Gianna, what do you want?" Lenny says, no emotion behind him.

"You know what I want."

"Fine, take it! It's yours. All of it. Just let Valentina and Lettie go."

Spinning to face Lenny, I shake my head.

But he stays firm.

"Lenny!" I beseech because he's just signed his death warrant. There's no way she'll let him live. He signs over everything to her, and in return, she'll make him dig his own grave.

Bria stirs, and her eyes flicker open. It takes her a moment to realize where she is, and when she sees me, she remembers why.

"You bitch," she spits, tugging furiously at her restraints.

Gianna arches a brow because Bria's not that good of an actress either. "You really did subdue her."

Gianna believed we were all in this plan together, but by Bria's response to me, she realizes that I knocked the bitch out. Well, Lenny helped, but she doesn't know that.

This may work in our favor.

She looks at Lenny, then back at me. "What little liars I raised."

"No, you raised us to be chameleons," I correct. "You forced us to be a dozen different people to suit your needs. We did your dirty work for years. What more do you want?"

This has thrown a spanner into the works.

I wonder if she's aware that I know who she really is to me. Did Francesco tell her?

Something is missing—I just can't pinpoint what.

"Francesco, free them both."

None of us have weapons, but it didn't matter if we did. I won't fight without knowing Lettie is safe.

Francesco does as he's ordered, and the moment Bria is free, she charges me, slapping my cheek. I don't have time to recover before she punches me in the stomach.

"*Mamma!*" Lettie cries, running for me, but Gianna grips her by the forearm.

"No!" I scream, dropping to my knees, interlacing my hands. "Please let her go."

Lettie begins to sob, her lower lip trembling as Gianna's fingernails dig into her tiny arm.

"I'll give you everything. Whatever you want, it's yours," Lenny says calmly, walking slowly toward her, hands raised.

Francesco now has his knife to Lenny's throat, but it's in vain.

Lenny could disarm Francesco if he wanted. But we're both powerless and at Gianna's mercy. Whatever she says, we'll both do.

"Oh, you tempt me, Lennon." Gianna mulls over his offer, knowing he means it.

Coming to a stand, I never take my eyes off Lettie, assuring her that things will be all right.

My brave little angel wipes away her tears with a snivel.

"There is one thing I want," she finally reveals.

The room is quiet because a storm is brewing.

"Playtime is over. It's time to leave the hard work to the adults."

"Done," Lenny says without pause.

But that was too easy.

"And I want you to choose."

"Choose what?"

"Choose who you sail off into the sunset with. Bria. Or Valentina."

I exhale slowly. I don't expect him to choose me, but I know that he will.

And so does Bria.

She bites her lip, stopping her tears. I actually feel sorry for her.

"Why?" Lenny demands. "You have everything you want! Why are you doing this?"

Gianna throws her head back, laughing. "Because, you silly, silly boy…I can."

There's no rhyme or reason. Gianna is torturing us because she can.

I risk a glance at Francesco, who still has the knife to Lenny's throat. But his arm is slack. He nods at me subtly.

He's on our side.

Gianna got to him as he feared, but it seems his loyalty isn't with her.

I can work with this.

"Take care of Lettie," I whisper to Lenny.

His eyes widen. "No, I can't. I—" But he's at a loss for words because whatever decision he makes, he will live with for the rest of his life.

"I'll make the choice for you. Choose your wife."

Bria's confusion is apparent, and she's waiting for the other shoe to drop.

"You heard her, she's making it easy for you. Or are you a coward?" Gianna baits Lenny who sneers.

"W-we can start again. Just you and me," Bria says, eyes wide, begging he does the right thing. "I'm sorry for everything. I love you. So much. Let's forget this life and run away."

But Lenny isn't moved.

"I can never forget," he says with conviction.

"My father trusted you!" she yells, tears of anger cascading. "You promised to protect me! You fucking lied! You son of a bitch! How can you do this to me? I have been nothing but loyal to you. How?"

Lenny doesn't retaliate as she spits abuse at him.

Gianna watches this shit show she created with fire in her eyes.

The commotion is what I need to gesture to Francesco that it's time. I'm certain Lenny is biding his time. When he sees the opportunity, he'll take the knife from Francesco and act in whatever way he can.

Lettie is watching me closely. She's waiting for instructions. She is Lenny's and my daughter after all. It shouldn't surprise me that she knows what to do.

I thought we created a monster.

How wrong I was.

I nod, and everything happens in a split second.

Lettie twists and stomps on Gianna's foot. Gianna topples over, unbalanced and caught off guard, which is my opportunity to charge at her. Lettie takes cover behind the altar. Francesco quickly hands Lenny the knife, then runs to protect Lettie.

Lenny grabs Bria by the waist as she fights like a wildcat, desperate to get to me.

Gianna grabs a pew to balance herself, but I bring my foot down, stomping on her kneecap. She buckles with a yelp.

I give her no time to recover as I elbow her in the face. Her nose cracks.

Her stilettos will be the death of her, as will her elaborate train. Both hinder her movement because every time she tries to run, her heels catch the train.

I use her poor wardrobe choice to my advantage and stand on the train, holding her in place as I punch her repeatedly in the face. She tries to fight me off, and usually, she'd be able to block me.

But my rage is animating me in a way I've never felt before.

Every part of me is humming, demanding I bathe in her blood and use her skull as a goblet as I bask in celebratory champagne.

She scratches across my cheek with her long nails. It only infuriates me further.

I hear Lenny ordering Francesco to take Lettie back to his home.

Bria is cursing at the top of her lungs to let her go.

Gianna manages to kick off her heels.

Her nose is bleeding, and her face is slightly swollen.

But it's not enough.

"Looks like I should win the fucking Oscar…bitch," I spit.

Gianna smirks. "I always knew you'd be my most worthy opponent."

"Is that so?" I ask, removing my foot from her dress.

Let's make it a fair fight, then.

"Well, as they say, the apple doesn't fall far from the tree. Does it…Mother?"

Gianna's eyes widen.

So she didn't know.

Something is amiss. Gianna came into this, thinking she had an advantage. But this puzzle has missing parts.

I can figure that out later, though, because now we end this.

"You're not my child," she cruelly spits as we circle one another. "I may have given birth to you, but I disowned you the moment I left you on these steps. You're nothing but a disappointment. Nothing but a sniveling little weakling."

Her words bounce off me because the days of being wounded are long gone. And I know she says this with intent because an angry fighter is a fighter who makes mistakes.

"Really? That's the best you've got?" I mock, reveling in her anger that I haven't fallen for her tactics.

She lunges and attempts to punch me, but I block her and spin, jabbing her in the kidneys.

"You taught me well."

"I haven't taught you a thing," she counters, placing a hand over her lower back.

"On the contrary, you've taught me not to feel, which is why I'll have no issues cutting off your fucking head!"

She nods, understanding that only one of us will be leaving here alive. "Let's do this, then."

Just as she taught me, we bow as a sign of respect, which seems ironic. But once we stand tall, it's every man for himself. Even injured, she charges me, kicking me in the stomach. I stumble back three steps.

Lenny is still restraining Bria, so all he can do is watch. However, he knows this is my fight. He'll jump in if necessary, but this bitch is mine.

When she punches, I block.

When I kick, she sidesteps.

We know each other's fighting styles, but I have something Gianna does not—years of pent-up anger because of her.

I won't fatigue.

I won't surrender.

I will beat her down until there's nothing for her to give.

We circle the other, eyes fixed, watching for an opportunity to strike. As Gianna taught me, I look for anything that can be used as a weapon because we don't always have a gun or knife on hand. And I see it in the large statue of Mary.

I slowly lead her toward it because if I can kick her into it, that statue which sits upon a pillar will fall on top of her—I hope. At the very least, it'll knock her off-balance, which will give me an advantage.

"All these years," I start, hoping to distract her from my plan. "I wanted to ask my mother, why? Why did she abandon me? Why did she leave me here to fall prey to the vile creatures inside? But now that I've met my mother, I know the answer."

Gianna listens intently, oblivious to the statue behind her.

"My mother needs to lie, cheat, and steal because she's nothing but a coward. And I don't want to be anything like that. If I'm to sit on a throne, it's because I earned it, not because I stole it. You're pathetic. A bitter woman who is terrified of being alone."

Gianna is offended by my barrage because the truth hurts.

And so does the Virgin Mary as Gianna bumps into the pillar, and the statue topples onto her back. Gianna buckles under the force, which is when I advance and slam my fist so hard into her face, a tooth is embedded into my knuckles.

Blood trickles down her chin.

With a roar, she charges me, but I'm faster, and I deliver a roundhouse kick to her stomach. She staggers backward, but soon regains her footing. She grips her dress and rips off the train, freeing her legs. She doesn't wait and comes running toward me, delivering a succession of punches.

She manages to land two.

One in the face.

The other in the ribs.

The bitch can pack a punch.

I shake off the double vision, and when she throws another punch, I grip her wrist and bend it back, breaking it with a loud crack.

She screams in pain.

It's the first time I've ever heard her scream.

She crosses her injured arm over her chest and uses the other to grab my hair like the catty bitch that she is. I try to break free, but she yanks on my hair like whipping reins. She tosses me into the side of a pew, the sharp edge digging into my flank.

Our fingers tangle as I try to pry myself free, but she only holds on tighter and heaves me into the confessional booth.

There's no way she's letting me go, so with no other choice, I pull away so hard, she yanks out a chunk of hair.

I use the confessional booth wall as leverage and kick her in the stomach.

She's hurled through the air and crashes into a tall brass candelabra. The lit candles roll along the floor, but one bounces on the altar, setting the linen altar cloth alight.

With the altar on fire, it sets the perfect backdrop as I elbow Gianna once, twice, in the face. She loses her footing and bangs her head on the side of the altar. The hit is hard, and she grips the edge, her feet slipping out from under her.

She tries to stand but can barely hold her weight, as she's only able to use one arm for support.

I walk toward her, and seeing her this way, I feel nothing.

I don't feel guilty.

I don't feel bad.

I reach down, and with my finger, I swipe the blood from her cheek.

Placing it into my mouth, I say, "The infamous Gianna Ricci is human after all."

Her eyes are filled with pure hatred. "I'll always be a part of you. You can kill me a hundred times, but that doesn't erase who you really are. You're my blood. You're rotten on the inside… just like me. And deep down, you know, even in happiness, you'll forever feel solace in the darkness."

"You're right," I reply, watching as she struggles to hold up her weight. "But I'll do my damnedest to try to stay in the light. If not for me, then for my daughter…something you'll never understand.

"You kidnapped your own granddaughter and used her as bait. You left me here to rot. You are the true monster in this story, Gianna, and whatever your backstory is, if perhaps you didn't get cuddled enough as a child, or maybe your parents were as heartless as you are, I really don't care.

"You had a choice to do better, but you chose to be a fucking cunt."

I hear commotion behind me, but I'm transfixed on the sight before me.

"You need me. That's why you keep coming back. You're nothing without me!"

"You arrogant woman. You came into this thinking you had won. Why? What ace do you have up your sleeve? I thought it was Lettie…but it's something else, isn't it?"

"You clever girl." She grins, revealing her missing tooth.

I yank her up, pressing us nose to nose. "Tell me what it is."

She instead laughs manically. "You can't kill me."

The small, slow-burning fire creeps closer and closer to the end of the altar, giving me a wonderful idea. I turn to walk into the sacristy, wishing to retrieve the consecrated wine, but am knocked to my ass when a loud pop rocks the chapel's walls.

Spinning, I see Lenny tackling Bria, who has a gun.

My bad for not checking if she was armed. Her ball gown allows ample space to hide a piece.

The gunshot throws me off, and Gianna uses that to her advantage as she rams something sharp into my ankle. Peering down, I find her jeweled hair clip sticking out of my Achilles.

And the bitch, just like Jesus Christ, has arisen.

Gianna gets a second wind as the playing field is somewhat leveled because an Achilles tendon injury is one of the worst to have.

She slams my head onto the altar, holding me down.

I drive my elbow backward, connecting with her stomach, winding her.

She releases me, but when I hear another gunshot, I know Bria didn't miss this time.

She hit the back of my shoulder.

A flesh wound, but Gianna jams her fingers inside and twists.

A scream rips through me because that fucking hurts.

"Bria, please, don't let it end this way."

"You're the one who made that choice! And now, deal with the consequences."

I'm trying to ensure Lenny is okay, but Gianna is punching me in the back. I can't fight her off because my arm doesn't work, and putting pressure on my left foot is excruciating.

However, I manage to turn and grab Gianna's broken wrist, slamming it onto the altar.

She howls in agony.

I grip her hair, and as the fire is burning on the altar cloth, I rub her face into it.

Her muffled screams are music to my ears.

The product she has in her hair instantly sets alight. Her scalp is on fire. I watch for a few seconds before dragging her toward the stoup and dunking her face into the holy water. Her hair sizzles as the fire extinguishes. I'm surprised she didn't implode when drenched with the holy water like in the movies when it touches something unholy.

I yank her back out and smack her cheek as her eyes flutter. "Wakey, wakey. I'm not done with you yet."

Death is too easy for Gianna. I intend to make her suffer and tarnish her name and reputation. Only then will I end her miserable life.

"Bria, no!"

I turn and see Bria break free and aim the gun at Gianna and me. I'm about to duck behind a pew, but the gun leisurely tumbles from Bria's hand, crashing to the floor.

It all happens in slow motion.

She looks at me and then down at the knife embedded into her heart, the knife Lenny threw to save my life.

"Looks like you made your choice." Those are Bria's last words as she collapses with a thud.

Lenny stands still, eyes wide open, stunned that he killed his wife.

Gianna wheezes, her lungs filled with smoke, but beneath her gasping for air, she cackles—cruelly.

"What's so funny?" I scream inches from her face.

Her face is burned, bloody, and swollen. Yet she's still in the belief that she's won.

"I...win," she manages to push out, her breaths labored.

"Wrong, you sick fuck. We all fucking lose."

I punch her in the face, and as she drops to the floor, I reach down and snag my fingers through her hair. Lenny stands over Bria, watching for any signs of life, but a knife to the heart usually means one thing.

Ironic, it seems, because I bet that's how Bria felt about Lenny's betrayal—metaphorically.

But now, it's literal as well.

I leave Lenny to grieve as I begin a slow hobble down the aisle, dragging Gianna by the hair. She has nothing left and lays still, groaning and mumbling gibberish under her breath.

I shoulder open the chapel door and limp down the corridor with Gianna trailing me. Every part of me hurts, but funnily enough, the pain spurs me on.

This place has caused me nothing but anguish, but it's time to end that once and for all. It takes me a while, but when I turn the corner and am greeted with terrified screams, it makes everything worth it.

People literally run away from me, screeching in horror. A man throws up in his wife's cocktail. And a woman faints, Scarlett O'Hara style.

What a bunch of crybabies.

The crowd parts, and I feel like Moses parting the Red Sea. Seems fitting, seeing as I am slathered in red—my blood as well as Gianna's.

I drag Gianna's body up the stairs to the stage, and thankfully, the sisters have ushered the children back to their rooms. I toss her into a chair and arrange it at the front of the stage for all to see. She can't keep herself up and slouches.

She's barely recognizable.

I tap the microphone, and it echoes over the speakers. "What a glorious affair this is," I declare, sweeping my arms out wide.

The pain in my shoulder is incapacitating, but I persevere.

"This here is your host, Gianna Ricci. And as none of you know because she's a gutless woman, she is my mother."

The crowd is unsure if this is halftime entertainment. Or perhaps one of those art house performances that make no sense. So they dare not make a sound.

"I am Valentina Ricci, and Saint Maria's Orphanage was my home until Gianna "saved me." But she only adopted me, her own daughter, to shape me into the person you see today.

"So thanks...*Mother.*"

The term of endearment is anything but.

Saliva dribbles from Gianna's chin as her head droops to her chest.

"Gianna is a drug dealer, she kidnapped her own granddaughter and used her as bait...and she's a murderer. Tonight's ploy was to raise money not for the orphanage, but for herself. But I suspect most of you knew that. I also suspect that most of you are liars, con men, and just all round fucking horrible people.

"The reason I know that is because no one has called the police. In a society where we're glued to technology, no one is posting a live feed on their socials for the world to see, and the reason for all this is because you don't want your peers knowing who you really are."

And this is why I know I won't suffer any backlash for this very public execution.

No one wants their name associated with tonight and the scandal that will follow. But like curious drivers who can't help but look when passing an accident, these perverts can't look away.

"So hear me now, forget this orphanage exists. Not a single child will be going home with any of you. You *will* donate, however, and your generosity is greatly appreciated. So please, dig deep."

My eyes flicker as unconsciousness tackles me. But I push past it.

"You will not forget me…because I won't forget you." I look closely at the faces in the crowd, and when my gaze lands on the only one who matters, I instantly feel better.

Lenny walks toward the stage, and I know it's finally over.

He climbs the steps, and in his palm, he holds the knife he killed Bria with. He offers it to me.

"My entire life, I always wondered what was wrong with me, and now, I see that…nothing is. I'll see you in hell, Mommy dearest."

Gianna smirks as I slash the knife across her throat. She doesn't make a sound. It doesn't surprise me. Even in death, she refuses to surrender.

Her blood gushes out, coating my face and chest. I stab the blade into the incision and begin severing through tendons and tissue as I cut off her head.

This elicits hysteria, and the crowd runs from the ballroom, afraid they're next.

Once the cut is deep enough, I twist and tear the head from her shoulders. Her body, which is leaning to the left, slides to the floor with a squelch.

With her head in my hand, I limp from the stage and through the crowd.

The remaining guests can't look away, but they don't make eye contact with me either. They know better—a new Mafia queen is in town.

Lenny walks beside me as we head back to the chapel. I don't know why, but this place grants me solace.

We enter, and I see Lenny has placed Bria on a pew. He's also put out the fire. I place Gianna's head on the altar. The macabre scene is one I commit to memory because the blood, the power—it's ours.

And just like always, the bloodlust claws at my skin, awakening the hunger that demands to be fed.

Lenny grabs me by the throat and arches my neck backward. He stares me deep in the eyes as he leans down and licks the blood from my face. Like a cat licking away the cream. To most, this act is revolting, but to me, it's carnal and animalistic.

He sweeps his tongue along my cheek before skimming it across my trembling lips. He's being gentle as I am severely wounded, but my body has suddenly forgotten that I am shot and beaten, as it wants to be manhandled.

"Fuck me," I demand against his lips. "And fuck me hard."

Lenny smirks, cupping my throat harder. "Since when do I take orders?"

"Since you're going to fuck me over the altar while Mommy watches."

He hums low before smashing his lips over mine.

This isn't a kiss filled with love.

It's a kiss where we want to eat the other alive.

He tears at my mouth.

I scratch at his face.

He rips off my already ruined dress.

I do the same to his shirt.

He spins me, giving me what I want as he throws me over the altar and tears off my underwear. He reaches down and hisses when he feels I'm already wet. Within seconds, his trousers hit the floor, and his cock plunges deep inside my pussy.

I grip the altar as Lenny fucks me hard. He holds my waist, helping to keep me standing as I relish his brutal strokes. He's ruthless, and each time he thrusts into me, I grasp the altar as he propels me up the marble.

The hard surface cools down my heated flesh. I take what Lenny gives as he drives into me, before pulling all the way out. He teases my outer lips with his cock, then thrusts back into me.

Leaning down, mid-thrust, he whispers into my ear in Italian, "My girl. Always and forever."

"Yes," I moan. "Don't stop. Don't you ever stop."

He turns my cheek as he fucks me, and we both take in the

sight of Gianna's head, watching us. It's sick and twisted, but it's the final fuck you.

Her smirk will forever be frozen in time.

Lenny groans, swearing in Italian.

I bounce back on his cock, but he presses me between the shoulder blades, making sure to avoid the gunshot wound as he rides me like I am his own personal toy.

This is possession and ownership.

This is obsessive love.

He is meant for me.

And I am meant for him.

Two broken pieces that make a beautiful mess.

"Ti amo."

My eyes are still locked with Gianna's as I come loudly, screaming, "I love you too!"

I see stars behind my eyes, and Lenny comes with a sated moan, spilling his seed into me. He collapses onto my back, but holds his weight, not wanting to hurt me. And here, we lay, breathless and spent, slathered in our enemy's blood.

What's next for us?

Well, for the first time in our lives…our life is ours.

CHAPTER 13

VALENTINA
ONE MONTH LATER

"*Guarda, Mamma!*"

I stop punching the bag and smile when Lettie comes bursting through the door, holding a pink box that is bigger than she is.

"What do you have there?" I ask her, dropping to a squat.

The outside of the box reveals that inside is a pair of LED light-up roller skates.

Lenny walks in a second later, carrying many bags in both hands.

I arch a brow, looking at him.

He smiles innocently.

"Is Lenny spoiling you again?"

Lettie sits on the floor, tonguing her cheek as she rips open the box. Lenny places the bags beside her and stands behind me, watching.

He doesn't want to crowd her as we've agreed it'll be too confusing for her if we just dump that he's her biological father. She still calls Nico *Papa*, which kills Lenny. But we're all trying to get along for Lettie's sake.

When she's old enough, we will tell her the truth, but for now, we're all one big happy family.

I couldn't just expect Nico to go back to Italy and forget about his family because that's what we are. Although the circumstances have changed, I'll never forget what Nico did for me. Eventually, he'll have to return to Italy as his visa will expire, but until then, he lives with us.

Lenny has been surprisingly good about it. I think he respects Nico, not that he'd ever admit it. Nico protected us when Lenny couldn't. So, in his eyes, he owes Nico.

But that's the sacrifices one makes for their child. Lenny can see how much she loves Nico, and Nico isn't pushing for any parental rights.

Lenny has put him behind the register at the store. He has no idea he's selling drugs inside those crystals. Not all the customers are buyers, however. It gives Nico something to do and to practice his English.

Our household isn't divided.

We sit at the same dinner table together.

We take turns looking after Lettie.

The only thing we don't do together is share a bed.

Lenny has made it very clear that Nico was welcome here, but he was to understand that I was Lenny's, and blah, blah… all that alpha shit which…yawn.

Nico respected my decision. Besides, he isn't lacking any female attention. The moment women hear his accent, they're a goner.

But I need to remember, just because I've checked out, that doesn't mean he has. I'm trying to be sensitive to his feelings, but it's a little hard when I finally have my HEA with the man I've loved for as long as I can remember.

Things are surprisingly…good.

It's surreal, to be honest.

After the very public display of cutting off Gianna's head, the orphanage was inundated with donations. No doubt hush money. But I'll keep to my word because I never want to see or deal with any of those assholes again.

I work closely with the sisters to ensure the kids are safe. The money has come in handy as the orphanage is undergoing a facelift. The kids will never go without ever again.

I visit Elena weekly. I wish I could adopt her, but I won't until I figure out what my future holds. It's a lot to take in and change must come. It makes sense to stay here, but it's hard not to feel like the "other woman."

Lettie asks Lenny to help her put on her skates. He attempts to hide his excitement that she asked, but fails miserably.

I leave them to daddy-daughter time and decide to go for a run.

Grabbing my earbuds, I decide to make the most of the day. Spring is coming, my favorite time of the year. It's time for new beginnings and rebirth. Seems fitting.

Selecting a playlist, I commence a slow jog around the gardens. Lenny's home is beautiful. But it's not my home. This is the home he built with Bria. Her spirit lingers. I can feel it. Her ghost roams the halls, and sometimes, I catch her from the corner of my eye.

I know it's just my guilty conscience playing tricks on me, but I feel uneasy here. Even sleeping in their marital bed at first gave me nightmares. She's haunting me. Or rather, what I did to her is.

Lenny had Bria buried with Aldo. No ceremony was held. Lenny had his men take care of it. He was the only one in attendance. We don't speak about her because I know it hurts him. He made a choice. But it's evident he did love Bria, just how I do Nico.

But it's a different kind of love.

I pick up the pace and venture into the thick, wooded area that extends around the back. The blaring music spurs me on.

I think back to Gianna and her death. I wish I could kill her again and again. But it'll never be enough.

This is the end, but I can't help but feel…incomplete. Like this ending is so…anticlimactic.

The bad guy loses, and we live happily ever after? I can't help but think, where's the catch?

After living a life filled with pain, perhaps I'm not used to being happy.

But something feels amiss.

I can't put my finger on it.

Something just doesn't feel right.

Like this was too easy?

Seems ridiculous because nothing has been easy thus far.

I'm just being paranoid.

Things are good. But too good?

I'm wrestling with my mind, and it's exhausting. Who needs enemies when you have the brain of an overthinker?

I try to ignore this bad feeling in the pit of my stomach and run faster. But my anxiety only builds. The faster I run, the closer I feel to falling into an abyss.

My smartwatch beeps as my heart rate is dangerously high.

I suddenly can't breathe.

I come to an abrupt stop and bend forward, placing my hands onto my knees. I'm still tender from my injuries, but this is different.

I feel sick. Like something is very, very wrong.

The same feelings overwhelmed me when I was in Italy. When Lettie was taken.

No, please, God. Not again.

I take off toward the house, focused on nothing but getting there. I get back within minutes. I run toward the gym, hoping they're still there, but they're not.

"Fuck!" I curse.

My feet can barely keep up as I sprint to the house and burst through the back door. I give the housekeeper the fright of her life. "Sorry, Betty, have you seen Mr. Shepherd?"

Betty looks afraid to answer. "No."

Panic turns to hysteria when I hear Lettie scream.

It's coming from the porch.

My sneakers skid on the polished floors as I shoulder open the front door. "Lettie!"

However, once outside, I don't understand what I'm seeing because it's not what I thought. Not by a long shot.

Lenny gives me a puzzled look, while Lettie happily waves. She's on her behind as she's clearly fallen while trying out her skates. She has a helmet and knee and elbow pads on. All the things a reasonable parent gives their child.

Nothing is amiss here other than me being psychotic.

"What's the matter?" Lenny rushes over, gripping my upper arms. "Are you okay?"

"Yes," I reply, pressing my face into his chest as he cradles me tight.

"*Mamma?*" Lettie asks, a look of concern on her beautiful face.

Wiping away my tears, I nod. "*Si, cara mia. Mamma* just missed you, that's all."

Lenny sees through the front I'm putting on for her. Thankfully, Lettie buys my story.

"Lenny taught me how to skate. But I fell. But he said you can stay up if you don't fall," she says in English with her cute Italian accent.

"He's right." I kiss her forehead, brushing back her soft hair.

Nico comes up the driveway, finished for the day.

"*Papa!*" Lettie screams, waving hysterically.

Lenny stands behind me, comforting me in his arms. I feel like an idiot, but I could have sworn something was wrong.

"*Ciao, bella.* How was your day?"

Lettie tells Nico all about her day. But he sees my face and reads that something is wrong.

I nod subtly that it's okay.

He thankfully reads my facial charades.

"Go with *Papa* and show him your other presents," I

suggest, as I need to talk to Lenny.

Nico takes her hand and helps her sit so he can take off her skates. Lenny and I walk down the stairs and take a walk. It's safer this way because I don't trust that the walls don't have ears.

When we're far enough away, he asks, "What's happened?"

"I don't know how to say this without sounding crazy...but I feel like something is wrong."

He arches a brow with a mischievous grin.

"Not helping," I quip with half a smile. "Do you feel like we're being watched?"

He arches the other brow this time.

I playfully slap his arm in response.

"I would hope not. Not after the things I've done to you."

"Maybe I'm just insane. Look at my family tree."

Francesco is still on probation. I've given him the benefit of the doubt after he saved Lettie, but he still betrayed us. So I'm watchful. One wrong move and he'll be joining Mommy dearest.

Lenny draws me into his arms. "You're exhausted and running on the defense. It's what we've done our entire lives. It's hard to accept that a happily ever after does exist for us. That's all it is. No one is watching us. Our house is under twenty-four-hour surveillance. Romeo is the RoboCop of bodyguards."

He's right. I don't even know he's there half the time.

I run my fingers through my hair. "I *am* exhausted."

"Go rest. Tonight, we're going out. I'm taking you out on a date."

I bite my bottom lip to hold back my grin. "I think we're past the dating stage. We have a child together."

"Well, we skipped the fun stuff."

This time, I'm the one to arch my brow.

"I mean the stuff like flowers and first dates and shit."

"You're adorable," I mock, suddenly feeling better.

"Go take a bath and listen to Enya."

I can't help but laugh. But all of that does sound amazing. "I love you. Thank you."

"For?" He kisses the top of my head.

"For not thinking I'm a complete psycho."

"Now, now. Don't put words in my mouth."

I pull away, faking horror.

"Oh, baby, you can put something else in my mouth." He drops to his knees and kisses over the front of my shorts. He slides them down my legs, and just like that, I'm feeling much better.

Lenny didn't give me a dress code, so a little black dress it is.

I do what Lenny suggested and take a bath. I listened to indie rock instead, though. I slipped into fluffy pajamas, crawled into bed, and slept like the dead.

I do feel a little better.

As I showered, I decided I'm probably jumpy due to…life. It's been a roller coaster for as long as I can remember. I'm not used to peace.

I'm applying the final touches to my makeup when the door opens. Lenny stops dead in his tracks when he sees me.

"Oh *Mamma*." He whistles, eating me up from head to toe.

I feel desirable, and my cheeks heat. This kinda feels like a first date, I guess. Not that I'd know. We skipped that part of growing up as we were too busy, well, murdering people.

"Too much?"

"No, never," he replies, coming up behind me and squeezing my ass.

He kisses the side of my neck.

My eyes flutter.

"Wear boots," he instructs.

I look at his reflection in the mirror, confused.

"Do what you're told." He slaps my ass, before taking off his T-shirt. Then his pants.

Who am I to argue?

"If I didn't know any better, I'd assume you're taking me out here to kill me and bury the body," I quip as we trek through thick forestry.

I now understand why he told me to wear boots.

I have no idea where he's taking me, but I trust him.

The sky is star-kissed, and the moon is bright. It's magical. Lenny and I don't have many memories such as this one, so I'll cherish it. And I look forward to making more for the rest of our lives.

We climb a steep hill with Lenny holding my hand the entire time. This reminds me of something kids would do, and I realize this is why he chose this location. We're making up for the childhood that we never had.

When we get to the top of the hill, I know the trek will be well worth it.

"Wow," I gush, staring at the twinkling lights before me in our town. "I didn't realize it was so big."

"I know. Looking at all that, it makes you realize we're merely a speck in existence. I used to come up here a lot when we were kids," he confesses, eyes focused ahead. "It was my place to get away and think."

"All those nights, I thought you were with girls."

"Some nights I was."

I'm quiet.

"But they were a substitute for who I always wanted." He runs his finger over my inner wrist. "And now, it's your place too."

"Thank you for bringing me here."

"What's mine is yours."

It touches my heart. It's too much, and my eyes pool with tears.

"That wasn't supposed to make you cry."

"They're happy tears." I sniff, feeling like a crybaby.

"Well, that's a nice change."

Tears soon turn to laughter.

My emotions are all over the place.

"I literally feel like I'm going crazy," I confess, blowing out a long breath.

"It's okay to go a little crazy. Besides, I like your crazy."

He pulls me into his side, and we stand staring at the town, which holds so many secrets. Every light in a home represents someone's story. It's a life lived.

"Marry me."

It takes me a moment to realize what Lenny just said because, what?

How?

Marry? *Me*?

What?

He leans down and whispers into my ear, "This is the part where you say yes."

Stepping in front of him, I stand on tippy-toes and throw

my arms around his neck. "Yes! A thousand yeses. Of course I'll marry you!"

His smile is so big, I don't think I've ever seen him so happy. We kiss fervently, pawing at the other, desperate to peel off one another's skin and become one. My heart is so full. All I taste is happy tears cascading down our lips from both our eyes.

After everything we've been through, this makes it all worth it.

Lenny's cell rings, and he hesitantly ends the kiss with a groan. Lettie is with Nico, but he would call me if anything were wrong. No one calls Lenny to chitchat.

"What's up, Romeo?"

Lenny's face changes within an instant.

He hangs up and curses under his breath. "Fuck. We have to go."

"What's happened?" I barely get the question out before he's leading me down the hill to our car.

"Opal Imports is on fire. It's arson."

I gasp. "How does Romeo know?"

Lenny doesn't stop, and he doesn't change his tone as he replies, "'Cause he found bodies inside. The fire is to conceal the crime."

I mirror his earlier comment as I fumble through my purse to find my phone. I call Nico and hold my breath until he answers. "Just checking in," I casually say in Italian, not wanting to rouse any suspicion.

He details his evening and that Lettie is safely sleeping.

But I have to be certain.

"Can you go check on her?"

"Why?" he asks in Italian, but I can hear his steps as he walks to her room.

"Just please go. And hurry."

He picks up the pace, and I hear her bedroom door squeak open. "She's sleeping. She's safe. What's going on?"

He always speaks quickly when worried, and now is one of those times.

"Just please, don't leave her alone until I get back."

"Valentina—"

"Please, Nico. Promise me."

He hears the urgency in my tone.

"Okay. I promise."

"Thank you. If anyone knocks on the door, don't answer. Just stay there until I get home."

I hang up, unable to explain anymore.

I've tried to keep Lettie and Nico safe, but now I see we're not safe wherever we go. "Who the fuck would do this? Gianna is gone."

Lenny shakes his head, as puzzled as I am.

We get to the car and take off toward the store. He knows better than to drop me off at home. We do this together because bad things always seem to happen when we're apart.

Lettie is safe. And I trust Nico.

The drive takes half the time it should. We are confronted by fire trucks and police. Police tape surrounds the smoking remnants.

This is bad. A detective in a brown raincoat sees our car and flags Lenny to park off to the side.

"It's okay. He's on my payroll," he assures me, pulling up away from prying eyes.

We park the car and get out. The detective's face says it all. "Three bodies inside, Lenny."

Lenny runs a hand through his snarled hair. "Who?"

The detective reaches into his pocket to retrieve a pack of Marlboros. "Tian, Kong, and Matias. Any idea who wants to leave you a very public message?"

The detective offers Lenny a cigarette, but he waves him off. "No fucking idea. The person who would normally do this shit is…indisposed."

The detective shields his smoke with a palm to light it. "Well, I hate to break it to you, Lennon, but you've now got someone else gunning for you. And this person is pissed. The attack was very personal."

"Why?"

The detective retrieves his cell and shows Lenny some photos.

"This is not good."

I shift to look at the phone and see the image of three men hanging upside down, the insides on the outside, just like Lenny's men who were slaughtered at the delicatessen.

"I suggest you be careful and reevaluate everyone."

It begins to drizzle.

"Thanks, Derrick. Check your front porch tomorrow morning at seven thirty."

He nods, flicking his smoke to the ground. "Keep your nose clean. I can't be cleaning up your mess no more."

"I don't want a mess," Lenny says, defeated.

"Well, just so you know, there was no sign of forced entry. The door was either left unlocked or someone has the key."

My stomach drops. Nico worked today. Did he leave the door unlocked on purpose?

Lenny shakes the detective's hand.

He stands staring at the burning rubble. White smoke rises into the night sky. Bystanders gather and no doubt all wonder why someone would set an opal store alight.

"It's not Nico," I say, reading his thoughts. "I know what it looks and sounds like, but what's he got to gain from any of this?"

Lenny never takes his eyes off the building. "The same thing we happily sacrificed our lives for."

Lettie.

We don't speak further.

Lenny doesn't bother going into what's left of the store.

We drive home in silence.

Nico is in bed with Lettie, both asleep. This was my entire world once upon a time, and now, I wonder if maybe that has all come crashing down.

I close Lettie's bedroom door and amble to our room. I'm exhausted. I leave my clothes where they fall and don't bother washing off my makeup. I slip under the covers and close my heavy eyes. The bed dips beside me, and Lenny's familiar scent comforts me.

We don't speak.

We simply fall into the darkness once again.

I jolt upright, slathered in sweat.

On instinct, I reach out, and a sigh leaves me when I feel Lenny beside me.

He's sleeping soundly.

Picking up my phone, I see that it's just after midnight. The house is dead still.

Gently pulling back the covers, I tiptoe from the room, grabbing my robe on the way out. I keep my footsteps light as I walk to Lettie's room. When I slowly push open the door,

Lettie's bedside lamp projects blue and green stars around her ceiling and walls. She's clinging to Nico, feeling safe in his arms.

Closing the door softly, I make my way to the bathroom. I don't bother turning on the light. I sit on the rim of the bathtub and just remain still. Tonight was a mixed bag of emotions. To go from experiencing one of the happiest moments of my life to feeling like I'm drowning once again has really thrown me off.

Nico isn't involved in this.

I know that he isn't.

How would he even know who Lenny's drug suppliers are?

No, it's not him.

It's a new moon, but it seems darker than usual. The bathroom has a large chandelier with matching wall sconces. The glass shower screen extends half the wall. The marbled double vanity adds to the opulence.

Every room in this house was designed beautifully. I wish I could love it here, but the air just feels...cold.

A shiver racks my body. But this is so intense, I feel nauseous.

Once I use the toilet, I flush it and make my way over to the sink. With a yawn, I wash my hands, sleep suddenly tackling me. Peering into the mirror, I yelp as the shadows play tricks on my eyes, and I see a figure standing behind me.

Turning over my shoulder rapidly, no one is there.

"You're losing your mind," I whisper into the darkness.

Drying my hands on a hand towel, I am ready to go back to bed. But the hair on my neck stands on end.

Their presence is oppressive.

I can feel their breath on the back of my neck.

And I suddenly realize that my eyes weren't playing tricks.

Someone was…*is* behind me.

Lunging for the ceramic decorative vase to use as a weapon is too late. I feel a prick on the side of my neck.

I want to turn, but my legs feel like they're made of cement. I lose control of my hand. The vase crashes onto the floor, shattering the quiet. Wavering, I grip the edge of the counter, but I'm going under.

Everything is blurry, and my tongue is heavy.

I can't scream.

The last thing I can do is look back into the mirror and see that my ghost stands behind me, and in the darkness, I can see it smile.

I don't remember much after that.

CHAPTER 14

LENNY

I wake to a thud.

The bed is cold. Valentina hasn't been in it for a little while.

I pull back the covers and sit on the edge of the bed, listening for anything out of the ordinary. Perhaps my mind is playing tricks on me.

Regardless, I get up and measure my steps as I walk through the house in search of Valentina.

She's not with Lettie. Nico is still sleeping beside her when I peer inside her bedroom.

I do a sweep of the house, but she's not here.

She probably couldn't sleep and is in the gym.

I open the back door and am about to walk down the steps, but I hear it before I see the devil. He was waiting for me on the porch.

I don't know who he is because he wears a mask like a coward. The mask is modeled after a Venetian-style devil. A sign of things to come. And perhaps, where I belong.

Before I have a chance to fight him off, he jabs me in the side of the neck with a needle.

I punch him in the face and stomach before I'm heavy on my feet. I'm now faced with four faces of the devil.

I try to fight off the heaviness, but the drugs…are quick.

I wake to the obnoxious chewing of gum.

I *must* be in hell.

It takes me a few seconds to catalog what I remember last.

"Valentina," I moan, forcing my eyes open.

She was gone when I woke.

I should have listened to her. She warned me that something was amiss. But my arrogance got in the way. With Gianna dead, I assumed our enemies were no more.

But I was wrong.

It takes my eyes a moment to adjust to the dim lighting, but I know where we are—we're at home, tucked away in the panic room inside the walls.

But in here, we have every torture device available. We built this room in secret. No one knows about this room.

So we're here because whoever that coward is beneath the mask has been watching us.

Valentina is tied to a chair next to me. Her chin drooped to her chest. She's out cold.

The man stands in front of me, sitting backward on a chair, chewing his gum.

I tug at the restraints, but they're done up tight.

I need to know my enemy so I can understand how to beat them. I need to know their weaknesses, and when he slowly removes the mask, his weakness glares at me…through one eye.

A ghost from the past is here, someone I haven't given a second thought to since the moment I left the orphanage.

"Surprise!" Hugo exclaims, hands out wide like this is some grand reveal. "Bet you didn't see that coming?"

"Neither did you, not with that one eye of yours."

Hugo the asshole, who I thought was dead after Valentina and I tortured him in the toilets after he defiled my girl, is here.

In my home.

He may be older, but Hugo is still a little runt.

My response to this is nothing but hilarity. I burst into

laughter, which Hugo doesn't appreciate.

"What's so funny?" he demands, standing slowly.

His attempts at scaring me make me laugh even harder.

"You," I manage to get out between laughs. "You're fucking lame. You're still holding on to some childhood trauma. Do you need a cuddle?"

Hugo launches and punches me in the face. "Trauma? She took my fucking eye! And the internal damage done to me when…"

"When I stuck a mop handle up your ass?" I finish for him. "Did you forget what you did to her? You tortured her for years! So if anyone needs a cuddle, it's her. But she's not a little bitch like you. *I'm sorry*!" I snivel, mimicking him from that night.

Hugo punches me in the stomach.

"Wow, you even hit like a little bitch," I wheeze with laughter.

Hugo inhales sharply before turning his attention to Valentina.

My poker face is fixed in a firm expression because he knows the only way to hurt me is through her.

A disgusting smirk tugs at his thin lips. "Just like old times, baby."

He licks her face like a salivating dog in heat.

I try to remain unmoved because he wants a rise out of me.

When he sees I continue to be passive, he licks down her neck and opens the lapels of her silk kimono. Her breasts are exposed. He takes them into his mouth and suckles them.

I shift in my seat, clenching my fists, attempting to break the restraints.

He slips a hand between her legs and molests her, never taking his eyes off me.

Rage animates me, and the wooden chair creaks beneath me. "I'm going to cut off your fingers and tongue and take great pleasure in watching you eat them."

Hugo snickers, thinking he's won.

But he's missed one vital thing—Valentina is awake.

She's playing dead until she sees an opportunity, like right now when he places his lips on her and defiles her mouth. He thrusts his tongue into her.

In response, she clamps her teeth around it and bites down hard.

Hugo's muffled screams echo loudly. He desperately tries to break free, but Valentina is like a rabid dog and violently shakes her head from side to side.

He tries pushing her away, but when he moves, she lets his tongue go and headbutts him. He staggers back and trips over his own feet, ending up on his ass.

She turns to look at me.

Her cheeks are flushed, and her pupils are pure black.

God, I love her.

"Are you okay?"

She nods. "Where are we?"

"At my home. In a panic room."

She takes a minute to take in what I just shared. "How does he know about it?"

I shrug because that's something I don't know.

Valentina looks at his boots. "*You're* the one who's been following me. Doesn't surprise me. You've always been a fucking creep. What do you want?"

Now, it's Hugo's turn to laugh. "Ready for it? Here's the plot twist!"

Nothing he says can shock me.

Or so I thought.

"Surely you didn't think Hugo was the mastermind behind this all? I'm insulted."

Both Valentina and I share the same reaction of utter shock.

"Hello, my darling. Miss me?"

"How? You're dead."

"Yes, I know. You killed me. Till death do us part. But you didn't think you'd get rid of me that easily, did you?"

"I'm not crazy. I *did* see you." Valentina seems relieved.

But now, we have another issue to deal with.

Bria is alive, and she's fucking pissed.

"This isn't possible. You were dead. I felt for a pulse. I plunged that knife into your heart."

Bria stands tall in a pantsuit, very reminiscent of Gianna.

"Yes, you did, but lucky for me, I was wearing a stab-proof vest. Very affordable and came in a day, thanks to Amazon Prime."

She's making jokes? She *is* fucking crazy.

"You felt for a pulse for two seconds. You were too worried about Valentina to check if you had finished the job. You know better than that."

"But I was at your service. My men told me it was all taken care of."

"I was too," she says, examining her nails. "That pathetic excuse of a burial was an insult to my memory. Thankfully, your men are easily bribed."

Her words cut deep because now, I understand. "It's been you this entire time, not Gianna, hasn't it?"

"Ding! Ding! Ding!"

Throughout this entire time, I believed Gianna was the one responsible for killing my men and overthrowing my kingdom. But it was Bria.

"The mole is you."

"Yes, darling, I can't believe it took you this long to figure it out. I thought you'd have worked it out long ago. When I saw the files my father had on Valentina, I knew you'd have the proof to convince her that Gianna was her mother.

"So I thought if I deleted them, you'd give up your little obsession with her. But it seems I was wrong."

"So you made a deal with the woman who killed your

father?" I shout, struggling in my seat to break free.

She flinches as my words have cut her deep. "If you can't beat 'em, join 'em, right?"

"Have you no loyalty?"

My verbal stab wounds her, and she lunges forward, slapping my cheek. "I was loyal to you! And where did that get me? Constantly living in her shadow! Do you know what it feels like to be second best your whole life?"

Valentina is quiet, and that's because she's working at the restraints behind her back. She must have enough slack to eventually break free.

In the interim, we need to stall Bria.

"I'm sorry! I was a fucking shit husband! But that doesn't warrant you to destroy everything I've worked so hard for. You killed good men, and for what? 'Cause you're upset we didn't go on date nights!"

"Don't patronize me," she snarls.

"I'm not," I counter, hoping she buys through my shit. "I acknowledge my mistakes in this marriage, but I didn't fucking go out of my way to destroy you! I loved your father. I loved you."

The minute I mention Aldo, tears fill her eyes.

"I know you're hurt. I fucked up. I went back on my promise. You never got revenge, and I am sorry."

"My father was good to you." She sniffs, her lower lip

trembling.

"I know he was. Everything we've built has been to honor his legacy. You're his legacy, Bria. And this is how you honor him? By siding with his enemy? The woman who killed him in cold blood?"

A tear trickles down her cheek. "I got my revenge in the end."

"How?"

"Gianna and I made a deal. I would overthrow you from the inside, so to speak, and in return, she would give me Valentina. I would give it all up for revenge on that bitch because she's the real reason my father is dead."

"That's the reason Gianna wanted me to bring you to her? In reality, she wanted me to bring you to her so we all would be in the same place at the same time?" Valentina asks, piecing things together.

"Not just a pretty face," Bria spits, walking over to a steel table with an array of tools.

She picks up a box cutter.

"But that's soon to change."

"You did me a favor killing Gianna. Yes, I was planning on killing you, but once I was done, I was going to kill Gianna and take her kingdom, which she stole from my father. This world is rightfully mine."

"You were aiming that gun at Gianna, not Valentina," I

say. "She thought you would 'save her,' but you were going to double-cross her the entire time."

"She was an ignorant woman, and her arrogance got her killed. We were both going to double-cross the other. I just got to her first. We both knew better, but our hatred for you both was far greater than the risk of working together. Poetic justice, really. She got what she deserved."

As Bria walks close to Valentina, I have to distract her. "You can't do this on your own."

"Who said I'm on my own?" she counters. "I disposed of your most loyal men. Now, the ones left bow to me. I have your kingdom as well as Gianna's. It's what is owed to me!"

"Baby, don't do this. You can't do this on your own."

From the corner of my eye, I see Valentina working subtly at the ties.

It won't be long.

"You've had your chance."

"You need me. You know we're stronger together. It's only a matter of time before the men revolt. They will find out what you've done, and someone will challenge you."

She pauses, mulling over what I said.

"You can't think Hugo the pirate is really a suitable candidate to sit on the throne next to you?"

Hugo stands guard.

His time is coming, however.

"Of course not! He's an imbecile with a childish need for revenge for something that happened a hundred years ago."

Hugo doesn't appreciate the insult.

"So who can you trust?"

When she doesn't answer, I smile.

"You know who. Let me make it up to you."

"Really?" she says, her eyes bright.

"Yes."

"How?"

"Whatever you want."

She taps her lip in thought. "Whatever I want?"

"Yes, baby, anything."

"I want what I've asked for…I want her dead. That's all I ask. Allow me to avenge my father, and everything will be over."

"Okay, you win. Untie me and I'll do it."

Bria looks for any signs of deceit. But eventually, she ambles over behind me. She places the box cutter at the rope around my wrists and slices through.

"I love you, Lennon…"

I feel a slash across my back.

"But you were never a good liar." She laughs hysterically, seeing through my ruse.

Blood spills from the wound she made, and I know this is merely the beginning.

"Your men are now mine. Gianna's men are now mine. I am

unstoppable. This entire fucking town will submit to me."

"Take it, it's yours."

"I don't need your permission. I have it. Your name is ruined, Lenny."

"Just kill me and be done with it."

"Kill you?" Bria questions, licking her lips. "Why would I want to do that? Killing you would be easy. I'd rather you live a life with shame as the once all-powerful, almighty Mafia king. Shame will follow you wherever you go. That's a punishment far worse than death. You're ruined, and nothing but an embarrassment. Overthrown by your own wife."

She's right. I would rather death than live with a tarnished reputation because once you commit to this life, there's no getting out.

The men who once followed me will see me as a coward. A man's honor is everything, and Bria is taking it away.

"I killed all your confidants. I burned down my father's store because I'm starting fresh. A new era approaches, and it's one I built myself. Everyone will remember my name."

She's doing all this for notoriety and believes she has something to prove. But her father has the respect he does because he was honorable.

His daughter is anything but.

"This entire time, I thought Gianna was the bad guy, but it was you. You're the one who kidnapped Lettie? You knew about her this whole time?" Valentina deduces.

"Yes. I came to Gianna with a proposition to use your bastard child as bait, knowing she'd take it because, look what she did to you. She was desperate and weak, and this was the only way to get what she wanted. Even until the very end, she believed she was going to win, that we were still in the sisterhood together."

"Don't you *dare* call my daughter that," Valentina snarls. "If anyone, you're the home-wrecker, you fucking psycho!"

"Why do you get to have it all? Lenny's love and his child. It was supposed to be me, not you! But I played all of you. I was under your noses this entire time, but I was underestimated. But never again. As Gianna says, to love is to be weak. And I don't plan on being weak ever again. A woman scorned is a dangerous thing."

She snaps her fingers, and Hugo jumps to command. He enters a moment later with a man I've never seen before. I assume he's one of Gianna's.

The other people they drag in, I *do* recognize.

He has Francesco and Nico.

"No!" Valentina screams.

Her anguish merely feeds the monster that is Bria.

"Hurts, doesn't it? To see the people you love suffer before you. I watched my father die because of you. And for years, I watched my husband be half the man he is because of you.

You're nothing but poison, polluting everything you touch."

If Nico is here, then where is Lettie?

"Any final words?" she asks Francesco, but he doesn't get a word in before she slashes his throat with the box cutter.

He drops to the floor, bleeding out and clutching his throat.

"No!" Valentina hollers, rocking back and forth in the seat.

Bria smiles at her pain. She turns her attention to Nico. "Time to eradicate your family tree and wipe your existence from the face of this earth."

"Take me…I won't fight you. Please don't hurt him."

Nico doesn't fight.

He doesn't beg.

And at this moment, I respect him profoundly.

But he will *not* die here today.

Lettie needs her *papa*.

She needs both her *papas*.

I need to get out of here, and I need to do so fucking now.

I think back to Gianna's lessons because the bitch knew how to fight. What would she do in this circumstance?

I'm tied, but Nico isn't.

We make eye contact, and I side-eye the table with the weapons.

He needs to be my hands when I cannot.

Valentina catches on.

Who knew this throuple would eventually come in handy?

"You're a fucking coward. Your father would be disgusted by your behavior."

Bria turns her attention to Valentina. "What did you say?"

"You heard me, you ugly bitch. All this because your father and your husband loved me more than you. No wonder you recruited cyclops. You're both pathetic. Great empire you're going to run."

"My father loved me!"

"Too bad you didn't love him enough to protect him. I mean, you fucking stole from him because why, he wasn't giving you enough attention?"

"Shut up!" Bria roars.

"You shut up," Valentina counters calmly. "I cannot believe this is the plot twist. A spoiled little brat ruins the story because she is throwing a tantrum. Boo-hoo, Lenny doesn't love me." She turns down her bottom lip, mimicking a whiny Bria.

Bria rushes over to Valentina and slashes her face with the blade.

It's deep and it will scar, but my God, it just makes Valentina even more brutal than she already is.

Valentina licks away the fallen blood from her lips. "You can kill me, but that doesn't bring back your father. Nor does it erase the fact that even dead, Lenny will love me more than you."

Bria shrieks, and when she attempts to slash Valentina's

throat, Nico runs at her, shoving her into the wall. The table with tools topples over, scattering instruments all over the floor.

Nico punches Bria in the stomach, which results in the box cutter falling from her hand.

Valentina furiously works at the rope on her wrists, and as Hugo charges for her, I trip him.

The other man pulls out a gun and shoots at me.

I rock my chair backward at just the right time, and it crashes as I hit the floor. I'm able to free myself, but my hands are still tied. Regardless, I charge the man with the gun and tackle him.

Nico is attempting to restrain Bria, but he's no match for her. She throws a punch that connects with his jaw.

Hugo is attacking Valentina, who is still tied. She uses her leg to propel backward and smashes her chair against the wall. She charges him and even with her hands tied, she beats the shit out of him. She kicks, bites, and headbutts him.

He doesn't stand a chance.

But we're at a massive disadvantage being restrained.

Bria charges Valentina, gripping her hair and smashing her face into a cabinet. She hurls her around the room like a rag doll. The man with the gun aims at Valentina. I kick him in the solar plexus, and when he goes down once more, I kick him in the face, knocking him out cold.

Nico runs over, blade in hand, and furiously cuts through

the rope at my wrists.

"Hurry!" I demand, and when it gives, I break my hands apart, the rope coming free.

I grab a hammer and instantly smash Hugo's fingers with it as he reaches for the fallen gun. I pick up the gun.

Bria still has Valentina, but when she sees me charging her, she spins her around and places a knife at her throat. "I'll give you a choice—walk away with Valentina and live your happily ever after. But in return, you leave me Lettie.

"A small sacrifice for happiness."

Valentina laughs, but it's not a happy sound. "That's not happening."

"Fine, have it your way, then."

Bria throws the knife at Nico.

He grips the knife sticking out of his chest, and his eyes widen as he drops to his knees. If unattended, he will die.

Valentina howls in pain, frozen and watching the man she loves bleed out in front of her.

I go to charge Bria, but Hugo smashes my kneecap with the hammer using his uninjured hand.

"Fucker!" I cry, kicking him in the face with my good leg.

I can't put my weight on the busted kneecap, so I hold myself up against the wall.

Hugo hobbles over to where Valentina is being held captive by Bria. Valentina looks at me because we're fucked this time and for real.

No army of men will come to our rescue, Bria made sure of it. The ones left standing are Bria's puppets. No one will help us. We're on our own.

Just how we were when our paths collided.

But I won't stand back and watch my family be destroyed.

We need a distraction, one that allows Valentina to break free.

And I see it in the form of a gun in my hand.

I place it against my temple. "Not the ending you were expecting?" I say to Bria, who gasps.

"Lennon, no, don't you dare play martyr!" Valentina screams, struggling against Bria.

"My life for hers?" I offer Bria, but she shakes her head furiously.

"No, that's not part of the plan."

"Well, I always liked to stray from the rules. I love you, Valentina. Tell Lettie her father loved her more than anything in this world."

"Lenny, no." Tears stream down Valentina's face because she knows me. She knows I am doing this for her.

The moment the gun goes off, Bria will falter, giving Valentina the window she needs to subdue her.

"You'd take your own life for *her*?" Bria asks, unable to comprehend any of this.

"Yes," I counter, feeling nothing but peace for the first time in my entire life.

I cock the trigger and the loud bang is deafening inside these concrete walls.

But the bullet isn't fired from my gun.

It comes from behind me, and standing, gun in hand, is my daughter.

Bria drops to her knees as she's been shot in her stomach. She clutches her bleeding torso, eyes begging I help her.

Oh, I'll help her.

Walking over to Lettie, I drop to a crouch and gently remove the gun from her hand. "Want to play hide-and-seek?"

She looks at Valentina, who shifts to stand in front of Nico.

"You go hide. I'll count to one hundred, and then I'll come find you. All right?"

Lettie appears afraid, worried she's done something wrong. "It's okay, my life," I say to her in Italian, touching her cheek.

She leans into my caress. The first time she's done this. "Okay, *Papa*."

My heart clenches. A moment surrounded by carnage and blood is the most beautiful memory I'll cherish forever.

She runs back into the house and does what she's told.

The men who entered left the door open, and my clever little banana figured out where we were. When she saw her mother in trouble, she acted on instinct—she is truly our daughter.

We created a brave little girl who will grow into a woman that'll change the world.

But now, I turn and finish this once and for all.

Hugo crawls away, but he can wait.

I hobble over to Valentina and draw her into my arms. I don't think I'll ever let her go. No words are spoken as we join hands and peer at the weapons at our disposal. Valentina opts for a mallet.

Without emotion, we walk to where Bria is crumpled over, bleeding out. She peers up, begging for mercy.

"Lenny, I love—"

"Oh, shut the fuck up."

Bria never gets to finish her sentence because Valentina smashes her in the temple with the mallet. Bria collapses onto her back, where Valentina straddles her and bashes in her face and skull. Bria's face is soon pulp.

The sight stirs a longing in me.

One down…

I reach down for the large hunting knife and make good on my promise. As Hugo is crawling away, I bend and slice off his fingers. When he opens his mouth to scream, I yank out his tongue and slice it off.

Kicking him onto his back, I stuff his fingers into his mouth and stomp on his face. He screams a gargled cry as I stuff his tongue down his throat.

He begs for compassion, reminding me of the time in the bathroom as he slinks away.

Reaching for the hammer, I yank down his pants, and without hesitation, I shove the handle in his ass. He screams in agony, his pinkie shooting out his mouth and hitting the wall with a squelch.

Valentina walks over casually, peering down at Hugo. "Just like old times, baby." She repeats his earlier comment before bringing her foot down on the hammer and driving it deep into Hugo's rectum.

This time, he won't recover from his injuries.

A whimper alerts us to one survivor.

Valentina links her bloody hand through mine. We turn, and the man shifts away, hands raised in surrender.

This world will always be filled with greed. And as I look at Valentina, my blood-splattered princess, I realize this world is ours. No matter if we want it or not, it's in our blood.

"Tell your men what you saw tonight. Spread the word that Lenny and Valentina are back, but this time, we fight together. You can either join us…or join them." I gesture to an unrecognizable Bria and an ass-in-the-air Hugo.

The man nods, interlacing his hands. "I pledge my loyalty, and I'll make sure all my men do as well."

I gesture that he should leave while we feel charitable.

He runs from the room, afraid we'll go back on our word.

Valentina and I are quiet—injured and blood splattered, but never happier or more alive.

Valentina's eyes soften when they land on Nico, but I'll be damned, the asshole's chest is rising and falling.

Valentina sees it too.

"We can give it all up and leave. We can be normal."

I pull her toward me, kissing her lips chastely. "*Tesoro mio*, this *is* our normal. We were born for this. As was our daughter, for our blood runs through her veins."

Valentina sighs before rubbing my blood across her lips. She reaches for my hand and wipes her blood from her face, and wipes it across my lips.

"For this is my blood," she whispers a Bible verse.

"A-fucking-men. I suppose we'd better take him to the hospital. And fire Romeo. Some bodyguard he is."

Valentina giggles.

"I'm ready!" Lettie excitedly cries.

"She gets her bossiness from her mother," I quip, dancing away from Valentina's playful wrath.

Hand in hand, blood slathered, we play hide-and-seek with our daughter because nothing is more important than family.

And for the first time in our lives, we are a family.

So here, on the throne, sits the Mafia king and his forever queen.

Long live the queen…

Subscribe to my Newsletter: https://tinyurl.com/mvjjk6k2
Die for You Playlist: https://tinyurl.com/4w3yr5u2

ABOUT THE AUTHOR

Monica James spent her youth devouring the works of Anne Rice, William Shakespeare, and Emily Dickinson.

When she is not writing, Monica runs her own business, but she always finds a balance between the two. She enjoys writing twisted AF stories, hoping to terrify her readers...just a little.

She is a bestselling author in the U.S.A., Australia, Canada, France, Germany, Israel, and the U.K.

Monica James resides in Melbourne, Australia, with her Unicorn, and her three crazy cats. She is slightly obsessed with red lipstick, heels, and crime documentaries, and is *that* person who always runs late.

CONNECT WITH MONICA JAMES

Website: authormonicajames.com

Facebook: facebook.com/authormonicajames

Goodreads: goodreads.com/MonicaJames

Instagram: @authormonicajames

TikTok: @authormonicajames

BookBub: http://bit.ly/2E3eCIw

Amazon: https://amzn.to/2EWZSyS

Reader Group: http://bit.ly/2nUaRyi

Newsletter: https://tinyurl.com/mvjjk6k2

Patreon: https://www.patreon.com/c/AuthorMonicaJames

Shopify: https://authormonicajames.store/